ALIEN DIMENSIONS
SPACE FICTION SHORT STORIES
ANTHOLOGY SERIES
#26

Mars Colonization 2033

Alien Dimensions Series

www.AlienDimensions.com

Edited by Neil A. Hogan

Published by Space Fiction Books, Melbourne
www.SpaceFictionBooks.com

Subscribe to the Space Fiction Books Newsletter

Receive the latest news about Alien Dimensions and other space fiction related titles.

Group giveaways, discounts and more!

Special Offer!

Download Alien Frequency: Stellar Flash Book One for free when you confirm your subscription.

Find out more at
www.AlienDimensions.com

Contents

Foreword

This Mars colonization special was inspired by a report by engineers at the NASA Jet Propulsion Laboratory, which you can find here: https://arc.aiaa.org/doi/pdf/10.2514/1.A35437 . Written by Hoppy Price, Robert Shishko, Joseph Mrozinkski and Ryan Woolley, the 2022 paper describes the science behind the possibility of a mission to Mars of a manned craft that would remain in orbit of the planet for about a month before returning. Published in early 2023, it has stimulated the current discourse on the possibility of landing on Mars within the next 10 years.

While astronauts have been talking about a human Mars orbit or landing in 2033, since at least 2013, the only thing stopping anything from happening is funding. We've (the world) got the experts. We've got the science. We've got the tech. We've got the designs. We've got the ideas. We've got the volunteers. We've got the passion. All we need is the money and everything can happen.

I would like to be optimistic, and believe that, even if NASA does organize a Mars orbit mission, private organizations with bigger budgets, like SpaceX and Blue Origin, might try harder for an actual human landing by this date, considering the huge saving on time and fuel in using Venus in a slingshot maneuver while the planets are aligned. This effectively makes 2033 a likely landing year. Also, with SpaceX planning robot landings to build structures for humans as early as 2029, 2033 may mark the first colonization year, perhaps by a private volunteer who would take a one-way trip to live in them.

Of course, cosmic radiation, and the lack of a uniform magnetic field on Mars to hold a thicker atmosphere, means anyone living on the surface is likely to be dead within 4 years, so whoever lands better bring a shovel. Currently, the only way for humans to survive long-term on mars is to live deep underground, or in habitats with their own magnetospheres, or in domes with a hydrogen outer shell.

Still, this is what the science tells us is probable. Science fiction is a bit more flexible. In this issue you'll read stories that are mainly set this century around the Mars colonization period, though some might be more alternate reality. Some stories reflect the confidence we all feel in there being remains of civilizations under the ground or in caves. And still others reflect one of our fears that dangerous microbes and viruses are just waiting for humans to land to give them a living host to resurrect themselves.

Will Mars be a death trap? A quarantine zone? A First Contact location? These stories explore some of these ideas so that the brave humans who do eventually colonize Mars can read them and perhaps plan for some of the less likely scenarios, just in case.

Looking forward to 2033!

Neil Hogan
7 May 2024

Mars City Space Port
By David Castlewitz

Off-Earth Enterprises, the sole company licensed to operate on Mars, claimed the recent outbreak of mental illness at the Equatorial Water Works on mass hysteria. George Levy didn't doubt the possibility, but the military had questions, so he was sent to investigate. After an hours long bumpy ride from Mars Central, he was happy to peel off his pressure suit – a "Mars Tux" – and store it in an assigned locker.

He turned off the beacon tracking his movements. If anything happened to him here, somebody at Central would figure it out when he failed to make regular status reports. An irritable tremor of trepidation wriggled through his slender frame as he paused to look out a window and watch the sand buggy that brought him disappear in the distance, swallowed by jagged rocks, gritty mounds of sand, and the brooding red tincture of a Martian day.

Reynolds's, the Works' manager, looked up when Levy entered the office. "You're a …. A what?"

"Senior Corpsman," Levy answered. He'd chosen his cover story and low ranking so nobody at the water extraction plant would fear him when he poked his nose into their business. "I'm here to help."

"If you want to help us, take our nut cases back to Central. We've got a small infirmary, and these malingerers are taking up seven of our ten beds."

"Then they're fit for travel?" The briefing Levy viewed told him otherwise.

"I think so," Reynolds said. "It's that Fran Kitt – Dr. Kitt – who won't release them."

Levy made note of the name. He hadn't heard of this doctor before. "Do I have to go through her to get to the men? I mean, to speak to them?"

"Do everything through her. I'm tired of dealing with this mass hysteria thing. We're got a thousand liters a day quota to pump up. Bots can't do all the work. Clear debris, change out drill heads, that sort of thing. And we're still doing maintenance. These snap-together buildings aren't foolproof. You must have the same issue at Central."

Levy never gave maintenance much thought, but he nodded to be agreeable. There were specialized robots for every aspect of maintaining the sprawling water works complex, which had been assembled from pre-fabs with the same rush-rush as Central. From what he'd seen, the buildings were aligned, the seams true, and every module and interconnecting passageway pressurized to account for Mars' minimal atmosphere.

"One question," Levy ventured, "were all seven men on the same crew?"

Reynolds pursed his lips, ran his hand across his bald pate, and glanced at the sound absorbing ceiling. "I don't know." His face began to redden.

"I'll track down this doctor you mention," Levy said. "Kitt, right?"

He found the infirmary by following the signs in the vast labyrinth. He also found Dr. Kitt, a short, redheaded woman with a lined face and green eyes.

"I guess someone told you I'd arrived," Levy said in a friendly tone of voice.

"Told me? Warned me is more like it. These men are dangerously psychotic. They're not fit to – "

"Wait, wait. Psycho?"

"That's a gross term, but I guess a corpsman wouldn't know any other."

"Doctor…" He paused, sucked in a breath. "I'm here to assess. I will include your opinion in my report. I'm not here to override your decisions."

Kitt released stream of air between her parted lips. "Why're you here at all?" Hands on hips, she seemed to await Levy's rebuttal. He offered none. "Go on then." She gestured at the closed glazed glass door into the ward.

He pushed it open, but was taken aback by the acrid smell of chemicals.

"The floor's mopped at least twice a day. Depends on how many times they vomit."

He glanced at the two rows of five cubicles facing him. Blue lights embedded in seven of the doors were self-explanatory. "Can I see the master conditions monitors?"

Kitt pointed to an open cubicle where two technicians sat in front of several monitors, each divided into seven viewports. Ragged lines zipped past beneath the views. Elsewhere, pulsating lights indicated heart rate, oxygen level in the blood, and pulse. The dizzy-inducing display told Levy the patients were well-cared for.

"I'd like to – "

Kitt cut him off with a nod of her head. She took him to one of the rooms where she gently woke up a skeleton of a man in blue and red striped pajamas. "Jonas. Ned," she introduced the patient. Hooded eyelids obscured his pale brown eyes. Damp threads of hair clung to his forehead.

Levy hurried through the requisite preliminaries, the introductions and the explanations. Then he turned to the single window in the cramped room. "Does that look out directly?" he asked Kitt.

"No. It's a viewer." She fiddled with the control and an image of the empty red desert appeared. Derricks in the background supported the drill-hammers digging into Mars' upper crust. Capped wells, sans-derricks, sat with spider legs of thick tubes sucking up the liquid and delivering it north from the equator.

"Tell me what you see," Levy said to Jonas. He wanted to hear for himself what he'd been told these men were claiming.

Jonas sat up in bed, his face glistening with an eagerness to please. He spoke of tall rockets with large fins, elevators carrying freight to the cargo bay and passengers entering near the nose cone. On the ground, three-wheeled vehicles zipped left and right at fast speed without colliding. No one wore bulky life-support outfits, as though Mars was totally terra-formed. That's what he saw, this comic book version of a space port, when he looked at a viewscreen.

Patient Number Two, a wiry elder whom Levy assumed had just managed to squeeze under the age limit, jumped up out of his bed and adjusted the view window controls himself. "Scooter," he said when asked his name.

"Danny Tunn," Kitt whispered to Levy, correcting the patient.

Scooter also saw tall rockets with fins, elevators, tricycles, and lots of people working outside in shirt sleeves and jumpsuits. The descriptions reminded Levy of museum displays of 20th century art.

Just for the sake of thoroughness, Levy interviewed the remaining five patients. The last man, a beefy guy with a shock of wild blonde hair.

"Mr. Gallagher," Kitt whispered as they entered the room, "is patient number one."

"Don't talk about me," Gallagher roared. He sat in a straight-backed chair at the side of his bed. When Kitt turned on the viewer, he didn't look at the scene, but he described what he saw using the same words as the other. A teeming spaceport with classic rockets that belonged to a bygone age of aspiration populated the screen.

"Do you remember what you used to see out there?" Levy asked.

Gallagher pointed a thick thumb at the viewer. "It's always been there. The spaceport's been there since I got here."

Outside in the hallway, Kitt told Levy how the men were caught trying to leave their dormitory without protective gear. First Gallagher, then the others in a span of three days.

"What sort of assignments were they on?" Levy asked. "Were they exposed to any chemicals that might account – "

"You're welcome to see the records. My job's been to keep them comfortable and safe."

"Just curious, Doctor. What's your specialty?"

Kitt laughed. "It's not psycho-analysis, if that's what you're – "

"Do you have a psychiatrist on staff?"

"You have anyone like that at Central?"

Levy shook his head. Medical attention on Mars was limited. Bone setters and aspirin pushers made up the medical staff for the military at Central. Privateers like Off-Earth had little more to offer their employees.

"Anyone else ever go off the deep end out here?" Levy asked.

"It happens. When it does, we ship them out if they don't snap out of it."

"Then why didn't you ship Gallagher home? What about the others?"

"Wasn't my call."

"Who made the call?"

"I guess it was Reynolds. He's the manager. Or it could've been someone from Off-Shore's Earth office. I got orders – from Reynolds – to solve the problem. On Mars. With help from Central Command if necessary." Her words shot out with a staccato beat.

A door suddenly opened. "How's my guy doing?" The intruder, tall with a sturdy build and wild black curls across his head, flashed a white-toothed grin at Levy. "You the one from the Ministry of Health?"

Kitt introduced Levy to Carlos Ortiz, the manager of a nearby archeological dig. "Which one is 'your guy'?"

"All of them. How's Gallagher doing, doc?"

"Improving," Kitt mumbled. Lines had returned to her face. Her vibrant red hair lost some of its luster, as did her green eyes.

What're you worried about? Levy wondered.

"Just like to check in on the guys," Ortiz said. "Gallagher's one of my best, you know."

"I don't know," Levy said in an even tone. "Did all these men work for you? I thought they were with the company."

"Loaned out," Kitt explained.

"And at a good price!" Ortiz laughed. Kitt cringed when the big man touched her shoulder. Color drained from her face. Even after Ortiz had gone, Kitt stood like a petrified puppy anticipating trouble.

"Do you want to tell me what's really going on?" Levy whispered.

She countered with a snappish, "After you tell me who you are. You don't act or look like the usual low-level corpsman."

A decision had to be made. Levy stepped close to Kitt, bent his head so she could hear him whisper, "You're right. Now, what are you hiding?"

Dr. Kitt didn't know as much as Levy had hoped. Her orders were to shelter the seven men until they recovered their senses. She was also told to send Reynolds any videos that were made of her patients' bizarre episodes. As to Levy: Reynolds told her to cooperate but oppose transferring the men to Mars Central.

"And that Ortiz character?" Levy pressed.

She flushed. "I don't know where he fits."

"What sort of hallucinogens do you have here?"

Kitt suddenly grinned. "We don't. No drugs. Recreational, I mean. And alcohol's limited to beer. All tightly controlled. Not like the early days. No endless kegs."

Levy visualized the pieces of this puzzle coming together, though nothing really fit. When he left the infirmary, he couldn't shake the annoying feeling that Dr. Kitt might not be the ally he needed. She didn't know – profess to know – very much about her seven patients. As head of the department, she should know everything, including how they got their crazy ideas about a thriving spaceport in the Martian desert.

At The Hub, where many of corridors met up, Levy applied for an overnight pass, some place to sleep, and a courtesy meal ticket. When the clerk at the admissions desk refused his requests, he took the matter to Reynolds, who grilled him about his intentions.

"I just want to know more about these patients before I report back," Levy told him. He sat in a wide chair in front of Reynolds's desk, his legs crossed. Act casual. Don't be intimidated, he told himself.

"Okay," Reynolds finally said after a few more questions. "Anything else to keep Mars Central happy?"

"Can I get a buggy and driver tomorrow morning?" The thought had just popped into Levy's mind.

Reynolds narrowed his eyes, pressed his thin lips together, and let loose a barely audible snort of derision. "We don't do that for guests. Anyway, where do you think you'd go?"

"On tour. You know. See the water works, the drilling platforms and pumping stations."

"There're drone views of anything you'd want to see. All real time."

"But I can't just go out there?"

Reynolds shook his head slowly. "Insurance. If something happened – "

Levy cut him off. He knew enough, He didn't need to hear a rubbish-filled round-about excuse. As he left the office, Reynolds sputtered another stream of reasons why touring the work areas wasn't a good idea. The men would become too curious. Work would suffer. Men on drilling crews in close proximity to the digger-bots needed to be sharp at all times. Distractions caused problems.

After he retrieved his carryall from the closet in the outer office, Levy found his way to the cafeteria. The shift-change bell hadn't yet sounded, so the large room was near empty. Just a few tables occupied. But with no one he knew. Judging by the color of the work overalls, he didn't think any of his fellow diners would shed any light on the issue, so he refrained from questioning them. Even the few base security personnel who lingered over coffee and threw suspicious glances his way didn't strike Levy as worth his time.

The facility's bar would be a better source of information. It was easy to find, first by using the directions on the corridor walls and then by following the boisterous voices and laughter from men and women capping off a full day of work.

Without a beer chit, Levy could only stand by the open door and take in the scene. Two burly women carrying shock-batons guarded the entry way and pushed him aside when he couldn't produce a ration code on his watch. Looking around, Levy spied the cause of all the laughter. Four of the five video screens above the bar showed images captioned "Kitt's Seven."

Gallagher was wrestled to the floor near a sally port. The one who called himself Scooter lay naked with two white-suited attendants on top. The other five, when they appeared in the video loop, entertained the bar patrons with plenty of demeaning antics. How would they ever live this down? Levy wondered. If they ever shook off their hallucinations, they'd have a hard time integrating back into the work force. Maybe Gallagher would do it, based on his weight and strength. Scooter might because he seemed to enjoy clowning around.

"Get your fill? Stick around. There's one where Dr. Kitt gets flung on her head."

Levy locked eyes with Ortiz. Refusing to blink, he glared harder. How many other eyes peered at him, he couldn't say. The crowd raised their glasses to toast the screen. After a few cheers, most everyone melted away, leaving only Ortiz standing nearby, one elbow on the bar. As a kid in boarding school, Levy often found himself sizing up adversaries – potential and real. He couldn't quite shake the childish practice.

Abruptly, he walked out of the bar.

Visitors' quarters were located in a module more than a klick away, and made even further by the roundabout directions that took him into a maze of connecting corridors. His assigned room, though adequate, offered no comforts. Narrow bed, hard plastic mattress, and a small desk with a comm-unit that lacked a port where he could plug in a scrambler. If he communicated with Central, it would be in the clear, unencrypted.

Lights out, he turned on his right side and faced the door. Footsteps passed in the corridor. Laughter exploded, then was squelched. Soon, even whispering on the other side of the door died out, but was replaced by shuffling shoes.

The door opened a crack and Levy sat up in bed, his feet on the tiled floor. He thought of the palm-sized rail gun in his bag, deep in a secret compartment. Stupid, he thought, not to have it handy. But it was a one-shot, and the sounds in the hallways made him think two or more were about to attack.

He pushed himself off the bed and dashed into the bathroom. A canister bounced into the room, twisting as it spewed a noxious smelling gas from its nozzle.

"That's a spaceport out there, guy. Rockets. Remember? Giant fins and people serving them, loading passengers and freight. Don't need a suit to go out. It's like Earth. Maybe not the gravity, but there's oxygen enough and the air pressure is just what you're used to."

Levy collapsed against the shower stall, Pictures of rockets waiting for liftoff swam through his mind. He grabbed a towel from atop the commode and spread it out in the crack between the bottom of the door and the tiles on the floor. His hallucinations faded to nothing, and he reinforced that by remembering how the Martian desert looked.

He sat in the shower stall, its door shut, a damp towel draped over his head.

He concentrated on seeing the water works as they actually appeared. He saw domes and above-ground tunnels and massive drilling rigs tended to by specialized bots, with workmen following along, all dressed in pressure suits, heads in plastic-fronted helmets.

In spite of his precautions, the initial whiff Levy got when he woke made his head spin with visions of a vast spaceport emerging from his drug-addled imagination. Reminding himself of the truth – of where he stood and what lay outside the walls – he dressed, taking short shallow breaths to minimize the effect of any lingering hallucinogenic in the air.

He sent a quick message to Central as his daily status report, providing just the code word for "No changes." Then, adding, "But I might signal for a half-dozen strawberry cakes. Food here is awful." That should get a rise out of whoever monitored his communications. "I'll send up a flare if I get desperate."

He looked for the spent canister, thinking it could be identified.

What gas? What chemical compound induced the hallucinations abetted by suggestive comments. In the back of his mind a memory of a stage magician using hypnosis and verbal commands lingered from when he was a boy.

Maybe Kitt knew something, but when he got to the infirmary, he was told her duty cycle began at 7AM Mars Tie. The ER tech on call offered his help. Levy asked, "Know anything about psychedelics delivered by gas?"

A nurse piped up with, "Yeah. They use those at raves. On Earth, I mean. Not here." She shrank away from the back of the counter, her face suddenly going pale.

Stepping close to the counter, Levy smiled to disarm the young woman. "Mind if I kill time using your terminal?"

The nurse shrugged.

For the next hour, Levy filled in the gaps of what he knew about Kitt's seven patients. The only significant thing he discovered was that they lived in a small dorm, the seven of them packed into tight quarters. A diagram showed 8 beds – one not labeled by an occupant's name – arranged in two rows and separated by short cubicle walls.

"Is there a reason you're back?" Kitt asked when she walked in.

"Somebody gassed up my room." He knew by her startled look that she understood what he meant.

They went into her office, and he explained how he avoided falling into the same trap as her seven patients. "Any way to figure out what psychotic they sprayed in the room?"

"Hallucinogen," she corrected. "And you heard voices while you were – "

"Someone kept trying to embed that spaceport imagery in my brain."

"Maybe they were joking." She looked down at her desk. "At any rate, what do you expect me to do? This should be reported to Reynolds."

"I want to see that dig."

"Why?"

"Because your seven patients who share the same delusion worked at this dig. Because when Ortiz was here yesterday, you looked frazzled. What's going on with that site? It's not even listed as an official project."

"Check it out. Why ask me?"

"Reynolds won't give me a sand buggy. I'm sure you could just check one out." Levy watched Kitt's face, saw her start to say, "No." He stared at her until her negative expression dissolved.

"Fine, if you think it'll help. The sooner you finish your investigation and let me get back to my real work, the better things will be." She sounded flustered just then, as though she had to argue with herself.

Signing out a sand buggy wasn't as simple as Levy anticipated. Kitt claimed she needed to make a safety inspection of the water works' drill sites. She spent several minutes at a terminal filling out forms and fielding questions thrown at her by an AI-driven monitoring app.

"Did you just send a message to Ortiz?" Levy asked when Kitt signed off and had her ID badge updated with an authorization chit.

"As a matter of courtesy. He's the manager there, even if the project's on hold."

Levy triggered his beacon as a precaution the moment the buggy headed for the dig, leaving the water works compound to fade into the red tinted distance after climbing a hill and sliding down the other side. The archeological dig didn't stand out. Not on the monitor in the buggy's center panel nor in the heads-up display that floated in front of his eyes. Annoyed by the shuddering icons and bright white letters across the bottom of the view, he turned off the monitor and relied on what he could see with his eyes.

"It's coming up," Kitt said, her voice ringing in Levy's helmet. He tapped for the heads-up display again and adjusted the speakers' balance and squelch. He leaned forward, the top of his helmet grazing the windshield.

A blue and red pennant atop a slender pole waved in the wind. Scooper-bots and diggers littered the area. Several exoskeletons sat mute, half buried in the sand, their usefulness relegated to another day. A pit surrounded by waist-high white piping as a barrier drew Levy's attention and he rushed towards it the moment Kitt stopped the buggy.

"Is this the site?" he asked. "Your seven patients all worked here?"

Kitt nodded. "So far as I know."

Levy opened a gate in the barrier and climbed down a steel ladder rooted to the pit's base. There should be answers here, he told himself, disappointed that all he saw was a large hole and discarded equipment.

"How long has the site been inactive?" he asked. When Kitt didn't reply, he glanced to where she stood next to the gate.

"Don't know," she answered.

He walked to a shed and tried the door. An electric lock winked at him. He pulled on the handle and got what he expected: resistance. "What's the pass code?" he asked, turning slightly to look at Kitt.

A tall figure sidled up beside her. Ortiz? A deep and menacing voice pounded Levy's ears. Of course, Levy told himself. Kitt shrank from the pit's edge. Ortiz grabbed hold of her Mars suit where the material bunched up at her shoulder, and pulled her back.

"I'm coming down," Ortiz said, and descended the steel ladder, his boots checking for purchase at each rung. The last meter down, he pushed off and hit the pit's floor with a soundless thump.

Levy stepped away from the door just as Ortiz approached and bumped him aside.

"Go on in," Ortiz urged. He keyed in the lock's code.

Levy stepped close to the threshold, the lamp on his left shoulder providing a bright white light that illuminated smooth yellow walls.

"You should've let the Divi-gas do its job." Ortiz muttered, and shoved Levy deeper into the underground chamber.

"Divi-gas? Is that what you sprayed in my room? Used that on Gallagher and Jonas and the rest?"

"Look around," Ortiz snapped. Levy stumbled when pushed. "You were so curious about my business, get a look and see."

Nothing but blank walls, Levy determined, letting the beam from his shoulder-mounted lantern grave his surroundings. He found an irregularly shaped hole in one corner. Peeking into the murky darkness at his feet, he adjusted the lamp on his shoulder to shed light on what lay below.

"There's a ladder. Go. Take a look." Again, Ortiz urged him on with a push.

Levy shook his head and turned to face Ortiz, who now held a palm-sized weapon in his hand. "You sure that railgun is calibrated for Mars?"

"It is."

"It's a one-shot, right? What're you going to do, aim for my faceplate?"

"Down the ladder."

Levy shook his head, his entire body twisting left and right with the effort. "Don't need to. Whatcha find down there? Evidence of – "

"Go!"

Levy expected a push or a kick. He got out of the way. Ortiz tipped backwards when his leg came up and hit – nothing. Levy used his newfound leverage to push the bigger man down on the ground and, at the same time, wrest the weapon from his grip.

"You want in?" Ortiz asked, "It's coins and jewelry. Metal plates. Tools. It's proof of a past civilization. We can all be rich."

"Like Gallagher and the others?" Levy scoffed. He tapped the inner red button on his utility belt.

"If you're trying to signal," Ortiz began, and then didn't bother to finish his statement.

"What is it? Lead? You saying we're in a lead box?" Levy backed up to the door. A sickening fruity smell filled the air. Ortiz crawled towards him, got to his knees, and rose to his full height.

"You cut out the seven guys who help you dig," Levy said. "How'd you even get the idea there was something down here?"

"What do you care," Kitt answered. She waved a railgun at him, a one-shot like Ortiz' weapon.

Levy stood his ground, stunned when a steel ball slowly flew from Kitt's hand. He caught the projectile before it hit his face plate and shook his head in the face of her stupidity. She'd never tested her weapon. On Earth, the 5mm wide ball would have zipped across the short space separating them. It would have shattered his helmet's faceplate, leaving him vulnerable to the planet's low-pressure atmosphere.

He body-slammed Kitt, knocking her onto her back. Ortiz hit him with a fist, but from an awkward position that sapped the strength of the blow. Levy skittered up the ladder and climbed over the barrier. He set off his emergency alarm; then he waited. He didn't doubt that the strawberry cakes he referred to in his message to Central would alert Security to what he really wanted.

After the two video-bots floated up from the underground cavern, Levy descended to see the artifacts for himself. A few oval pieces of metal with holes in the middle looked like coins. Thin plates of a different metal showed faint images of what looked like horses with horns. Goblets and parts of a sword's hilt, along with necklaces made from smooth nodules that were once strung together, completed what could be found on the ground. How many more artifacts were buried beneath?

"It's at the nascent stages of revealing Mars history," Reynolds said when Levy walked into his office. "And there's good news about the seven patients."

"I heard. Gallagher's out there fighting anyone who looks at him sideways. And Scooter's cashing in on his celebrity getting people to buy him beers in exchange for his stories."

The other five patients were taking longer to recover. Maybe, Levy thought, they were hit harder by the mind-alerting gas. If the dig hadn't been investigated, Kitt and Ortiz would have had the found relics all to themselves because no one would've believed Gallagher or Scooter or any of the others if they talked, not after watching them ranting and raving about a space port; anything they claimed would be suspect.

"Well," Reynolds said, "I imagine you're anxious to – "

"In a hurry, actually. I need you to sign off on the buggy."

Reynolds nodded. A cold sheen came into his eyes. "This should be a friendly parting, Levy."

"Why? I've been told the whole thing's being buried. I don't care if Ortis and Kitt are in prison for the rest of their lives, but why not continue the dig? Why not – "

"Not my call," Reynolds said with a sigh. He glanced at the virtual screen rising from the edge of his desk. "Your valise is at sally port four. That's where you'll find your buggy."

Not for the first time, Levy wondered if Reynolds had been involved with Kitt and Ortiz. No evidence connected him to their scheme. The water works manager was well above the storm.

"I hope you never have to come back here," Reynolds said.

"You and me both."

As he left the office, Levy felt a weight lift from his chest. When he passed a window looking out at the red tinted desert, he grinned at the thought of a comic book space port peppered with finned rockets pointed at the stars.

--

A retired techie, David turned to a first love: writing fiction. Living north of Chicago, David enjoys wonderful winters that keep him inside and splendid (though short) summers for walking, biking, and fishing. All three give him time to contemplate new story ideas. He has published stories in Farther Stars Than These, Future Syndicates II, Martian Wave, SciFan, Bonfires and Vanities (an anthology) and other online as well as print magazines.

The Trouble with Truffles

By Humphrey Price

Mira DeMayne and Jack Marchak floated together in his phone booth sized personal quarters following an intimate interlude. They were en route on a commercial transport ship for a seven-month transit to Mars and engaged in a disposable relationship of convenience. Mira had doubts about the wisdom of this space fling, but Jack was an interesting and rakishly exciting sort of character.

"This has been a fun trip to Mars, Jack. Much more entertaining than my previous one."

"And I am all about entertainment."

"So I've gathered, and it's been a delightful way to pass the time. Now, just two more weeks and we'll be landing."

"Yep. The zero g stuff is pretty sweet, but I'm looking forward to standing on solid ground again. So, Mira, I have to ask, have you ever tried any of the Martian truffles?"

"You mean like eating those slimy things?"

"Well, yeah!"

"Besides sounding gross, that would be a serious violation of protocol. Why would I do that?"

"Because they're incredible. Why do you think they sell for two hundred thousand dollars a gram on Earth? So, you scientists never snitch a little for yourselves?"

"No, of course not," she replied. "We collect tiny samples using sterilized robots to take back for study in the lab. Planetary protection protocols are important, and our directives are to not damage, interfere with, or contaminate the native microbial mats."

"You're such a goody two-shoes scientist."

"And you're a harvester," she said in a harsh tone. "But you have your subsurface site at Phlegra that's been allocated and licensed for commercial extraction."

"Yeah, but the mats are thinning out now. The quality is getting crappy. We have to keep digging deeper to find new zones with good material. The mats grow on the underside of the glacier where it meets the regolith, and we're having to go into thicker layers that are harder to drill through."

"Oh, you poor babies. You're killing off the mats, because your greedy company has contaminated the site. It's a good thing your operations are limited to Phlegra and isolated from the rest of the Mars ecosystems. I can't believe you make a profit from this. Who can pay two thousand dollars a gram?"

"We have no shortage of wealthy customers. They buy up all the truffles that Nisei Data Company can supply, and we're planning to raise prices. The company is making a killing, and the truffle business has far outstripped what we get from our bio data products. I know you've got some great stuff at Arcadia. Most of our mats are brown, and those are excellent, but we've found a few patches of the gold-colored microbes. 'Martian Gold' is primo, and that brings twice the price. I've heard you have a lot of the gold at Arcadia. Just the thought makes me drool."

"Why do you need to bring the Martian microbes all the way back to Earth? Can't Nisei Data synthesize the active ingredients?"

"They've tried. It's a complex mixture of chemicals and enzymes. No one really knows how it works, and it hasn't been replicated. You have to get the real stuff from Mars. Mira, you should really try the truffles."

"What are they like?"

"For cooking, it has an intoxicating scent and flavor. A thousand times better than Earth truffles, and you only need to use the tiniest little pinch. Plus, it's the perfect drug. It only takes a few milligrams to get off. It doesn't impair cognitive function or make you drowsy. You get jacked up without any negative health effects. The truffles are non-addictive in the sense that there are no withdrawal issues, and it's incredibly euphoric."

"Sounds kind of like what we've been doing here in your cubicle."

"Maybe. Let's give that another try, and I'll let you know."

The Mars lander set down its crew of six at the international Mars Base at Cerberus. From there, a Nisei Data LOX-hydrogen hopper craft transported Jack and Mira to the spartan science station at Arcadia where Mira was dropped off before returning Jack to Nisei Data's commercial site.

"Mira, I'm going to miss you. When you get some time off, I can send the hopper here to bring you over to my hab at Phlegra and show you around our operations. I can guarantee a good time."

"Thanks, Jack. I'll think about it. Good luck with your truffle hunting."

"Yep. I'm gonna be going for the Martian Gold. In any case, I'll see you on the return trip to Earth in a year and a half." Then Jack whispered in her ear, "You gotta try the truffles."

"I'll take that under advisement. Bye, Jack. Stay out of trouble."

"That's a hard one for me."

Mira waved goodbye as the hopper lifted off with Jack for Phlegra.

Following the faded remnants of dust-covered wheel tracks from previous visits, Mira and her crewmate, Otto Otabe, steered their pressurized rover down a safe entry point into the huge crater, then down toward the bottom, through a flat area, and finally over rougher terrain toward a depression that looked like one of the thumb indexes in the side of an old dictionary. The gleaming vertical wall of Arcadia Ice Scarp #27 lay exposed at the end of the depression. Though they had both ventured there before on previous Mars stints, the two explorers were still filled with awe staring up at a cliff face of pure water ice that was a hundred meters tall and almost a kilometer wide. Scarp #27 was unique in that a portion of the bottom of the ice sheet had separated from the underlying regolith, forming a cave that provided entry deep into the underside of the ice.

As they approached the cave, Otto said, "I still can't get over how extensive the microbial mats are inside the cavern."

"Yeah, it's astounding. Those little one-celled critters have formed a highly connected community, just like the ancient microbial mats on Earth."

"This site is unique in that tendrils of mats creep out from buried portions and are exposed to the Martian atmosphere. They seem to survive just fine out in the open. Of course, in the cave they're still shielded from UV and radiation."

"There are lichens on Earth that can survive in vacuum for a long time, so it's not surprising that the microbes could have evolved to thrive even in this thin air."

"These mats are different than the specimens that are totally underground. Sure, they grow in the ice interface with the soil, living off chemical energy from minerals, and they give off oxygen, just like the subterraneans, but these open-air tendrils grow quickly, like they are probing around and exploring their environment. I get the feeling that they are aware of our presence."

"Oh, Otto, that's ridiculous."

"I'm not so sure. The mats remind me of terrestrial slime molds."

"There are similarities. So what?"

"Microbial colonies on Earth can perform some pretty intelligent functions. Slime mold cells communicate with each other and can learn from experience and exhibit memory."

"There are hints of collective cognitive function, but that's a far cry from being sentient."

"Terrestrial microbe colonies decide which direction to grow. Slime molds can solve mazes. Some fungi have neural-type electrical activity and are capable of learning. There are even creepy fungi that can invade insects and turn them into controllable zombies."

"Okay, Otto, you're freaking me out now."

Mira parked the rover near the opening to the cave and prepared to deploy the sterilized Axel rover that was secured on a flatbed at the rear of their vehicle. Then she noticed something worrisome.

"Otto, look over to the right of the cave. Tracks."

"I see them. They look fresh. No dust coverage. An undocumented rover was here not long ago. Within a few weeks at most. They must have timed their visit to avoid reconnaissance orbiter overflights. Looking at the wheel track width and the treads, I'd say it was an M-3B unpressurized rover. A four-seater. Pretty limited range."

"And who has those?"

"Nisei Data."

"Damn! Truffle pirates."

"Looks like it. How would they get here? Phlegra is too far away for driving."

"An M-3B will fit on one of their hoppers. They must have landed nearby in a flat area and then driven over in a rover through the rough spots to get to the cave."

"We need to check out what damage has been done to the colony."

Otto teleoperated the two-wheeled Axel 5 robot to roll off the flatbed and drive over to the cave opening. It was connected to their rover via a power and data cable that spooled out from the central axle of the remote-controlled robot. The two scientists monitored telemetry and observed the video feed from Axel 5.

Mira said, "Steer Axel clear of the footprints leading from the M-3B tracks to the cave opening. We don't want to mess up evidence that Nisei has violated their agreements and planetary protection protocols."

"Copy that. I'm getting visible and LIDAR images to document the intrusion."

"We need to get this info back to base ASAP."

"We're in a relay dead spot. No birds overhead. The last one just flew over, and the next recon and Comsat pass won't be for another three hours."

Images from the Axel showed that the boot impressions disappeared at the entry to the cave.

Otto said, "The floor of the cave is free of dust, so no more prints to follow. Let's steer Axel to where exposed mats were seen the last time this was explored. Then maybe we can determine what was disturbed by the pirates."

"According to the logs, we should find some mats about twenty-five meters ahead. There might be a few shoots of growths emerging from the edges into the open cave. Scan the headlight beams from side to side so we can check for exposed material."

"There! Up ahead on the left. A little tendril from an underground mat. A nice gold one."

"Yeah. Get Axel close so we can examine it. Crap, you can see a cut where some of it was hacked away. Otto, use the arm to collect a tiny sample from the cut area. Back in the lab, we can assess the level of contamination from the pirates."

Otto worked the arm. "Okay. Got the sample. Hey, it looks like the tendril wiggled a little bit and felt around our sensor. Maybe the microbes' receptors are tasting us to identify and remember if we're a threat or not."

"I think you're imagining things, my friend."

Otto shrugged. "Let's drive deeper into the cave and see what else we can find."

"We're approaching the branching point in the cave," Mira noted. The live video from the Axel displayed six narrower passages leading in different directions. "Let's take the branch that's almost straight ahead. That way it will be easier to back out if we need to."

"I'm good with that. Here we go." The Axel drove another twenty meters, and then the image from the video feed went dark.

"Loss of signal from Axel," Mira said. "All telemetry flatlined. Holy crap! We've got nothing."

"Now what do we do?"

"Nothing we can do. Abandon in place for now. We'll have to send in another rover to investigate on the next site visit."

"We need to recover the Axel," Otto said. "Without it, half of our science explorations are out the window. I'm going into the cave to take a look."

"You'll contaminate the site."

"I think the Nisei Data pirates have already done that. I'll put my suit in non-effluent mode to minimize any further contamination."

"I'll go with you."

"No, I need you here in the rover to drive Axel, if I can get it going again. It should be safe. From their rover tracks, we know that the pirates have left the area. You'll have live audio and video from me. I'll drop comm relays along the way to maintain contact while inside in the cave."

Against Mira's protestations, Otto climbed into his EVA suit through the rear entry suitport hatch. After getting his arms and legs into the suit, ducking his head up into the helmet, and checking diagnostics, he actuated the hatch closed and separated from the rover.

Mira monitored Otto's suit telemetry and the video feed from his helmet cam as he entered the cave. Lights mounted on the helmet illuminated his path.

"I'm dropping the first relay pod now. Do you have a good link?"

"Roger, Otto. I'm reading you five by five."

"Copy that. I'm pressing on, following the cable to the Axel. Everything looks nominal so far. As soon as your signal starts getting weaker, I'll drop another relay pod."

Mira monitored Otto's telemetry as he progressed farther into the cave and positioned another relay unit. "Looks like you're nearing the branch point to the other passages."

"Affirmative. There are loose sections of mats on the cave floor that the pirates hacked off and left here. I'll try to avoid stepping on them. I'm carefully moving them to the side next to where some of the colony's tendrils are poking out. And now, one of tendrils is slowly moving toward the mats and joining them back up to the colony. Whoa, what's this? A tendril coming down from the roof is touching my helmet. I can't believe they're moving so fast."

"Yeah, I see that. I'm glad we're getting this on video."

"Maybe they *are* tasting me to label as friend or foe."

"You're reading way too much into this, Otto."

"I guess so. Well, back to business. I just tugged on Axel's cable, and it seems slack. No tension. I'm not sure what that means. I've just reached the branch point and am continuing to follow the cable toward Axel."

The video feed, voice, and telemetry from Otto abruptly terminated. Mira saw from the link data that the second relay pod had gone out. Otto and his suit might still be fine, but data wasn't getting back to the pressurized rover with the relay link having failed. *That's unusual*, she thought. *I've never seen a relay pod malfunction like that.*

She waited another fifteen minutes and decided something was terribly wrong. *Otto has to know that communications have been lost, and mission safety protocol would mandate aborting the exploration and returning to the pressurized rover as soon as possible. He should have been back by now. I'm going to have to go in and find him. If his suit has suffered a failure, time will be critical.*

Mira left a status message for transmission to Mars base on the next relay satellite pass. She exited through the suitport and soon entered the cavern. With the passage illuminated by the side lights on her helmet, Mira followed the Axel's cable toward the location where contact with Otto had been lost. She looked for his comm relay pods along the way and was alarmed that she didn't see any. *That's weird. Where did they go?* When she reached the branch point where multiple passageways converged, she was struck by the extensive nature of the microbial mats overhead, clinging to the icy roof of the cave. *I'm sure there weren't this many sections of mats overhead in the images I saw from Otto's video feed. Could they have grown that fast? I must just be imagining that there are more of them.*

Following the cable farther into the cavern, she found where it had been severed, and Mira was struck with a rush of fear. It was a clean cut that had been made with a tool. *Definitely foul play.* Since she hadn't seen anyone leave the cave, it was certain that the perpetrators were still inside the network of passageways. *The Nisei Data rover must have dropped off the pirates, then left to hide from the reconnaissance orbiter's last overhead pass. The rover will be coming back soon to pick them up.*

Mira scanned through all of the available comm channels and heard voices on one of the rarely used frequencies.

"…really got some good stuff here. Primo Martian Gold." It was a male voice, but distorted by the weak signal.

Mira was surprised it was not encrypted, but unencrypted links were more reliable, and the pirates probably figured they were unlikely to be overheard inside the cave. They must be not far away for her to pick up their comms.

Then she heard a female voice. It was clearer, so they were getting closer. "We have a good haul here. This is the mother lode retirement fund for both of us. We're gonna be livin' high on the hog the rest of our lives. When we get back to Phlegra, we should dose some and have a little fun together to celebrate. Man, I just can't wait to get back home on Earth. I'm so sick of this place. These truffles are the only thing worth a damn on this God forsaken planet, Jack."

Jack? Mira thought. *What the hell!*

"I'm just going to cut off this last juicy gold truffle here."

"Whoa. The mat recoiled and thrashed around when you cut it, like it's feeling pain. Then it reached out and touched your helmet."

"No way, Anne. It's just some kind of reflex reaction. We've seen this with the truffles at Phlegra."

"Whatever. Wrap it up. We need to hustle, 'cause the recon orbiter non-coverage window's going to close. Our ride will be back soon, and we need to skedaddle outta here."

"Okay. We'll finish filling up the cart with truffles, then make it look like the NASA guy got killed in an ice fall over where we cut that two-wheeler rover cable. Make it seem like the ice cut the cable too."

"It's gotta look like a convincing accident. We'll plug the oxygen hose back in, then make sure the ice fall smashes his helmet visor. His data recorder needs to be damaged beyond recovery. And Jack, there's gotta be someone in a rover outside that was operating the two-wheeler. What'll we do about that?"

"Gonna have to wing it. We'll cover our haul with the tarp and warn them about the ice fall. If we can swing it before the relay pass, we can make sure their rover has an accident. A ricocheting rock from the ice fall broke their windshield causing depressurization and tragically killing the crew. We were exploring near the cave area and responded to a distress call. We'll figure out a good story."

Mira wasn't sure if the pirates were ahead of her or behind in another passage. She was panicking and breathing hard as she followed the next section of cable after the cut. There was a curve in the passage up ahead, obscuring what was around the corner. Mira picked up the cable and pulled it. It immediately went taut, so she knew the Axel was not far away, probably just around the bend.

She steeled herself to advance farther into the cave, not knowing if she would run into the pirates. Rounding the corner, she discovered Otto's body crumpled on the ground, just in front of the Axel rover. It was obvious that his air hose and the power cables had been disconnected from his portable life support system, the PLSS, and he appeared lifeless. Staring at her companion in horror, she noticed that slimy blobs of the gold-colored Martian microbes had fallen onto Otto.

She looked up and saw a section of microbial matting overhead, glommed onto the solid ice sheet. The shadows in the cavern were shifting, and lights were shining from behind her. The pirates were coming.

"Well, look who's here," Mira heard Jack say over the comm. She spun around to see two people in EVA suits. They both had guns pointed at her. Behind them was a four-wheeled rover wagon with its cargo bin stacked full of microbial mats.

"I was afraid it was going to be you," Jack said as he read the name tag on the suit and saw the face behind the helmet visor. "This is really unfortunate, Mira."

"You killed Otto!" she screamed. "How could you do this?"

"He was in the way, sweetheart. You two science chumps just had to come by and mess with our operation, didn't you. It's a crummy deal for all of us."

"Stop yappin', Jack" Anne said. "Let's get this done. Our exit window is closing."

Jack leveled his gun and said, "Okay, Anne. You go around to the side of our NASA friend, while I keep a bead on her."

"So, you're going to murder me in cold blood after all the time we spent together. I thought you liked me, Jack."

"Oh, I do, Mira, and I will treasure my memories of all the fun we had. But now, here you are in the wrong place at the wrong time. I'm really sorry it worked out this way, but business is business. There's no way I'm going to jail and giving up my life's fortune."

Mira thought, *They're going to pull my oxygen hose just like they did to Otto, then make it look like we both died in an ice fall.* She muted her microphone and started breathing quickly to hyperventilate and get as much oxygen into her blood as possible. From her decompression training she knew she would have at most fifteen seconds after exposure to vacuum before losing consciousness. Mira also tried to focus on putting her Jiu-Jitsu exercise practice to use. *It's my only chance. I can't make a move yet, though, with a gun pointed at me. Maybe they'll be off guard after they think I'm dead.*

Anne was at her side fiddling with the oxygen feed hose from the PLSS. Mira kept hyperventilating until it was disconnected. Then she exhaled sharply to empty her lungs of air so she wouldn't get an embolism as her suit vented to the near vacuum of the Martian atmosphere. Mira fell to the ground, feigning death, but orienting herself to be able to see Anne. Her eyes were burning, and her skin felt like it was boiling.

As Anne turned to walk away, Mira grabbed her foot, pulled her down, and got her in a twister hold. Jack shot his gun toward Mira but was firing wild, having been taken off guard and disoriented by the sudden turn of events. Mira angled Anne in front of her to use as a shield and Anne took three hits from Jack. Mira was fading fast as Anne's body went slack, and she scrambled for Anne's gun. Still using Anne's body as a shield, Mira got off some shots in Jack's direction as she began losing consciousness. She missed him, but Jack backed away, bolted, and fled around the bend in the passage.

Mira's disconnected hose had been blowing out oxygen, which may have exhausted the supply in her PLSS. In a half-awake fever dream, wracked with pain and with the last of her strength, she disconnected Anne's supply hose and plugged it into her inlet connector. Oxygen immediately rushed into her evacuated suit, and she breathed it in with desperate gulps. Her ears felt like knives were piercing them as Mira swallowed and worked her jaw to equalize them with the sudden increase in pressure.

She fought to clear her head and pushed her tortured body up from the ground to be on her knees. The oxygen hose from Anne's suit was stretched taut, so Mira turned Anne's body to provide additional slack. She momentarily fixated at the nametag on the Nisei Data Company suit which read, "Anne Lufford."

She shook her head to clear it and tried to prepare for Jack's return. Mira figured he would wait until he was sure she was dead from exposure to vacuum. While still anchored to Lufford's body by the oxygen hose, she positioned herself to point the gun down the passageway. She saw a light moving and knew Jack was approaching. When he rounded the corner, Mira fired, but missed. It was pretty hard to aim a pistol in a spacesuit looking through a visor.

Jack was surprised, but got off three shots. Two of them missed, but one of them shattered her helmet visor in a glancing hit. Mira's head was uninjured, but her suit was rapidly evacuating air once again. She thought she was hallucinating as she saw movement in a microbial mat overhead. While struggling to remain conscious again, Mira aimed for another shot at her former lover, but a huge section of truffle matting let loose and fell on Jack, covering his helmet, blinding him, ensnaring his arms, and immobilizing his movements.

Mira dropped the gun, pivoted, unlocked Anne's helmet, removed it, and then took off her own damaged helmet, completely exposing herself to vacuum. She hastily secured Anne's helmet on her suit just before she blacked out.

She awoke to an audible alarm from Anne's PLSS, unsure of how much time had passed. It was the low air supply warning. Her breathing was labored, her lungs were on fire, and blood was oozing out of her eyes and nose. She checked the oxygen supply and saw only a few minutes of air remaining. Mira forced herself up and removed Anne's almost empty PLSS still attached to her suit by the oxygen hose. She carried it and stumbled over to Jack's motionless body to check his condition.

Kneeling before him, she pulled on the section of microbial mat covering his helmet visor and was surprised to see that it easily fell away. Jack's face was white, and he looked quite dead. He was definitely not breathing. With her mind set in survival mode, she felt no immediate grief at his demise. Matting was tightly constricted around his lower neck, just below the helmet ring, and around his entire torso. The mat had contracted powerfully and strangled him like a python.

Mira gently tugged at the mats, and they relaxed and separated from the suit. The microbial colony then slowly retreated away from the body, back toward the edge of the cavern to join other sections of matting.

Checking Jack's PLSS, she saw that the remaining air supply was good, so she closed the valves, unplugged the cables, and detached it from Jack's suit. Mira ditched Anne's PLSS and plugged into Jack's. She daisy chained the supply hoses together so that she wasn't on such a short leash with her oxygen supply. *How am I going to carry all this out of here? Maybe on their truffle truck. I hope I can work it.*

She carried the PLSS over to the cargo rover that was filled with pilfered truffles and tenderly removed the severed microbial mats to set them down near the side of the passageway. Tendrils from the underground mats gradually slithered out to join with them, as if they were rescuing a friend. *These mats are way more active than we could ever have imagined*, she thought. *They're like slime molds on steroids.*

The controls were a standard layout, so she guided the cargo truck over to Otto to transport his body out on the vehicle. She bent down to see his face, which had turned blue, and noticed that the suit was inflated. *That's strange. How could that have happened?* Mira inspected the disconnected oxygen hose and discovered it was completely stuffed and plugged with microbial sludge. *The microbes generate oxygen. How did those critters get in there? What an incredible coincidence.*

She plugged Otto's power cable back into his PLSS, which still had battery power remaining. The body temperature sensor indicated 1.6 degrees centigrade. Incredibly, there was a slow faint pulse. The suit pressure reading was 17.1 kilopascals. The microbes that had filled up Otto's hose were definitely generating oxygen. Mira unplugged the power cable to keep the suit heaters from coming on. *There's a chance he might be saved, like drowning victims in icy cold water. I need to keep him cold and get to the AutoDoc in our rover as soon as possible.* In the one-third gravity of Mars, she was able to pick up Otto and place him on the cargo truck.

Mira walked alongside the rover as she steered it toward the cave's exit. After her two exposures to near vacuum, her lungs were burning, and she could only take shallow breaths. The sharp pain was still in her ears, her skin was raw, and blood crusted in her nose and around her eyes. Mira's head was throbbing, her body ached, and the vision out of her left eye was blurred.

In extreme discomfort, she struggled to focus on her surroundings, but she did notice that microbial mats had emerged to cover much of the walls and ceiling of the cavern. *This was not here when I entered the cave. This level of activity is astonishing.* Mira wished she could examine and document the phenomena, but it was all about survival now.

Emerging from the cave into the Martian sunlight, she saw that a new visitor had pulled up – an unpressurized rover from Nisei Data. The driver leveled a pistol at her, and Mira responded in kind with the pistol she had taken from Anne.

Mira set her comm to broadcast on all of the standard proximity frequencies. "Nisei Data rover, this is Mira DeMayne from Arcadia Station. It looks like we're in a standoff here." She expected no response and received none. "Jack Marchak and Anne Lufford are inside the cave. They are both deceased, and their bodies are at the end of the Axel rover cable. If you want to retrieve them, you can use their cargo truck just as soon as I'm done with it. Everything here is being recorded, so if you shoot me, you will likely be convicted of murder."

The rover driver set down the pistol and waited. Mira took her chances and put away her weapon to focus on saving her friend. Being tethered to Jack's PLSS, and with Otto unconscious, she couldn't use the suitports for entry. Instead, she pumped down the rover's internal air and opened the vehicle's side hatch.

She struggled to carry Otto inside, and again the one-third Martian gravity helped. With the hatch closed and the rover repressurized, she removed their spacesuits and got to work trying to save Otto. Mira hooked him up to the vital signs monitors, the CPR equipment, and an IV feed from the AutoDoc system. There was a pre-programmed routine available for reviving victims from a cold state, and the AutoDoc got to work.

She finally had time to check on what was happening outside. The Nisei Data guy and the cargo truck were gone. He had ventured into the cave. The recon orbiter would be tracking overhead in twenty minutes, but that probably didn't matter at this point. *Nisei Data is totally busted. I hope they get run out of their Phlegra operation, but big money and political connections will probably keep them in business, even after this debacle. They'll find scapegoats to punish and claim no company involvement.*

Mira heard Otto cough, so she rushed over to the AutoDoc. His eyelids were fluttering, and the vital signs on the screen were encouraging. The respirator had automatically turned off, and Otto was breathing on his own. She reached down and held his hand, still cold, but no longer like an icicle. A few minutes later, he woke up, but was shivering violently, so she got a space blanket from the emergency kit to cover him. The shivering subsided, and soon he was able to talk, sit up, and engage in a functional capacity.

Otto considered Mira's injuries from her two decompressions and insisted that she connect to the AutoDoc. She said, "I'm actually feeling better, but I'll hook up in a little while. First, we need to follow protocol and record a debrief while this is all fresh in our minds."

The two began a video recording recounting the horrific events that had transpired. Mira was stoic while describing Jack's death, but she knew she would break down later and shed tears over the treachery and loss.

Otto had divided his attention to watch the ice cavern with binoculars and interrupted Mira's part of the debrief. "The pirate is now just inside the cave entrance. There are no bodies on the cargo truck, but it's piled with microbial mats."

"Greedy bastard."

"It looks like he's cutting off a few more sections just to make sure he has enough."

Suddenly, there was a loud rumble that carried into their vehicle even in the thin atmosphere, and the ground was shaking, rocking the pressurized rover back and forth. Mira and Otto were shocked to see the cave opening collapsing with ice tumbling down from above. The cave-in continued in stages for about a minute, and then the dust began to settle. The ice cave was completely sealed off.

They stared in silence for a time, then Otto said, "It had to have been caused by the microbial mats. Perhaps they went into an exothermal survival mode and melted the ice overhead to cause the cave-in and protect themselves. I'm convinced they are an intelligent colony. They saved my life and then protected us from the murderers who were ripping out pieces of them."

"I don't know, Otto, but I agree that the slime mold things are extraordinary. We need to be even more careful about how we treat them. Whatever motivated the microbes – intelligence, reflex, learned instinct, or something else – they did rescue us from those cutthroats. And now the pirates are buried inside forever with their precious truffles."

--

Humphrey Price is a space systems engineer at NASA JPL who has contributed to robotic exploration missions to the Moon, Mars, Jupiter, and Saturn. His goal is to introduce interesting plausible ideas for space travel, aliens, and the future of the human race through highly realistic hard science fiction stories. You can catch up with his Sci Fi exploits at humphreyprice.com.

The Nerine Seven

By Zachary Taylor Branch

"Wadda ya think, Colonel? Alien attack?" asked Lieutenant Union, shining her torch on an ataxic steel device about the size of a beer keg, but with some sinister-looking protrusions and conduits penetrating the tank casing. Jane was in deep space vacuum gear, on what should have been a routine inspection of the reaction mass tanks. "Frankly, it looks more like a German or Dutch device to me."

"They're our allies, more likely the Entente Cordiale or Maritime Powers using PanWestern design," replied Colonel Glenn. "Definitely not alien. I know our Exochemist will be disappointed." The Colonel was about 30 meters from Jane in the strangely narrow space between the building-sized reaction mass tank, and the even larger Interstitial, the 150-meter-long pylon that connected the main disk of the Nerine Seven with the aft Drive Section.

"This tank will be going active again in less than five minutes," said Jane. "If it's disabled or destroyed, we could shoot right past Mars."

"Possible, but I don't think they're targeting the tank itself, Lieutenant," said the Colonel. "It's opposite the main coupled matter control conduit to the Ion-Electrics. If it blows and severs the conduit, we'll lose control of gravity decoupling and transmitted power from Earth."

Jane immediately took Glenn's meaning, and dialed up Loadmaster Dooley on the comms while her Commander continued his inspection of the limpet. "Mr. Dooley, how quickly can you jettison Reaction Mass Tank Three?"

"That tank is three quarters full, Lieutenant," replied Dooley. "Most of our reserves. We might not be able to brake into orbit on return to Terra, if we lose active gravitics, or…"

Col. Glenn broke in. "Problem for a later date, Loadmaster. The device we've found on Tank Three is dug in like a tick, and the Deep Scan indicates a timer mechanism and remote thermal energy coupler. It's a Tesla Bomb, no doubt. Fire explosive bolts and peroxide thrusters on Tank Three. Now!"

"Sir, the tank load is not equalized," responded Dooley, his usual condescension giving way to anxiety. "It's going to tumble on separation, you could be..."

"We can take care of ourselves, Loadmaster!" yelled Glenn. "Push the button now!"

Union and Glenn saw the small explosions as the bolts fired, and the bright white jets of the peroxide rockets straining to push Tank Three away from the Nerine Seven. But the rockets weren't all firing, and the tank was pivoting toward the Interstitial. Glenn was pulling himself toward the airlock, when one of the heat transfer fins of Tank Three started to scrape along the Interstitial, and caught his left foot in a tangle of debris pushed ahead of the pinch. Jane heard Glenn shout some very atypical profanities over the comms, and call for help with his suit breach.

The Nerine Seven was heading ass backwards into the Mars system. Jane was forward of Glenn, and estimated it would take at least a minute to climb back down to him through the debris field. The bright purple exhaust jets of the ship's ion-electric engines, even at low thrust station-keeping, were almost obscuring the red disk of Mars, and the slightly smaller silver disk of her big moon, Nerine. But Tank Three was moving aft at an increasing relative speed just a few feet overhead, so Jane kicked off and caught a ride toward her Commander.

Glenn's profanity shifted from distress about his foot to threats about prematurely ending Jane's career in First Fleet when he saw her near-suicidal maneuver. But within seconds, she had pushed back over to the Nerine Interstitial and was applying tactical sealant to Glenn's ruined boot, even as she helped haul him the remaining meters to the airlock.

"God, I hate it when Dooley's right," said Glenn, after a long wait for the airlock pressure to equalize. "I'll get Tom to patch up my foot, should be good to go in a few days for the landing. I would be much obliged if we could leave that one detail out of our report on the attempted sabotage of Tank Three."

"Not a problem, Colonel," said Jane. "Just a routine tank inspection. Well, other than the fact that someone tried to blow us out of the sky, and we completely lost the tank. Wouldn't mind taking a few shifts off, though."

Two days later, July 19, 1954, The Nerine Seven was approaching areosynchronous orbit above Syrtis Major. Jane and Mission Exochemist Peter Protean, looking like a couple of school kids trying to keep a secret, were the last to return to the bridge. Jane slipped a photo of a little girl to Chief Scientist Tom Congress with a wink and a grin. Tom touched it lightly with crossed fingers and handed it to Pilot Al Shepard.

"Wish us good fortune, little Janie," he said, handing the photo to Colonel Glenn.

"Lord, spacers are a superstitious lot," he said, but he touched Janie's pictures with cross fingers nonetheless and handed it back to Peter, as he strapped in next to Jane at the Survey station. A hand-drawn note above his crash station read:

Life? Maybe
Chemistry? Definitely

"I've never failed to return to my little girl, Colonel, don't intend to jinx a spotless record now," said Jane, tucking the picture back into a thigh pouch.

"Indeed, I would not dare disappoint Janie and her Grans. Approach report, Al," said Col. Glenn.

"It's Route 66, John, and we're about five minutes from Santa Monica," said Captain Shepard, with his usual mischievous grin. "Re-vectoring, tweaking ion drives to 0.12g decel., on target for orbital insertion 11,017 miles above Syrtis Major, t-minus 350 seconds."

"Lieutenant, any anomalies showing on the telemetry from the remote drones?", asked Glenn. He and Jane had quietly re-purposed almost all the Nerine maintenance drones for exterior scans of the ship after the attack on Tank Three.

"All clear, sir," replied Union. "Some intermittent contacts trailing us. Could be debris from the Tank Three explosion, trying to get some clearer returns."

"Keep on it, Jane, don't want any more rude surprises to mess up our big day. Loadmaster, any imagery or telemetry from HMS

Cabot?" asked Col. Glenn, over a noticeably increased vibration felt in the chest and static heard over the comms as the ion-electric drives pushed the last of the outward-bound aqueous reaction mass through the electrohydrodynamic tubes.

"No, sir," said James Dooley, the Logistician, the only commercial contractor aboard the Nerine Seven. There was some debate about his proper title. "We've had no signals from the Cabot for three days. If they made Mars ahead of us, they've said nothing about it."

The Whiteboards on the port and starboard bulkheads of the bridge flickered to life, with the projected image of Major Gus Grissom, the Nerine Seven Flightmaster. Gus was very reluctantly dirt-side, directing a mission that he'd hoped to command. "No word from the British Admiralty on the fate of the Cabot, John. They should have achieved orbit three days ago. We're assuming the mission was lost, the limeys would have lost no time announcing the first successful landing on Mars, and their claim to unreasonable swaths of Martian real estate."

"Thanks, Gus, we'll try to do better than the Brits," said Col. Glenn, in an immediate response, since there is no time lag in coupled matter communications. "Drivemaster, gravitics and power report, if you please."

"Tesla-electric coupling to Earth at 95% efficiency, more than sufficient power for orbital insertion and normal ship functions," said Engineer Elsa Watt. "We have gravity decoupling, but no active gravitics. We will require the Ion-Electrics to thrust out of orbit. And the Whitehall generator on the surface is still not operational, base camp is functioning on solar-electric power only."

"No Dutch Process, and no Whitehall power," said Col. Glenn. "Just gravity decoupling and remote transmitted electrical power, the same Tesla technology we had 60 years ago during the Second Western War. Could be worse, I suppose. We're on final approach, Gus... Orbital insertion in five, four, three, two, one, engines stop."

The ship slipped back into free fall, and the rumble and static from the main drives ceased. After a brief silence, Lt. Union said, "Well, that was anticlimactic."

"Not the first words from Mars that we want share with the rest of the world," said Col. Glenn. "Gus, we have stable areosynchronous orbit, we will assume a lower orbit if...."

"Sooner rather than later, Colonel," said Jane with deceptive calm.

"I have bogies now, several dozen, small, but making over 100 km/sec, our terminal velocity out from Earth. Direct intercept course with the Nerine, 45 second to collision."

"The buggers targeted our orbital insertion point, probably how they got the Cabot as well," said Col. Glenn. "Drivemaster, Loadmaster, Delta 27, if you would be so kind."

The crew was still strapped into crash stations, and glad of it. The port Ion-Electrics restarted, and the Nerine started a hard pivot on her center of gravity, as her bows turned directly towards Mars. The groans and pops of the over-stressed Interstitial were transmitted through the bones of the ship, so the crew could hear the Nerine trying to tear herself apart, even over the din of klaxons and collision alarms.

"Al, thrusters at your discretion!" yelled Col. Glenn. Shepard fired the forward starboard thrusters, trying to keep the Nerine from going into a spin. She began to make an arcing course towards the surface of Mars.

"Bogie spread increasing, three still on collision course!" yelled Jane, barely audible over the comms.

Drivemaster Watt threw a few more toggles, and the crew was pushed backed harder into their seats. The rumble of the engines increased, and Mars, which had been little more than a reddish dot for most of the two-week crossing from Earth, was now a curved wall of mountains and craters getting closer at an alarming rate.

A few seconds later, the crew heard, and felt, a sharp bang and low rumble from the aft of the ship.

"All engines stop," said Glenn, back in a normal tone of voice as the ship's noise began to return to its usual low rumble. "Al, stabilize our orbit and engage gravity decoupling. Drivemaster, damage report."

"Telemetry still coming in, looks like we lost some meteorite shielding and hull plating in the Drives section... Indication of hull breach, loss of pressure near Engine Two, minor control system damage... Doesn't look like anything I can't fix," said Watt, as she sealed her flight suit and made for a long, lonely passage through the Interstitial to her damaged engines.

"What the Hell is going on up there!" yelled Grissom, his face near crimson on the big Whiteboard.

"Sorry to ignore you Gus, we've been kinda busy. Let the Big Brains know their hunch on the follow-up attack was correct. The limpet probably attached while we were booming out of Earth orbit two weeks ago, it didn't have enough relative speed for a kinetic attack. The bogies that just hit us must have also used negative gravity acceleration from Terra, targeting our orbital insertion point at full transit velocity. Any leads on who the Hell is shooting at us?"

"Nothing yet, John, most of the Big Nine are officially shocked and pointing fingers at each other. But not a word from the Brits. If they know what got the Cabot, they're not saying. Are you still mission capable, or do you need to scrub?"

"Scrub my ass, we're going to Mars, Gus. Mr. Dooley, make ready Lander Romulus, Captain Shepard and I will crew the first landing, and I want to be ready for descent as soon as we reach working orbit. We are currently on Mission Profile Alpha 4: single lander, two-man crew, four hours on the surface at Campus Martius, return to the Nerine with minimal collections. If successful, we will attempt landing in force. Now back to work, Al and I don't get to be famous until we land on this damned planet and return home safely."

And famous they became. Col. Glenn delayed landing for a few hours, having finally gotten word that the British Admiralty was about to announce the loss of HMS Cabot. It was a terse, cryptic dispatch, and the Brits were clearly still baffled about the sudden disappearance of an erstwhile successful mission that was on track to beat the Americans to Mars. And they had not replied to the classified dispatch from First Fleet about the attacks on the Nerine Seven.

"Nerine, this is Romulus," came Col. Glenn's voice over the comms, about two hours after the lander had undocked from the Interstitial. "We are hovering 1000 feet over Campus Martius. Gravity decoupling is still active, but no active gravitics. We have sufficient reaction mass for an Ion-Electric return-to-orbit launch when needed. The base looks to be in good shape, we are reading active telemetry from the Castellum and the ETV, time to go down for a visit. We are targeting an exposed basalt patch, 100 feet in diameter, approximately 3-degree pitch, about 150 yards from Castellum. Smooth ride, slow descent, Romulus responding well to Captain Shepard's commands. 500 feet now…400 feet, seeing some dust now, odd since our thrusters are at low power. Visibility still good. It's local dawn here, a new day at Syrtis Major. 200 feet…100 feet, dust diminishing, landing site is flat basaltic slabs, no boulders or large rocks. 40 feet…20 feet…10 feet…contact, engine stop."

The comms went quiet, a stray solar flare creating more noise on the networks than the billions waiting for word from Mars.

"Flightmaster, this is Colonel John Glenn of the Nerine Seven, the Romulus has landed."

Every communications network in the Solar System erupted, and the rest of the crew could barely hear Major Grissom trying to send instructions and demand status reports, until they switched back to a private band. They still had to get Glenn safely onto the surface and back to the Nerine Seven in one piece.

Like most gravity decoupled aircraft and spacecraft, Romulus was disk shaped. She was about 80 feet in diameter and was actually hovering about 10 feet above the Martian surface. The landing legs were not load bearing, a gravity decoupled ship didn't need that, but they had sunk concussion anchors into the black Martian rocks to provide stability should a freak dust storm suddenly pop up. Within 30 minutes, the main lift was cycling downward from the lower center of the Romulus, carrying Col. Glenn in an armored expeditionary suit. First Fleet was taking few chances with the first American on Mars. The lift pad came to a halt just a few inches above the Martian surface.

"Flightmaster, this is Col. Glenn. The main lift is deployed, and even with Romulus overhead, I have an excellent view of Campus Martius and the surrounding Martian terrain. Syrtis Major rises gently to the west, and to the east, I can see the flat expanse of Isidis Planitia. It's a study in contrast. Syrtis is all broken black rock, though Dr. Protean will be glad to know that I'm seeing some rather thick frost in the shade of the larger basalt slabs. The Isidis is a flat expanse of deep red sand, and even at this distance I can see the finer sands blowing over the tops of the dunes at the foot of Syrtis. A thin cloud of reddish dust appears to be blowing up the flank of Syrtis, but not enough to impede visibility. The surface directly below Romulus is broken basalt sheets, but not flat black, I'm seeing some granular texture, and flecks of color, reds and greens. Should keep our Exochemist occupied for a while. I'm preparing to step off the lift now."

After a few seconds, Col. Glenn spoke again. "Mankind has Come to Mars."

Most people on Earth did not hear what came next, as thousands of commentators and well-wishers overwhelmed the comms, but Glenn carried on. "We dedicate our first base, Campus Martius, to the brave men and women who have given their lives so that we lucky few may explore a new, possibly living world. We bring our industry and curiosity... "

The crew aboard the Nerine Seven knew the speech, and they had other priorities. In a profound violation of flight protocols, a liter of Imperial Romanov vodka was suddenly produced. And then another. The first American crew to Mars was somewhat in their cups when their commanders returned triumphantly six hours later. Glenn and Shepard polished off the third bottle themselves.

"You are go for landing in force, assuming any of you can see straight," said Major Grissom over the Nerine Seven Whiteboards, early on the second human day at Mars.

"Great news, Gus," said Glenn, nursing his third cup of coffee. "The rest of the crew is bouncing up and down like a bunch of toddlers on Christmas morning. We are now on mission profile Beta Three: Congress, Dooley and Watt will land at Martius in Lander Romulus, and prepare the base for permanent occupation. Tom, you'll return to the Nerine in the Expeditionary Transport Vehicle as soon as the Drivemaster and Logistician have certified that she's ready for flight. Should be a nice break from your Chief Scientist duties, but remember, this is the first solo human flight in the Martian system, a high-risk mission profile."

"Not to worry, John," said Dr. Congress. "I helped design the ETV; she's hardly a spaceship at all, more like a tank. She's slow, doesn't maneuver worth a damn, but very reliable. Remote telemetry shows all redundant systems are operational. I promise I won't wreck the car, Dad."

"Very good," said Col. Glenn, continuing with his mission briefing. "Once off-loading of the Martian water and volatiles is complete, and the ETV is cleared for return flight capability, Union and Protean will take Lander Remus to Martius, to begin geological and chemical surveys. I must emphasize that all future mission profiles require at least one lander or transport at the Nerine and Campus Martius at all times. So Jane, no expeditions beyond range of the flying rigs, because we're not going to send another ship out into the wild to save your asses - too much risk to the rest of the crew. Understood?"

"Crystal clear, sir," said Jane. "With your permission, Dr. Protean and I will retire for mission consultations while the rest of the crew makes ready for our triumphant arrival on Mars."

Shepard and Congress were chuckling, Dooley looked annoyed, and Watt just shrugged and headed alone to the lander for pre-flight checks. Glenn rolled his eyes and told everyone just to do their damned jobs. Which they all did, even Pete and Jane, after a fashion.

Within a few days, the Nerine Seven (crew and ship went by the same name) were firing on all cylinders. The Castellum was fully operational, with pre-positioned foodstuffs and provisions to maintain a crew of three for 18 months, by which time at least two more Nerine missions should arrive at the Campus. There was a steady flow of water and nitrogen from the air factory, and oxygen from the cracking plant, which was converting native water and carbon dioxide into O_2 and basic sugars, in a man-made version of the photosynthetic process. Most of the sugar was going to a modified yeast reactor, which was primarily producing nutritional fats and proteins and vitamins, but which also produced a fair amount of ethanol as a well-received by-product, Martian Moonshine. The algae plant got all the waste products, and helpfully produced more oxygen and pressed algae cakes, as long as the carbon dioxide and water kept coming. Which was not a problem, so far.

Drivemaster Watt had even gotten the Whitehall Generator working, though she had travelled alone over a mile of rough terrain to coax it back to life. Like all coupled matter technology, Whitehalls were fussy, and had an annoying habit of shutting down or blowing up without humans in close proximity.

Tom Congress got the fully stocked ETV launched, and off-loaded enough water to provide reaction mass for the Nerine to brake into Earth orbit, in the unlikely event that Dutch Process (active gravitics, not the cocoa) failed in cis-lunar space, and the Nerine Seven was unable to use negative gravity to bring herself safely into Earth orbit. All of which meant that it was finally Jane and Peter's turn to begin the first human exploration of Mars.

"Lander Remus ready for launch," said Jane from the pilot's seat.

"Go for launch," responded Col. Glenn from the bridge of the Nerine. "Dr. Protean, you have Coupled Matter Radio connection to the PanWestern Exchange, and may begin your mission update."

Peter was looking a bit nervous until Jane gave him a wink and a big thumbs up.

"This is Dr. Peter Protean aboard the Nerine Seven Lander Remus.

We are leaving our gravity-decoupled working orbit, other coupled bodies in the Solar System are experiencing decreased gravitational attraction as we re-establish our gravitational connection to Mars. Active gravitics, also mediated through the coupled matter built into the lander, are still not active here in the Martian system, so we will use the ion-electric engines for our return launch."

"Remote-entangled coupled matter, first discovered on Earth in iron/nickel meteorites in the wake of the 1859 Carrington Event, provides the instantaneous communications, energy transmission and gravity exchange that has allowed mankind to travel this far through the Solar System."

"My colleagues at the Virginia Institute and I also believe that it could be the basis of alien life. Remote spectroscopic analysis of Mars indicates abundant ataxic iron/nickel and platinoid on the surface, and my published work argues that coupled matter life may in fact be more robust and widespread than the carbon-based life of Earth that we currently take as the norm. Mars will be our first opportunity to test this thesis. When Pilot Jane Union and I land at the verge of Amazonia Planitia, we will begin a survey…"

Jane made an overly dramatic yawning gesture and toggled her comms over the NBC Blue Network broadcast of Glenn Miller's latest Little Band compositions. Peter was holding forth in his Bold Scientific Explorer mode, and he didn't notice at all.

After a leisurely two-hour decent to the surface, and an obligatory stop at Martius to check in with a vaguely hostile Logistician Dooley, Jane and Peter took Lander Remus down the slopes of Syrtis to the transition zone between the volcanic mountain and the sandy plains of Isidis Planitia. Things did not go as planned.

"Nerine, Martius, this is Dr. Protean. Lander Remus is hovering at the foot of a shallow incline near the base of the Syrtis Massif. Lt. Union is at the controls of the lander. I have just stepped off the lift platform, and I'm walking to the base of the incline. Treading through this very fine, deep red sand makes for slow going, like trying to walk up the dunes at Kitty Hawk. And with this armored suit and gear, I have an effective weight of almost one hundred and ninety pounds, even in this low Martian gravity."

"There are well-defined dark streaks on the incline; I'm headed toward one, very good chance that it's a water seep. There is a jumble of rocks at the base of the nearest seep, and it's a strange collection.

I'm seeing dark basaltic blocks with the red and green inclusions that Col. Glenn observed. I'm also seeing reddish rocks, quartz-based, that look like terrestrial jasper. I'm in the middle of the rock field now, seeing something new. A number of the red stones have a silvery mottling, I'm moving closer so you can see the images from my helmet camera, preparing to take a sample."

Back aboard the Nerine, Tom Congress was intently studying the new images Peter was sending, as they were projected on the big starboard Whiteboard. "Pete, use the X-ray fluorescence spectrometer before you take a sample, I want an elemental profile of the rock and the mottling first."

"No problem, Boss," said Peter, "I've just unslung the XRF, getting spectra now. The base rock is rich in silicon and aluminum, lots of iron, traces of nickel and titanium, looks like a Martian variant of terrestrial jasper. I'm moving to the silvery patch now. Totally different spectrum. Abundant phosphorus and sulfur, very weak returns for carbon and nitrogen, but this unit's not sensitive to light elements. And Wow! Look at all the nickel and iron and platinoids! I know this profile, Tom, it's…"

"Close to what you described in your last *Extraterrestrial Sciences* article, but don't start preparing your Nobel speech just yet," said Tom. "There's a lot we need to establish before we can declare the existence of coupled matter life. Energy management, reproduction, motility…"

"May just have obliged you, Boss," replied Peter. "The silvery splotch just moved!"

"I saw it, too, Pete," said Jane over the comms. "It's raising filaments right along your XRF beam line. It doesn't seem to mind X-rays at all, it's acting like a plant seeking light."

"And it sounds like something I do not want on my ship," said Col. Glenn, now also studying the Whiteboard images intently. "Back away from the anomaly, Pete, and turn your camera a bit to the right, something strange is showing up on the Whiteboards here."

Pete contemplated disobeying for a moment, he was inches away from sampling the first alien life found in the history of humanity, but then he saw what Col. Glenn was asking about.

"I'm seeing it now, Colonel, but I sure as Hell can't explain it. There are some new features in the rock field now, they look almost like stalagmites, but that couldn't be since we're not in a cave. And they're… not solid, I can see through them, they're like ghost rocks. And Jesus, they're moving too, they're growing, changing colors."

"Pete, this is Jane. Your comms are starting to break up. Move out of the rock field, and get back to the Remus. Now!"

"I concur, Pete," said Col. Glenn. "Make for the Remus immediately, and Jane, close with Pete at best possible speed."

"Colonel, this is Logistician Dooley. We've just lost communications with the Remus, and I can't raise Drivemaster Watt. We're starting to acquire some rather strange images at Campus Martius, as well."

"Mr. Dooley, patch your external cameras into the Nerine bridge," said Col. Glenn. "Jane, are you in contact with Martius? Do you have Dr. Protean yet?"

"Negative on both, sir," said Jane. "Our feed from Martius has gone dead, but Pete is only about one hundred feet away. Boost your gain, sir, we are beginning to lose your signal. And we're seeing more of those translucent rock towers. They look like cypress knees to me, smooth texture but knobbly, and growing fast enough to see in real time. They're becoming more solid. I'm seeing very complex coloration, speckles of primary colors moving across them, shifting patterns, like a…"

"A cuttlefish!" said Pete, cutting in on the comms. "Definitely surface chromatophores, I think they're signaling to each other! A purely visual language, we should have brought a painter or a Gestalt psychologist. The alien formations are increasing in number, and they're definitely becoming more solid. Haven't had to try to walk through any yet but wouldn't want to risk it. Almost at the lift platform now, any word from Watt and Dooley at Martius?"

"We are still receiving their transmissions, but signal strength is decreasing rapidly," said Col. Glenn. "Loadmaster, do you think you can safely make your way with Drivemaster Watt to Lander Romulus?"

"I'm not sure, sir," said Dooley. "I assume you're seeing what we are, and Drivemaster Watt reports by courier drone that she's seeing the same thing, so if we've gone mad, we're having the same delusion. There are men out there, lots of them, in battle armor, but ghostly, translucent, you can see through them. I'm seeing vehicles as well, and banners, it's like an Army unit on maneuvers. They're marching up the flank of Syrtis Major. And I can see their insignia now, it's becoming clearer, but like nothing I've seen before. It's a broken black cross on a white circle, all on a blood red background. I don't think they can see us yet, sir, but there are a number of them between us and the lander."

"Colonel, this is Jane. I have Peter, and we still can't hear Martius directly, but I just heard the Loadmaster's last transmission over the comms from Nerine. We're making our way back to base camp; we'll pick up Dooley and Watt at Martius and return them to the Nerine."

"Negative!" yelled Col. Glenn. "You and Dr. Protean are to return directly to the Nerine, now! Whatever trouble Dooley and Watt may be in, we don't need you and Pete in the same mess. Is that clear, Lieutenant?"

"Your transmission is breaking up, sir," said Jane. "Following last instructions: Proceed to Campus Martius, recover Loadmaster and Drivemaster and return all crew to the Nerine Seven." And then she flicked off the comms.

"That's not what he said, Jane," said Peter, as he entered the cramped bridge of the Lander. He'd shed his armor and paltry collection of samples, none of which appeared to be anything more than common Martian rocks, in the isolation chamber.

"Don't care, Pete," said Jane, "Not going to abandon comrades in the field."

Col. Glenn cursed under his breath, the pain in his foot reminding him not to swear over the comms again. "If any of us survive this thing, I will see Union in the brig for a decade. OK, we're stuck with failing communications, two very different sets of emerging anomalies and an unauthorized rescue mission. Al, Tom, what in blazes is going on down there on Mars, and how do we get our crew back in one piece?"

"John, I think there is more than one Mars down there," said Dr. Congress, rubbing his brow, and writing out short text messages to Dooley and Watt telling them to sit tight for now. "There's been a lot of speculation at the Virginia Institute about these types of phenomena for years. In the early years of modern astronomy, when we looked out at the planets and asteroids, the images were always fuzzy, and it wasn't just bad optics. We now know that we were looking at multiple versions of these worlds, from innumerable parallel realities. It's one of the reasons there was so much debate about the moons of Mars and Venus. Some observers said Mars had no moon, or two small asteroidal moons, and it took time for consensus to develop that Mars just has one large satellite, Nerine, our namesake."

"Of course, the 1859 sightings were definitive," said Glenn, recalling his astronomical training at Purdue. "But how does a dusty old debate about whether Nerine actually exists or not help us to rescue our crew?"

"It's critical, sir," said Congress. "Like with Nerine, there must be different versions of Mars, and they're in play on the surface right now. We landed on a fairly barren one with primitive life at best, and I think Protean and Union are drifting into another Mars with a complex ecosystem, possibly based on coupled matter. Dooley and Watt seem to be drifting into yet another Mars, one with other humans, almost certainly from Earth, but another version of Earth, with different nations, different flags. We need to get everyone back to the Nerine soonest and beat feet back to Earth while we still can."

"Bullshit," said Shepard, with an uncharacteristically somber expression. "Those Savants at the VI have been trotting out those fairy tales since the early days of manned space flight, at least since Admiral Byrd first achieved high orbit in '37. This has got to be some sort of mass hallucination, maybe some contaminant in the food supply, or mild anoxia, we may have the oxygen titers dialed down too low. Or some type of psychological attack by the buggers that tried to blow us out of the sky. The Russians are masters of unconventional warfare. John, have the crew take some hyperbaric treatment at Martius, get a good sleep, and we'll start comprehensive environmental and intel surveys, and get to the bottom of this. We can't abandon Mars. Protean may well have found alien life down there, and it could be the most valuable thing ever found by humans."

Col. Glenn was obviously torn between the opinions of his two most trusted advisors, but he didn't remain that way for long. "Colonel, this is Logistician Dooley. There is more movement down here. The troops out there have definitely seen us, they are emplacing weapons, something like grenade launchers. Transmissions are fading and we've lost almost all telemetry from the Nerine. I believe the alien troops are preparing to fire, Drivemaster Watt and I are going to make our way to…"

The comms from Campus Martius went dead. All evidence of Loadmaster Dooley and Drivemaster Watt on Mars simply disappeared.

"Dear God," said Dr. Congress. "We have no audio, no video, no telemetry or movement or heat signatures from Dooley and Watt. Martius and Whitehall telemetry is normal, all systems operational, and the alien anomalies are also gone. But it's like Dooley and Watt never existed. "

"Al, raise Lander Remus, even if you have to fire a missile with a note attached into their bridge," said Col. Glenn.

Captain Shepard started working the comms without a word, obviously shaken that the Nerine Seven (Nerine Five?) were facing something far more serious than anoxia or food poisoning or psy-ops. The Remus responded almost immediately.

"Colonel Glenn, this is Lt. Union, we are approaching Campus Martius. Are the Loadmaster and Drivemaster aboard the Castellum?"

"Jane, boost your signal, your transmission is very weak," said Col. Glenn. "Dooley and Watt have disappeared, as have the anomalies they were seeing. Do not attempt rescue, do not disembark Lander Remus. Make for the Nerine, crash climb, immediately!"

Pete responded before Jane could. "Aye, sir, I'm priming the Ion-Electrics for a 1g emergency climb. We're very sorry about Dooley and Watt, but check your Whiteboards again, sir, we have a lot of anomalies at Campus Martius. And some of them are flying."

The alien troops had disappeared, but Martius now appeared to be overgrown by the Martian rock knobs. The images on the Nerine Whiteboards showed that the ghost rocks had reappeared, and grown to the size and shape of trees. It was an odd semi-solid forest, like a children's picture book of the deep, dark forest drawn, or read, by someone on particularly good hallucinogens. The trunks were curving cylinders covered in ever-changing patterns of colors, streaks and splashes of bright primaries here, and subdued black/white speckling there. And the multi-colored crowns were sprouting fronds, which may or may not have been swaying in the Martian breeze, the instrumentation on Remus appeared badly conflicted on the composition and density of the outside atmosphere. But regardless, the tips of the swaying fronds were twisting, and with wild splashes of color were pinching off to form somewhat amorphous floating blobs of color, which slowly resolved into more solid, disk-shaped flyers.

Peter was staring slack-jawed through the main viewing port and whispering to himself, "Most beautiful thing I've ever seen…" Jane was distracted by other matters.

"Col. Glenn, this is Jane. We are losing gravity decoupling, and remote electrics are failing. I'm maneuvering over to the Castellum, we'll dock and recharge the capacitors, go for a 2g crash climb on battery and transmitted power."

Tom didn't like the sound of that at all and went to the Ion-Electrics control station. "John, the Nerine is also losing gravity decoupling and Tesla electric power from Earth. Jane needs to launch immediately, and we need to punch out of orbit in less than two hours if we're going to make it home."

Glenn was preparing new orders for Union and Protean when Major Grissom's image appeared on the Whiteboard. "John, I hope we've been misreading your transmissions, because none of us here can believe what's happening up there. Any word from Dooley or Watt?"

"No, Gus," said Col. Glenn, "I'm afraid we've lost them. I'm inclined to believe Dr. Congress' interpretation; I think Dooley and Watt have translated to a parallel reality, and we're in danger of losing Union and Protean. It appears that as they drift into another reality, we lose communications and coupled electrics and gravitics. Remus is going to attempt a crash climb..."

Jane broke in over the shared channel. "Tommy, it's about connection! We need to stay in contact with Earth, with home! Victoria and James were loners, no immediate family, no lovers... Get the Grans and Janie on the Exchange Line. Now!"

Dr. Congress and Jane were second cousins, and both doted on Jane's daughter, now staying with their grandmothers, sisters Crystal and Beryl, back on Earth. Tom was very familiar with Jane's tones of voice and did not hesitate. Seconds later, Whiteboards on the Nerine and Lander Remus were showing images of two older ladies, wearing identical sundresses and with impeccably styled gray hair. A young girl, the spitting image of Jane, was zooming back and forth in front of them.

"Janie, Tom, what a pleasant surprise," said Crystal. "We thought you'd be busy with the mission, it's all anyone here in Winchester can talk about. Imagine, two members of our family on the first mission to Mars." Little Janie had now stopped, and was waving to the little Sprite floating in her grandmothers' living room, and transmitting their images to Mars instantaneously by Coupled Matter Radio.

Jane felt her tension begin to unwind as she waved back at Little Janie. The connections were sharpening, she could virtually smell Beryl's pork roast. Power indicators on the Remus began to move back into the green, and Jane flipped the emergency launch toggle with great enthusiasm. She and Pete were pushed down into their crash stations as the lander leapt into the pinkish Martian sky, which quickly darkened to deep purple, then black. A few minutes later they saw a bright light ahead. It was the Nerine Seven, her main drives engaging, as she pushed into a rendezvous with the Remus, on a trajectory for Earth. Pete turned to Jane, who was not looking entirely pleased to be going home.

"I can't believe I left them behind, without even a second thought," said Jane.

"You're getting us home, Jane. We'd be of no use to James and Elsa if we disappeared, too. We can plan now, figure out how to move between realities deliberately. Maybe even learn how to communicate with those beautiful flying creatures. We're going to need something way fancier than an XRF and sampling kit on our next survey."

"The next survey…," said Jane, removing her helmet and gauntlets. "Won't include me. I'm crossways pretty bad with Glenn, my piloting days may be over. But I can be your anchor, Pete, like Janie and the Grans were for me. The Big Brains will let you come back to Mars, you're the most famous scientist in the world now. Just promise me you'll make them look for James and Elsa, while you go commune with the aliens."

"It's a deal, Jane," said Pete, taking her hand. She squeezed back hard. "You can't get lost if you know how to get home."

--

Zachary Taylor Branch, a.k.a. Mark Brickhouse, Ph.D., is a semi-retired scientist and consultant, enjoying the good life in Lorena, TX. He is currently supporting food security and community resilience efforts at Baylor University with his wife Nancy. "The Gray Horizon" was his first professional fiction sale, his short story "The Gateway" is in process for the B Cubed Press Alternative Truths series, and "Doctor Decon" received an Honorable Mention in Allegory's Fall 2023 issue. His non-fiction and fiction writing are profiled on his webpage, www.brickhouseconsultancy.com and blog, www.zacharytaylorbranch.com His family has deep roots in Virginia, the basis of his fictional New Elisia, and his children David and Elise are too far away in Saint Louis and Houston, pursuing careers in counseling and medicine.

Birthing the Unborn

By Kellee Kranendonk

The excitement built as we made our way down into the underground cave. The leader of our excursion, and my friend, Dr. Cris Jones, stopped a few minutes later, turned to face us, and put a finger to his mouth to stop our eager chatter.

"Listen," he said softly. Some didn't hear and they leaned in closer. "That hum. Do you hear it?"

A murmur ran through our small group, then each one of us nodded. We could all hear the staticky hum in the air, which almost felt electric. I'd thought it was just me.

"That's them," he told us.

"Communicating?" I asked, just as softly.

Cris nodded. "We believe so." He turned and continued leading us below ground. Not only did the hum grow louder, but the air grew warmer, not colder. We'd been told at the surface that these crystalline creatures created high temperatures. Heat intolerable to humans for lengthy time periods. We were just going to observe for a few short minutes.

Then we entered the cavern.

Giant, elongated crystals hung from the ceiling and rose up from the ground, some singular, others in clusters. Most were a pearly white, but others were an opalescent pink or blue. The heat was excruciating, the hum deafening.

The beauty made me want to stay and observe, but knowing that the heat could boil me from the inside out if I stayed too long severely dampened that desire. I turned to leave with the rest, but suddenly I was somewhere else.

The sky was red-orange, the land a bleak brown. I'd seen images from the Mars Rover, so I recognized where I was. The atmosphere was reasonably warm, though I could sense a greater heat beyond my scope of feeling. Clearly the crystals had done this, but how?

All around me was a chattering that sounded like whispers. Then someone called my name.

"Wanda!"

I spun toward the sound. There stood a white crystal, throbbing and nearly too bright to look at.

My heart and my breathing increased. I couldn't keep my eyes on whatever creature this was, yet not doing so gave me a sense of guilt.

"Wanda?"

How did it know my name? Was it reading my thoughts? I didn't even know how to respond so I forced myself to look, but there was no discernable face. I wasn't sure where to focus.

"We are in the time frame known to you as 2027, is this correct?" Where was it speaking from? "Yes, that's correct."

"We believe you are ready now."

"Me?"

"Your kind."

"My kind?"

"Humans."

Oh, right. "Ready for what?"

"Us."

What did that even mean? I had no idea what the creature was talking about nor why it chose me. I looked around again, this time noticing that the other members of my group were here. Yet they weren't here. The forms I saw were like ghostly images, frozen in time. Did they see me in the same way? Had we just been in the "right" place at the "right" time? What was it these creatures wanted from us? I could only hope they were peaceful.

"What? You… Who are you?" I stammered.

"We are the… " It paused. "I believe in your language you would say crystals. We are not, but we accept your name for our kind. My individual name is … Jhi. Your kind would be unable to pronounce our names for ourselves. This is my true form."

The crystalline body began to bulge and stretch, something that was both repulsive and fascinating. A sort of carved face formed on the upper end. Round eyes like opals, barely distinguishable from the rest. No nose. The mouth was a slit. The cylindrical body faded to an iridescent lilac and tentacles emerged, long and soft, almost like hair except for the small suckers on the underside. It was on these suckered appendages that it propelled itself from place to place.

"We feel you are ready to accept us for what we really are. You have overcome most of your phobias, and have become a more accepting society. You are ready for first contact."

Why now? I thought about that hum. Were these creatures really trying to communicate with us, as Cris had said. Or were they just listening to us, getting to know us?

Before I could ask, I was back in the cavern and Cris was already herding us out of the heat. Back on the surface, we all stood just breathing and looking at one another for a moment. Cris spoke first. "Did you all experience that?"

Everyone nodded.

"They said we were ready for them," I mentioned.

Nods all around. Jhi had informed us all.

"What do you think they want?" asked one of the others named Gayla. I had only met her since joining this research team, but we'd hit it off and become friends.

This time shrugs from each one. Like me, we couldn't imagine what such creatures would want from humans.

"Surely they're peaceful," said Cris. "They've been here for a very long time and haven't done anything harmful yet."

"Except that heat," said a woman named Jill. "But they wouldn't need us to be "ready" in order to wage war. They could simply overtake us."

Not only that, but they could have killed us where we stood. Instead, they opened themselves up to us, showed us who they really were. We were excited to get to know them better.

Not everyone shared in that excitement. After an amazing explosion, which we and the crystals had planned along with a few government officials, many humans went around shouting how it was the end of the world. Those of us who were 'woke' now, and wanted to know this strange new creature who'd made itself known to us, called them crazy, conspiracy theorists. Essentially, they were a harmless bunch who stuck to themselves. That was fine with me.

We welcomed the crystals, wanted them to feel accepted and loved. After all, isn't that what we preached, what we had been striving for? Eventually some of the 'theorists' switched sides. But the rest only got worse after hearing the crystals' tale.

Jhi and all its heat-exuding friends explained how the crystals had come to earth from Mars (that really blew the theorists' minds) on a ship which had crashed. Over time, the lay of the land had shifted, covering the crystals. Between the shift and their own heat, the cavern had formed. How long had they been here exactly? It was impossible to tell because they had a hard time explaining in our terms. But we knew it had been a long time. Much longer than it should have taken for the human race to be accepting of that sort of thing. For me it was kind of like opening a massive geode. Rough and ugly on the outside, precious beauty on the inside.

It actually brought tears to my eyes to think how hard the crystals had tried, every time some scientific group had gone to visit, or some tour guide led tourists in to get a glimpse. For so long we *weren't* ready for them.

Soon, the crystals became part of our everyday life. They opened spas and clinics. They soothed rattled nerves, eased mental health issues, and healed physical diseases. Sometimes the tentacles were involved, but mostly it was just that vibrating hum – somehow, they kept that and the heat at levels humans could tolerate. But at night they went back to their cave, and anyone who tried to approach couldn't take the heat they released. Their hum had changed too, and I wondered if they weren't releasing the toxins they pulled from our bodies in the daytime. We considered them miracle workers. Of course, in a way they were.

The sound of bass guitar and drums drifted out onto the street where I stood. Out behind the bar, the gas station, restaurants and apartments that lined the street, there was a new airport strip. The crystals had it built for themselves, and now their ships lined the tarmac. The ships took off vertically, so no extensive runway was needed for that.

They'd fallen in so easily with all of our traditions, our ways, that I was certain they'd never been communicating as Cris has said, but rather I'd been right about them listening, getting to know us. Even Cris was beginning to agree with me. But although we had no problems with that, we couldn't help but wonder what they'd want in return. Surely all of this couldn't be free. I had no doubt that the theorists were off their rockers, but there had to be a price. Everything came at a price.

It wasn't long before I found out what that price was. Yet it wasn't so much a cost as it was a plea for help.

They planned a games night - Bingo, Texas Hold 'em, Blackjack and games no human had ever heard of before. Everyone eagerly attended. Throngs of people crowded every bar, restaurant, anywhere these games could be played. We didn't know at the time we were being tricked, but neither did the crystals think they were tricking us. They thought we understood. We didn't. Not at first.

Nearly everyone went home that first night a winner. It kind of reminded me of kids in school getting participation awards. We each had our ticket with a number and a date. We were to show up on the air strip on that date. This went on for about a week. No one thought to question it.

We all gathered on the proposed night. The street behind me was now quiet and nearly empty. Like most of the streets in town tonight. We were all winners, and we were all here. The crowd was abuzz with questions – why were we here? What was happening? What was *going* to happen?

I looked at the bright orange ticket in my hand. Other than the number and the date, the writing on it wasn't any language I knew. I'd heard rumors that it was Arabic, ancient Persian, even elvish. But the most popular one was that it was the crystals' own language, (Marsian? Marsish?) which made the most sense. It could have said anything on there. I slapped it against my fingers, my brain whirling with questions and anxiety.

Finally, a door opened on one of the ships and a set of stairs proceeded to descend. Once the process was finished, a crystal – a green one, shorter than any we'd seen before - came out, limping along on those appendages, almost swaying back and forth. If they weren't so friendly, it'd be creepy.

It held a bullhorn up to its slash of a mouth, but from the sound inside my head, I was certain the device was for looks only. The crystal was speaking inside our minds.

"You are all winners," it proclaimed. "We have awarded you not only with our spas, clinics and treatments, but with this trip to our home planet of Mars.

"We do not wish to harm you, but we have a big ask of you."

And there it was. The price.

"Please understand that you are free to leave. You do not have to participate." It lowered the bullhorn and watched the crowd. Some of us squirmed a bit or shook our heads, but no one left. The chance to go to Mars had long been a dream of many of these people. There were movies and documentaries about it. We watched footage of the Rover eagerly. No one wanted to miss the chance. And we were curious.

"What are we being asked to participate in?" shouted Cris.

Agreement rippled through the crowd. We all wanted to know.

There was a shift in the air around us and we were back in that place where Jih had first taken us. Not on Mars, not on Earth, but suspended somewhere in between.

What looked like mesas dotted the rough brown surface. A pinkish hue on the horizon. Somehow, we were whisked to the foot of one of the mesas. I noticed it had a door. Of course! Crystals came from the earth, why wouldn't that be where their cities and towns were. Then the door whipped open. Bright light flooded out and we were "led" into it.

Gleaming stairs carved from what appeared to be ruby and sapphire led us down to a large chamber of lustrous opal walls and a purple quartz ceiling. Obsidian chairs ringed the room. A darkened entrance opposite the stairs led out of the room. It was to this we were once again "led".

We were pulled back to our present location on Earth. The green crystal raised the useless bullhorn once more.

"What you will see next is not enjoyable, but is necessary. Again, I'm telling you that you can refuse to assist us if you wish. We will not be angry."

Again it waited while many conversations buzzed in the multitude.

"What do we do?" asked Gayla.

Cris shrugged. "What could be so bad? They've been nothing but kind to us. If they need assistance, I say let's assist."

"What if they're tricking us?" I asked.

"I don't think they'd do that," answered Cris. "First contact has gone pretty good so far. I, for one, am going to stay and see what they need."

Gayla nearly left but curiosity, or maybe a sense of duty, got the better of her and she stayed. A handful of people did go, but most stayed.

Back in that shifted area between here and there, I could hear a faint hum as we were shown the hall, extravagant rooms on both sides of it. Each one looked like a one-person apartment. Then it got bad.

The vibrating hum was the loudest I'd ever heard it. From our dimension we could see dark mining tunnels, hear a constant but faint ring of metal blade on stone. Pickaxes were being swung by humanoids and crystals alike. Even within this shift, this dimension or bubble, I could feel the attitude change. I looked around at the crowd. Most faces were an oval of surprise. Gayla was crying. She reached out to me, but was unable to touch me. And we were currently stuck here. This wasn't a place we could just leave, not unless the crystals wanted us to.

A soft white glow garnered my attention. I turned back to the scene before me and watched it unfold. Suddenly beings gathered around the glow, picking gently with axes and fingers. The crystals stood back, seemingly helpless. Until someone lifted something from out of the glow. A small white crystal, sans tentacles. An infant? The little crystal was handed off to one of the larger ones who cradled it as it left.

Then we were back again.

The crowd went crazy, screaming and dancing themselves into a frenzy.

"You lied to us!"

"You tricked us!"

"Is this all a game to you?"

"I thought you were trying to help us! You just want prisoners to do your dirty work!"

A large group took up a chant – dir-ty liar, dir-ty liar.

Cris, Gayla and I looked at one another. Tears still streamed down Gayla's face. She shook her head and moved toward the chanters. I noticed the crystal standing stoic and unmoving at the top of the stairs. A small group of others joined Cris and me.

"What's going on here?" a woman asked. "Aren't you guys the ones who found these things?"

"We are," said Cris. "But I don't think—"

The woman cut him off. "No, you probably weren't thinking when you allowed them freedom to join us."

"We didn't," I reminded her. "They said we were ready. I guess they were wrong."

Embarrassment flushed the woman's face. "I just meant –"

This time I cut her off. "I know what you meant. But these crystals need our help."

"By forcing us to work in mines? Digging out more of them?" replied a male from the group. "How do we know they're not building an army."

"They could have harmed us at any time," Cris said. "They didn't."

"So, we're just supposed to trust them? Work our –" Again someone else was cut off. By me.

"No. We have ways of digging in mines that don't require a lot of physical labor. These machines can be calibrated to recognize these. . . these. . . infants?"

"Is that what they are?" asked someone else.

I shrugged. "It looked like it to me. But I'm saying we can make this easier for them. Show them new ways to do things."

"And how to you propose to get this equipment to Mars?"

Cris pointed at the ships. "They have the technology. If we work together, we can improve on that. Create a ship that will deliver equipment."

"How do you even know they'll go for that?" More people were beginning to speak up.

"They gave us a choice," I said. "If they were going to "force" us to do anything, they wouldn't have done that."

"I'm going to talk to it," said Cris, pointing. "Before this gets out of hand."

"What makes you our spokesperson?"

Ignoring that remark, Cris grabbed my hand and we threaded ourselves through the crowd toward the stairs. As we started climbing them, the crowd broke and rushed us.

The crystal, seeing what was about to happen, opened the door and lumbered inside, Cris and I right behind it. I heard shoes hit the bottom of the metal stairs, rush upwards. Green crystal slammed the door closed, and did something that made a snicking sound. Locked?

"Please tell me what is happening. What have we done wrong?" asked Green crystal, turning towards us.

"I think there's been a misunderstanding," said Cris.

Fists pounded the door making a sort of echoey thrum in the foyer we stood in. Feet kicked, but the door held firm.

Several other crystals appeared behind the green one. Jih was among them. They remained silent.

"My name is Yox," said the green crystal. "Jih and I will speak with you. Will you be okay if we take off?"

"Uh, sure," started Cris. "But those guys might not be." He pointed toward the door.

"The stairs will detach when we take off," said Yox, and I swear somehow it smiled. "It's a safety feature on this ship."

"Then let's go," I cried.

Yox turned to the others and uttered what sounded like commands. Everyone but Jih left.

"Shall we go where it's more comfortable?" offered Jih.

They took us to a largish room with white shag carpeting and off-white walls. There was a fireplace, but it was obvious that the flames were fake. They were too smooth and too quiet to be real. Vases of plastic flowers lined the mantel. The smell of roses and woodsmoke lightly tinted the air.

Jih and Yox sat on a white sofa fronting a painting of blue sky outside a window frame. Sat is a somewhat relative term. They just sort of parked the bottom of the crystal on the cushions, tentacles drooping and dangling.

Another white sofa, this one curved into a half-moon shape sat opposite with a coffee table in between, draped with a circular, beige tablecloth, and decorated with more vases of plastic flowers.

Despite the fire being phony, the room was comfortably warm.

"Please sit," said Yox. "I hope this room suits you."

"Very nice," said Cris, and I nodded my agreement.

After Cris and I settled on the sofa, Yox immediately asked his question again. He was genuinely confused, even a bit angry and hurt. I could sense it, feel it.

"They think you lied to us," Cris told him, leaning forward, as if this nugget was a secret.

"We did not!" Haughtiness filled Jih's voice. I couldn't say I blamed him for feeling that way.

"But you treated us so well," I said, a strange feeling forming in the pit of my stomach. "Your kind was so wonderful, but then you dropped this bombshell."

"Bombshell? We carry no weapons." This from Yox.

"Sorry. What I meant was you surprised us with this request. It's like you only treated us nicely because you wanted something in return."

Again, I swear I saw emotion in those non-faces, and their tentacles quivered. "But," said Jih, "is this not the way of this world?"

"Did we get something wrong?" asked Yox.

"We were certain you were ready for us." Jih.

"We are ready for you," said Cris. "At least some of us. But you did get it wrong." He got up and walked to the fireplace, holding his hands out as though there was warmth coming from it, then fingering the plastic petals. Signs he was getting agitated. I knew he didn't want to scare this race off. He'd been the most excited when they'd spoken to us, had joined us.

I started to speak, but decided not to. I wanted to tell them they should have just asked for our help in the first place. But would we have given it? Maybe, maybe not. I like to think we would have. On the other hand, would we have done anything different? If we'd been willing to give our help, we too would have wanted something in return. Considering the circumstances under which they wanted us to work, things could possibly have turned out much worse.

"Those crystals you dig from the ground, those are your infants?" asked Cris.

"They are. It is the way we reproduce. In the past we took prisoners, slaves, and made them do our work. But we learned that it was wrong. We did not mean to trick you; we only wanted your service. We thought you would comply."

Jih looked at Yox, and they began to converse in their own language. Then Jih spoke to us again. "I'm sorry. Yox informs me that I have used the wrong words. Comply is not correct. And perhaps neither is service. Forced compliance is no longer our way. But we still wish for you to work for us. I promise you will be treated well."

"Assistance?" said Cris, now kneeling by the fireplace like he was warming himself. "Like working together instead of master and slave."

"Assistance, yes," said Yox.

"Very well," agreed Jih. "We require your assistance."

"You could have just asked." Cris voiced what I would not.

"Would you have assisted willingly?" Jih's statement echoed my own thoughts. Were they? Or were they his? Maybe both. I began to think that they thought they had only one choice, once chance to recruit assistants to carry on their race.

For a moment there was silence. Awkward silence. Tentacles wavered, Cris air-traced the pattern of the flames. My mind whirled. What to say now?

I stood. "Look, we mind gems here on Earth. We have machines that can break up the rock. If you speak to the right people, I'm sure humans would be willing to help. You said it yourself; slavery was wrong. I understand why you did what you did and maybe there was no other way, but you undermined our trust in you."

"We meant no harm," insisted Jih.

"How can we fix it?" asked Yox, softly.

"Make a public announcement. Admit you went about things in the wrong way. Humans can be assholes, but we can also be kind."

"You, Cris and Wanda, are willing to help us with this endeavor?" Jih was on its tentacles, limping towards us. Yox was close behind.

"Yes, yes, of course!" Cris reached out his hand and met one of Jih's outstretched tentacles. They didn't shake on it, but did more of a medieval friendship grip. When Yox reached for me, I did the same.

The heat was nearly unbearable. The air scrubbers purified the air, and there were fans, but nothing could relieve that heat. Both my tank and my short shorts were soaked. So were Cris's. And Gayla's. And the clothes of a half dozen other humans who'd opted to come to Mars, and were now on this shift. Day and night we worked side by side with the crystals, the tunnel-borer chewing up rock, its drone competing with the crystals' hum. Some genius by the name of Edwin Gabriel had worked with the crystals to calibrate the machine to stop when it detected infants. Otherwise, it would have chomped right through them.

We walked beside the machine, waiting for it to stop. When it did, that hum took over. But by now most of us were used to it; we wore ear protection but even so, the sound remained, like background noise.

Cris and I were on pickaxe duty. The borer backed up, allowing us to crack stone from around the soft white glow that had begun to emanate from the ruptures in the rock wall.

As more stone was pulled away from the newborn crystal, the heat rose, and the hum grew louder. When tools were too dangerous, we used gloved hands to pull away chunks to help birth the unborn. The crystals waited patiently. Their tentacles were hardly suited to aid us, but they used soft brushes curl-clutched in one or two limbs and did the best they could. Then, once the infants were lifted from their rocky wombs, they used the same brushes to sweep away any remaining dust particles. Infants, born limbless (apparently the appendages began coming in around the time the little ones were what humans would call teenagers, kind of like puberty) were rushed away, usually by a purple crystal named Huz.

All infants were also born white, the color coming along with the limbs. As I pulled this one free, Huz took it from my hands. Tentacles wrapped around the baby as tenderly as any human parent.

"Thank you," said Huz, as it always did, then lumbered away to wherever they went once a newborn was birthed. This was something they never showed us, and we never asked.

Before the borer started up again, our forecrystal announced it was time for a break.

I dropped the axe and pulled the doo-rag off my head to wipe sweat and dirt from my face. We all headed for the nook where containers of cold, clear water with a salty-sweet taste were handed out. As we walked, I reflected on this friendship. It could have gone wrong, so wrong. But because a few of us were willing to take the time to listen, we now had allies. First contact had been rough, but worth it. The crystals continued to run their shops and spas on Earth. Most people got over being angry and were laughing now at the silly mistakes we all made.

"What are you smiling at?" Gayla asked.

"Just first contact and friendship."

She smiled back and we took our places in the water line.

--

Having spent a lifetime writing, editing and/or doing other writing related things, Kellee made her first sale over twenty years ago. Now she has numerous pieces published, most of which can be found on her websites:
https://sites.google.com/silverpen.org/krkranendonk/home
and www.facebook.com/profile.php?id=100082330346438
. She's very bad at updating them.

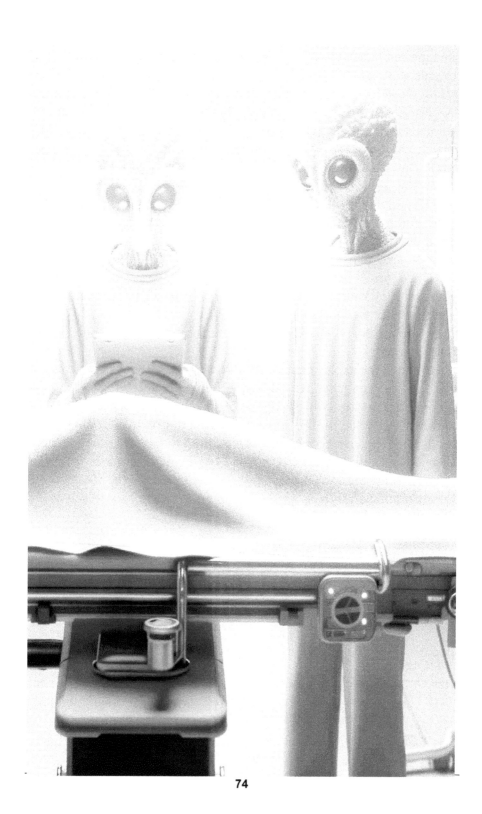

The Pathogen

By Lawrence Dagstine

The long road to becoming a Martian scientist began in a room filled with over two-dozen corpses. To learn of the human anatomy, and how their immune systems were susceptible to the dust in our planet's air, it was necessary to take their bodies apart. It was necessary to note their nerves, muscles and organs that became liquefied after a contamination period of days rather than weeks. It was necessary to study their brains and its complex patterns, in hopes that our own race could evolve and explain their sudden dissident and aggressive behavior. Yet the vision of twenty-five alien life forms, each on a silver-top hovering slab, was so overwhelming that I almost had to turn back into the warmer part of the corridor.

The long-gowned doctor of progress, Zyrok, stepped forward and comforted me. "You're not going to lose your lunch again today, are you, Durgess?" he asked, blinking his purple eyes and contorting the many wrinkles in his spongelike face.

I held my tongue back and swallowed. "No, I don't think so."

He nodded. "Good."

Still, it was *this*… The invasion of the privacy of death in another species, and on such a nearby world, which was so disturbing. We had to perform an almost infinite number of autopsies and encamp among these Terrans for several years, which was about how long our geoscientists suggested the winds carried the plague. How could the few that were left ever survive it? How could the Martians survive the constant reminder that it was our world that embraced and killed these people? I grabbed my face. I could not breathe, let alone look upon them, for there were hundreds more underground morgues and domed facilities across the planet which housed their corpses. I closed my eyes, overcome by nausea.

"It's obviously some kind of virus *we* can't catch," Zyrok said. "Something airborne amongst the red sands for who knows how long: centuries, millennia, eons." He looked around him. "Bishop Kalesk, horticulturalist and probably the most skeptical of all our researchers, had been arrested with a liquid form of the contagion. Megalomaniac. It isn't enough that we're being blamed for genocide. Still, he yielded to the evidence of healings from plantlife from the biodomes, which could not be explained by any other reason. Only that, when the internal filters swept the plague onto tree barks, they absorbed it and in turn produced a curative sap. A great variety of Martian illnesses have been cured by the same simple means, and the cures have been effected quickly even in serious illnesses that had resisted medical treatment for a long time. Before he lost his mind though, these facts seemed to Kalesk the sure foundation on which to base the research in which he at last acknowledged the aggressive behavior of the contaminated. Nevertheless, he was jailed. And we have yet to learn what *he* learned, then take over from there. In his brilliantly reasoned texts, the bishop submitted his own judgment to the judgment *our* planet should have taken when the Terran population first succumbed to the outbreak."

"Call nighttime executions on those exhibiting signs of the virus," I said, thinking long and hard to myself. "But in droves? Now *that's* genocide."

"Perhaps. But this is no ordinary pandemic. It's a microscopic pathogen which seems to grow, attack and destroy once inhaled by these creatures. For pity's sake, they even attacked *us* at times." There was a moment of significant silence. Zyrok could see the expression on my face. "It's not just in the air but the blood," he said, pulling me next to him. "The whole colony has been pickled in it. The pathogen awakens a diseased but dormant cell in their bodies, then somehow multiplies. It pumps through the blood to all the major organs, and then, finally, does something to the brain's oxygen levels, thus affecting motor skills and thinking processes. Everything begins to break down. At first, they exhibit signs of fever, and their behavior is zombielike. But then, within days or hours, a feral nature manifests itself, and…" He paused and put a webbed hand on my shoulder. "Well, that's what we're here again today to find out."

The morgue droid rechecked our passes and assigned us as a group, and we were given a platform in which to work. Zyrok psychically summoned a medical examination tray over to assist us. Frantically I looked around. Hovering nearest to us was the corpse of a young female who had had her eyes removed. Suspended next to her was a tall dark-skinned male who looked like one of the colony figureheads who first disembarked that great ship many, many moon cycles ago. 2035? 2040, was it? Never in my wildest dreams would I have thought that one of the most recognizable of their leaders would be among the dead—he had shaken my hand as a sign of goodwill and peace—and never, I thought, would I be able to touch either of them now.

"We killed them," I muttered, feeling sick once more. "A whole species on the verge of extinction."

"I said stop that." Zyrok put his scalpel aside and waved an angry digit. "Stop blaming yourself and get back to work. You can either stand here and bawl, or you can try and make a difference for the few thousand that are left." He nodded to the rear end of the room. "Why don't we start where it's a little less gory? We've got *him*," he said. "Seems to have expired in his prime."

Him was a light-skinned male, no blotches, all there—thank goodness—young and well-proportioned. His eyes reminded me of some of those middle-aged, well-groomed astronauts that introduced themselves upon landing here. They were blue and green. The hair brown, of course, and, if not slicked back, usually curled off to the side.

As a team, we were required to extract cells and assigned an arm or a leg. Then, using Kalesk's texts to guide us, we'd punch our own findings along the way into a small systemic reader in the side of the floating table.

Zyrok and I drew the right arm. "You want to start off?" he asked.

"No, you begin it. I'll pick up and pass you tools as we go along."

Zyrok began. "Here," he said. "Hold the wrist then."

I gripped my cold and clammy talons around it, then instinctively pulled back.

"What's the matter?"

"I'd rather you hold it yourself," I said.

"You know, you've done this before. You're only holding yourself back. Even students with promise must overcome things of this nature, submit to scientific growth and development. You and I know it is the only path for a Martian."

"Glory can wait for another day, if that's what you mean."

"Bah, you're just squeamish! I've had hundreds of pupils just like you. You possess the genius, but not the fortitude."

"And Kalesk?" I asked.

"He might have been deranged," Zyrok noted, "but he was still an excellent mind. He found his niche and went for it. I wish you'd concentrate more and do the same. I see a greatness in you."

Regardless, I did not touch a single body part that day, nor the rest of that cycle. I refused to. But gradually, as Zyrok and I visited more corpse-laden facilities and searched endlessly for a cure, I began to lose my shyness and do my share. Zyrok was very considerate, as were the other scientists I'd met along the way. I eventually came to enjoy his running sense of humor, which helped us through some dark times, such as when we had to draw samples from still-living specimens. He became my ideal—a researcher of grace and courage and wisdom. His knowledge of the human anatomy was astonishing. The ability to remove and put back nerves, vessels, muscles, bones and other tissue seemed an absolute part of his vocational makeup. And to do it with such precision, especially in those who were violent towards us, showed me just how bold and innovative he was.

"They call that the carotid artery," he'd say during our examinations, showing me one major internal vessel after another, summoning a thin wire-like pair of forceps down from the ceiling above to do work between the neck and ear. The utensils always adhered to his instructions, and always through telepathic communication. A gift only elder Martians from the heart of the core possessed. "Oh, that's the parotid gland. Exquisitely designed, don't you think?"

"Yes," I'd reply, along with the other things he showed me—the lessons never got old—wondering how one could witness the infinite complexity and beauty of the human body and not marvel at the negative effects this plague had upon it.

"Are you ready to examine the brain, Durgess? That's my personal favorite."

And it had become my favorite, too, for the challenge of that first cycle of research was not confined to just speculation over mounds of cadavers. In Martian physiology, it was normal to look for answers by dissecting animals belonging to the other race: dogs, cats, mice, frogs, lizards, even insects. We considered every possible solution and sought every possible clue, all for the sake of a species not our own.

We could have given up at any time and watched them wither out of existence. We could have stuck long needles through their heads and ripped open their spinal columns, only to see how the virus would react when the nerves and muscle fibers were exposed for long periods to *our* air. Why, we could have even gone one step further. We could have performed transplants. But we chose not to.

This work, within *some* living beings, rather than among mostly dead ones, allowed Zyrok and I, and the teams of researchers who helped us, to look at other alternatives. Slowly, through the first, second, and third cycles of my passage to becoming a respectable scientist, I became familiar enough with the aggressive pre-death aspects of the illness to know what to expect. I took Kalesk and Zyrok's findings with me, as if they had been my own. I prepared myself to do what every scientist must eventually do—leap from the known to the unknown and back again.

After much training, I was ready to leave the desert morgues and work with the terminally sick. The provincial hospitals on the darker side of the planet were small—one or two laboratories and operating rooms to each, crumbling architecture and ancient technology for the staff, which included seven assistants. One of the security droids introduced me to the head nurse on duty and soared off. Lying on a nearby gurney was a human female of about fifty, red hair and brown eyes, with the rugged, muscular build of one who had probably carried the immense burdens of her home planet with her. She had been recently infected. Her vinyl suit was ripped in shreds and matted with froth and blood. "Did something bite her?" I asked.

The nurse responded by compressing her eyelids and shaking her porous head; as a female drone, she was voice incapable.

Still, by some miracle, the woman's face had not been torn off. There were claw wounds everywhere else. She had regained consciousness, but was in shock from blood loss. To ease her suffering, we administered plasma injections. I wondered what had happened. Nobody could single-handedly fight off an army of crazed people showing signs of the virus. Not even this tough looking lady.

But she had. Another scientist had told me the story. A dozen or so colonists had been feeding on the intestines and brain matter of her livestock. The moment she came outside to stop them she was attacked, then the hospital's patrol had traced the assault and dispatched a unit. Security droids had smoked them off the farm. "You mean the people in these parts are tagged?" I asked.

"You kidding me? We have to," the scientist said. "The way this thing's become so widespread, they'd not only eat each other up but tear *us* apart along with them."

"How did you handle the other contaminates?"

"In the end we did the usual, sent in flame tanks, releasing firebombs and igniting them but not bringing them down. With the disease eating away at their insides, the wounded looked like charred remains but still raced away, looking for refuge in the outlands." The scientist looked down at the woman, then faced me again. "By the way, I'm Jingren."

"Durgess."

"Ah, yes, of course. Zyrok's pupil."

"Doctors of progress," I laughed. "That's us."

"Then your academies and domes are aware of the situation."

"The severity of it," I said. "What is the female's name?"

"Her tag says MARY 578. According to the task force that *pre*-taped it—over here, we don't take precautions—she heard her milk distributors *mooing* vulnerably. She went to the door of her living unit just as the aggressors crawled underneath the electric terrafence sealing off her property. They crept along the shadows and bounded for the farmyard. She barely had time to recognize what was happening before they leaped for the only flesh meal they'd probably had in weeks."

"Do you mind if I examine her?" I asked.

"No, go right ahead."

I approached the gurney, and the first thing I noticed was the bruising. "She must have fell backwards with one of them on top of her—powerful hands and sharp teeth got her good at the abdomen. She might have held her attacker's throat away from her face while her legs were hooked around his lower body. In murderous embrace, they probably rolled about. Mary here probably drove her thumbs into her attacker's windpipe—that would explain the missing fingernails and broken digits—while the others, just as hungry, lashed wildly at her from the side. Then she went limp from the pain."

"The droids found her on the sand, unconscious, the contaminates trying to make a break for it."

"See that she is given a room. Make sure she sleeps well, and have her monitored constantly. The first sign of weird or aggressive behavior, have her destroyed."

Jingren nodded and saw the patient to a room. When he returned, he said to me, "Never in my life have I seen such a field of human suffering."

"What do you mean?"

"Here. Follow me."

I was led down a long steel-walled corridor, then, eventually, outside. The courtyard to the hospital was just as old as the main building, filthy and falling apart, surrounded by large barrack-type structures. It was here that they recharged the security robots and housed the humans who were ultra-violent and on their last limb. Jingren parted with me momentarily, promising to return and finish his tour of the grounds. Impatient, and curious of the environment I would be working in, I wandered into one of the sparsely lit halls on the other side, drawn by the strange, muffled, exhausted cries. I had dealt with still-living specimens before, but never anything like this. At that point, I knew, that the *nature* of the virus was worse than any could ever have imagined; not even Zyrok would have been prepared for what my eyes were about to see.

I opened the hatch of a large, high-ceilinged ward filled with small cots that had electric cuffs and iron-barred sides. In each bed was a human child, all less than ten years of age, suffering late stages of plague and other *surreal* deformities. Some lay with backs arched like pulled bows, spasming and drooling blood while clawing at the railings. Others had rotted limbs stretched out stiffly in paroxysmal extension, their faces frozen, and only the eyelids moving normally. A few sat upright, not yet wholly deformed, jumping up and down in their cage-like beds in primitive rhythm; it was as if what remained of their intelligence told them to escape if they could from the horribleness that was soon to claim them.

The fact they were children only seemed to magnify the pain of watching this once great race, the waste of the promise and fulfillment of terrestrial life. Over it all rode the plaintive cries and sobs of my own people, fused into one long, unending wail. The corridors of their hell must echo with such sounds, I thought.

At the rear of the ward were two female Martians soaking up thoughts on what to do this shift, one of them an elder nurse with telepathic capabilities who was making a young Terran girl in white levitate for a medicinal puncture. Hovering behind her was a security droid. It had been placed there as a precaution.

Jingren had returned. "We can't get too close to them," he said, startling me. "We must always have magnetic syringes and other nanorythmic devices at the ready. Like the adults they, too, bite."

"I've been performing autopsies on this species for many cycles now," I said, deeply saddened. "I...I've never..."

"Never seen a strain of the virus this bad?" Jingren finished for me. "With the recent increase in malformations, dome leaders now suspect that this whole mess was industrial-based from the beginning, rather than a germ of dust and wind."

"Listen, I don't care how smart the leaders are, or how good your technology and security is. This should have been contained sooner!" I reprimanded him. "How could your tribes allow the outbreak to become so extensive? It's spread past Olympus Crater!"

"Lack of intelligent research. Funding, too. The science is there when it wants to be, but the financing, like all other worlds, just isn't."

"Have you searched your dome flora for answers?"

"Sure, on many occasions."

"Then you *must* have come up with some kind of antibiotic or stabilizer."

"Ah, you reek of *new* resident," he laughed, and at first, I could not understand why. "That's not a bad thing, mind you. But on this side of the planet the virus has entered a more critical stage." We both watched the nurse psychically put the sedated child back in her cot, then refit the bars and cuffs.

"What are their chances?" I asked.

Jingren shook his head sadly. "We rarely get them early enough. They either die immediately or become confrontational vegetables first."

On our way out of the ward we stopped to talk to a young boy, who seemed without infection and malformations whatsoever. He was jumping up and down, singing, "Twinkle, Twinkle, Little Star", a popular Terran nursery song. He wore a white and blue-striped elastic jumpsuit. And as he bounced about the dimly lit corridor, his eyes seemed to shimmer a ray of light, too. "That's OSCAR 183," said Jingren. "He's the luckiest of the bunch. Personnel were nice enough to let him stay here."

"More than just lucky," I said, kneeling forward and putting out a gloved hand. "A phenomenon! Oh Oscar, I hope you'll come here."

"I bet you do," he replied with snarky laughter.

"Where are your parents?"

"Dead. The plague took them."

"And of all the little boys and girls on the face of Mars, the plague never bothered you?"

"Nope." He flexed his tiny muscles for me. "I'm *invincible!*"

"I'm sure you are," I said, staring up at Jingren. The staff scientist began thinking the same thing I was. Only *he* wished the thought had come to his hospital many cycles sooner. Where research into human anatomy and dome plantlife was too often regarded, and ultimately failed, here was this amazing child with the word HOPE written all over his face in big letters. His body makeup *must* have been different from all the rest.

"So, you think there's something about Oscar we don't know about?" Jingren asked. "Something we've overlooked?"

"Of course. Look at him," I said. "Not a single sign of virus in him, and it doesn't seem as though he'll be exhibiting any symptoms soon. We need to build a sterile environment, and we need to extract right away."

"But the boy is still alive. To perform medical examinations of that magnitude on a living subject is not only sinister but—Well, it's *unethical.*"

"Zyrok and I conducted such tests on still-living specimens hundreds of times. I am already experienced in the area. Remember, I had one of the best teachers. He even taught me how to overcome medical malpractice and other obstacles."

"Yes, I understand that. But the boy would have to be subjected to postmortem stasis, and there's no guarantee we could bring him back."

"You underestimate the medical and scientific perfection of our race."

"Still, that isn't the way we handle experimentation detail," he argued. "Martians have their own laws, their own moral codes." He looked worried. "Think of the controversy."

"Think of the *benefits*," I said, trying to convince him once more. "Think of the positive rather than the negative. What if the doctors of Mars *could* save the people of Earth? Or would you rather sit back and watch what could very well be the death of all humanity?"

He did not answer. After all, how could he?

He knew I was right. If a brutal medical procedure was required to save the lives of thousands, then so be it. It had to be done.

In the right atmosphere, with the right tools—and this included the immediate quarantine and constant presence of five-year-old Oscar— I sought a cure to the viral nightmare around us. I had four other wards in which to extract. Jingren made sure permission was granted; given the laws of the other domes, this also provided a challenge. In the malformation cases, he and I occasionally removed nerves and muscle fibers rather than whole organs, and experimented with what could be had. However, my real interest was in what was already missing, and this had stemmed from that one ward which overflowed with the plague's tinier victims.

When we had successfully done fifty examinations, experimenting on the half-turned or already deceased, each case increasing in complexity and duration as technology and team became more coordinated, I was ready to accept the risk of anesthetizing Oscar and putting *his* body on that slab for the first time. Yet before this could happen, I had an appointment with one of life's crueler events.

The death of a teacher.

Early one morning in the sterilized chamber that had been prepared for me, word had come of Zyrok's passing. "If you want to see the body before Morgue Law goes into effect, you must leave immediately. There's not much time."

I looked down at Oscar's naked form on the slab, as one of the nurses was putting him under. "Count backwards from ten, child," I said, tapping his hand. "Everything will be all right." Facing forward again, I answered, "Tell the elders I'm not coming. Tell them to honor the body without me."

Jingren pulled me aside. "Are you sure about this? He would have wanted you there."

"He would have also wanted me *here*," I said.

Doubt was my oldest enemy. I knew it well. Yet with the thoughts of Zyrok's passing filling my mind, I had never expected it to arrive with such force at this crucial point. For the first time I was aware that we were actually going to perform an autopsy-like medical procedure involving an unacceptable science. The plan was to get what we needed and get out of there, then resurrect the boy. Or at the very least catch him in Near Death Mode. Instead of looking for the cause of death we were now looking for the cause of *life*. And in this, *hopefully,* we would find the cure.

Jingren, who would be on my team collecting what we needed from the boy's temporarily oxygenless body, wanted to make sure of the timing. "We'll get the child ready for telepathic resuscitation, in case his organs start to fail before us. We won't open him up until you say. Okay?"

"Yes," I said. "Then you come in and excise the essentials."

"Don't you want to do it?"

"No. If I do it alone, you'll never be able to follow me. You'd better know it from the beginning, and watching each other's movements and taking turns will help in case something goes wrong."

There was anxious silence as the team surrounded the slab.

Finally, Jingren and I drew the right arm. "Do you want to start?" I asked.

"No, you begin. I'll pick up and pass you tools as we go along."

I began. "Here," I said. "Hold the wrist then."

Jingren gripped his webbed talons around it, then nervously pulled back.

"What's wrong?"

"I'd rather you hold it," he said.

"You know, you've performed medical procedures before. Maybe not on this scale, but you've contributed your share. I've heard even students must overcome things of this nature, submit to scientific growth and development. Otherwise, you do yourself a grave disservice."

Once we had extracted what we needed, I passed the cellular snippings on to two nurses, who were at the ready holding trays. "Take these to the laboratory straight away. The boy won't hold on much longer. We have but a few minutes to let Oscar's samples intermingle with the other infected ones we've collected from the ward."

I felt a chill, thinking, oh no, everything's going to go wrong somehow. Any other impressions as to what would happen next rested on how much time we actually had.

Still, time would not be enough.

This was to be Oscar's last dawn, and the last one for that incredible young mind as well. Attempts at maintaining the stasis had failed. From birth, my life had built toward one moment: examining and perfecting the anatomical imperfections of other races, and a scientist was born. My life had found its meaning there, nowhere else, and now in the dying of this one untainted life was my own death, too. My vocational makeup did not matter anymore. At least, not to me.

"We were working on very little time," Jingren reminded me afterwards.

"We crashed because of my mistakes," I said. "I pushed too hard."

"We were working in the dark, Durgess, feeling our way across. We'll know more next time."

"I don't know if there'll be a next time. We're still in the dark, Jingren, and I've become afraid of it once more."

"Your confidence will come back as you work. You have to try again. You have no choice."

I could take no more and hurriedly left the chamber. Finally alone, I could no longer contain my overwhelming sadness and began to weep at the terrible tragedy of that young boy, so alive and ready to live, to grow up and experience our culture and way of life, to be surrounded by us. Yet *unable* to bring him back.

Where was their god when all this happened? Where was their god when they first became infected? If there was a reason for this, what was it? Leaving the hospital, I had no answer for any of it. Overcome with grief, I went for a walk into the red sands alone. Hospital staff wanted to follow and comfort me, but I was beyond approach. I wept for Oscar, and I wept for myself. I wept at how I had failed all those who wanted more from me than I could ever give them. There was no answer that I knew, yet there *had* to be one somewhere. I was sure I would find it if I went on long enough, so I wept alone. I knew that. But as painful as it was, for now, I must return to those wards.

When I arrived back at the hospital, I saw Jingren talking with one of the other scientists. His expression was one of elation. "What's going on?" I asked, curious.

He rushed over. "It's remarkable, Durgess. It's absolutely remarkable!" He forwarded me a smile. "When Oscar's samples were combined with those of the children and adults in the other wards, a metamorphosis occurred. It wasn't a complete transition, mind you. But it's a start."

"Well go on, tell me."

"We've won a seventy-five percent victory," he answered gleefully. "Now we must replicate those tissue samples and cells, strengthen them, and fight for the other twenty-five percent. The Terrans might have a chance after all."

Surprised, I looked from Jingren to the other faces that had been part of my team. Each one nodded, or in some way said to me: "Well done, Durgess."

At that moment I had my answer, and I began to build hope again. The first attempts, with all their pain and sorrow, had been leading up to this very second. I knew if I turned back now, I'd only deny Oscar a meaningful sacrifice and a rightful place as hero to his people, as well as my own chance for complete medical triumph.

--

Lawrence Dagstine is a native New Yorker and speculative fiction writer of close to 30 years. He has placed around 500 short stories in online and print periodicals during that period of time. He has been published by houses such as Damnation Books, Steampunk Tales, Left Hand Publishers, Wicked Shadow Press, Calliope Interactive, and Dark Owl Publishing (of which he has a new book out called The Nightmare Cycle). Visit his website, for publication history past and present, at: www.lawrencedagstine.com

High Seas

By Frank Dumas

Mars. Meridiani Planum, Mid-2033. Sol 1076

Marsha Sparke led a foot patrol near a cluster of pressurized habitation units, feeling like a damn fool.

Everyone wore self-sealing padding over vulnerable pressure suits. Everyone but Marsha carried a Steyr AUG rifle.

She was the only one armed with a pistol.

You should lead the search party, they said. You're the only one of the seniors with a military background. An officer.

I was missileer on a boomer! Want to vaporize a city from beneath the waves? I'm your girl. In a gunfight? Not so much.

The search party had travelled five hundred klicks by convoy to Maedra crater. They had patchy overhead imagery. Scraps of SIGINT.

And a distress call.

Five Years Earlier: San Francisco, Amber Enterprises Headquarters, 2028

Marsha arrived first in the anteroom to Leonard Amber's office. Two other project managers joined her, taking seats around a coffee table devoid of refreshments.

Vincent checked his phone repeatedly. Fernando stared at the linoleum floor as if it were his personal nemesis.

Waiting…

She pined for an old-fashioned conference, instead of one of Leonard's private sessions. At least with everyone at a table in a room together there was the hope, however fanciful, of ganging up on him. Perhaps he felt the same, hence the one-on-ones.

The door opened to admit a fourth project lead. Marsha bristled to see the last to turn up: *Daniels*. Effing Daniels with his effing Stoney Drive.

Daniels made straight for her. "Hey, Marsha!"

"Rodney."

"My team has made great progress on reducing the Stoney concept to practice."

"Really."

"We could use help with the gnarly plasma physics bits, though…"

In a low hiss Marsha said, "If you were thinking of asking Mr. Amber to transfer Vanessa to your project, know this. *I will break your arm.*"

Daniels crumpled like a wadded-up tissue.

"Don't you have somewhere to be right now?"

Daniels fled. Marsha composed herself.

Lose the feral rictus. Retract the claws. Turn the snaky locks back to perfectly coiffed hair….

Her phone throbbed. Incoming text.

"Heads below the parapet!" she said. "Mr. Amber is in the building."

The door to the hallway burst open. Leonard Amber strode into the anteroom, personal assistant in tow.

"Mr. Guzman. With me," said Leonard. Fernando followed him into his office.

Muffled shouting leaked through the massive door.

The office door opened. Fernando appeared, shutting it behind him carefully.

"Fernando?" Marsha put a hand on his arm. He looked at her with the eyes of a dead man.

"I asked him to postpone further field tests of Full Sapience for Rossum. It's nowhere near ready to turn loose behind the wheel."

"Oooh, bet he didn't like that!" said Vincent. "Wait. He didn't fire you, did he?"

"*No!*" Fernando's face darkened. "He ordered me to proceed and make Legal swat away lawsuits."

Fernando left to lick his wounds. Marsha flipped through her notes for the third time. Fourth? Vincent yawned and turned off his phone.

The door to the Sanctum Sanctorum opened and closed.

The assistant summoned Vincent. "Tell Mother I love her!" he whispered as he passed Marsha.

The door remained closed a long time. Behind its mahogany veneer all remained calm.

Vincent emerged. He told Marsha, "He's in a good mood. Break a leg."

The door opened. "Miss Sparke?" asked the assistant.

Dr. Sparke!

Wait...why is he in a good mood?

Did something just happen on the moon?

Vincent had been waiting for Marsha until Leonard finished with her.

"Only half-a-dozen action items," she said. "He usually shows more interest..."

"Something I need to tell you," Vincent began, just as Leonard emerged from his office.

"Oh," he said. "Still here. Time for my presser! Wanna come with?"

Not a request. Marsha and Vincent trotted behind Leonard. In the elevator, Leonard had a furious *sotto voce* go at Vincent over something she couldn't catch, Leonard having turned his back on her.

Ground floor. Short walk to the exit. Beyond that, the sanctuary of Leonard's limousine, its engine idling.

A pack of journalists lay in wait, held at bay by nothing but a velvet rope and beefy men with dark glasses and bulges in their blazers.

The minions of the press shouted questions. Leonard ignored all but one.

"Would you care to comment on Department of Transport's report on the recent fatality caused by the fully autonomous chauffeur feature of the Rossum?"

"There are no defects," said Leonard. "Rossum performed flawlessly."

"Is that all you have to say to the deceased's grieving relatives?"

Marsha's face burned.

Leonard opened the limo door and took his seat. "Why," he asked, buckling a seatbelt, "is everyone I meet an idiot or an asshole?" He slammed the door. The limo roared off.

"I take it that was a rhetorical question," said Vincent.

"Lucky us," said Marsha, "except for the feral journalists. What did you want to tell me?"

Vincent said, "Not here."

Lunar Highlands, Ray from Tycho Crater, earlier that day

Ben Dowling was finding it a strange experience to be walking on the moon. It wasn't the spacesuit.

It was the harness that allowed him to walk as if he were in Earth's gravity.

The harness contained five times his combined body and spacesuit mass in lead, and a power assist when he put one foot before the other. His muscles could not move several hundred kilos forward on their own.

Weird.

Ben hated to admit it: The silly thing worked.

He picked his way across a plain littered with debris that reminded him of briquettes, strewn from the mother of all charcoal bags. In the distance he saw mountains. So many mountains…

"Surface covered with clastic debris, but local regolith firm, as advertised," he said for the record. "Stopping to collect samples."

Jake Costello lounged in the shirtsleeve luxury of a Martian habitation unit prototype, deployed on the moon for testing, following advice of the late Stephen Hawking. He monitored Ben's transmissions in part as a scribe, but mostly to make sure the guy wandering over the Lunar surface was Ok.

"*Ooofff!*" was a sound he did not want to hear.

"Ben?"

"Oh, great!" said Ben. "How do I get up?"

The harness display showed Jake readings adding up to nonsense. Ben's video feed showed rocks. His spacesuit, however, hadn't complained of leaks.

Yet.

"Ben! Status?"

"Did a faceplant. No injuries, save to my dignity."

"First step. Get out of the harness," said Jake.

"Walk me through it."

Once unencumbered, vertical Ben said "Had it with that damned thing. Declaring it a casualty…Grit musta got into the gearbox. Or something. I brought my samples, data tablet, anything I care about, with."

"No argument here," said Jake. "But it might break Mr. Amber's heart. He spent months and a fortune on that gizmo."

"Amber's heart? That bitty thing!"

Both men whooped.

PARDON ME

I am totally, completely, one hundred percent calm.
Must be shock.

"Jake, you getting this?"

"You mean the creepy voice…Whoa! What is that?"

Before Ben stood a figure in a spacesuit.

"Not from around here, are you."

NO

Has to be shock.

The clear visor revealed a visage almost human, if you ignored the eyes and the skin colors: The former faceted and 'way too big, and the latter found nowhere outside class *Aves* on Earth.

Ben had the once-in-a-Hubble time opportunity, the privilege, the *responsibility*, of being the first human to speak to a representative of an extraterrestrial civilization.

"How do you make that *voice* sound in my headset?"

UNIVERSAL COMMS PROTOCOL INTERFACE. YOURS IS IN THE CATALOG.

"Oh…who are you?"

WE ARE THE 'nKLOMMAR

"May I ask, what you are doing here?"

As in, what are your intentions regarding Earth?

EXPLORATION, A BIT OF PROSPECTING. WE COULDN'T HELP OVERHEARING YOUR CIVILIZATION'S RADIO TRANSMISSIONS, AND DROPPED BY.

WE'D LOVE TO VISIT YOUR HOME PLANET.

"I'm sure that can be arranged."

AE Headquarters, Same Day

Marsha read "Encountered extraterrestrials exploring moon…"

and clicked on the attached video clip to see an alien creature in a spacesuit, waving at the camera while mugging a rictus presumably meant for a smile, with mountains in the background, or possibly hills, hard to tell on an airless world.

"Well, I'll be…," said Marsha.

"*I'm* sure you will!" said Vincent.

"…must sit down. When did this come in?"

"Coupla hours before Leonard's seance. Long enough for me to figure out what to tell him."

"No wonder he wasn't interested in our private session. Why did he even have it?"

"Probably didn't want to telegraph that anything out of the ordinary had happened."

"Went to the ground station, didn't he."

The terminal made a prim *ding!* "Another video from Ben," said Vincent.

"Oh my…Speaking as a girl who designs spacecraft for a living," said Marsha, "It hurts my eyes to look at that."

For weeks it seemed audiences worldwide couldn't get enough coverage of the 'nKlommar and their doings.

"Today is a day like no other in human history. Astronauts from Amber Enterprises encountered the first known extraterrestrial beings to visit the solar system. The 'nKlommar, as they call themselves, have accepted a formal invitation from the United Nations to visit Earth…

"A tour group of the 'nKlommar spent the day at Parkes Radio Observatory in New South Wales …"

"…Members of the 'nKlommar mission in New York were seen exiting Axel Daffyd's bespoke tailor shop with numerous packages and bags…"

"…'nKlommar photographed in front of the *Genbaku Domu,* Hiroshima …"

"The 'nKlommar paint London red, seen leaving the Color

Workshop after hours…"

"…A representative of the 'nKlommar addressed the UN General Assembly tonight. They expressed a desire to establish full relations—including trade and technology transfer— between Earth and the rest of the galaxy. This would require erecting something called a waypoint for their faster-than-light technology in the solar system, which would allow Earth routine access to FTL travel throughout the galaxy.

There is, however, a condition that Earth must satisfy. Humanity needs to establish a self-sustaining colony on, or in orbit around, another planet, without any form of technology transfer from other intelligent species. The 'nKlommar explained this accomplishment is used galaxy wide as a reliable proxy for the long-term viability of technological civilizations…"

"Has Leonard seen this?" asked Marsha.

"Just wait!" said Vincent.

"It has to be Mars. You know how he is about Mars. He'll go supernova."

"For sure. He's still torqued over Offworld sandbagging him with a crewed mission."

"Which has yet to launch. Bet a nickel that'll change! Any way I can talk with these 'nKlommar folk? I really want to learn about their FTL capability."

"You'd better," said Vincent. "I have them on speed-dial."

Leonard sat behind the imposing desk in his office, fingers steepled together, and gaze unwinking. Marsha, centered in the crosshairs, sat on a rickety chair before him.

"They travel faster than light by manipulating dark energy inflaton fields," she said.

"Have you heard of this before?"

"Only in crap science fiction…"

"Really," said Leonard, "Can you explain how it works? Simply?"

"I think so," said Marsha. "During cosmological inflation the space between distinct neighborhoods of spacetime expanded at enormous speed, while the neighborhoods themselves remained locally at rest. It's like someone blowing up a balloon. Consider two points on the balloon. They separate even though they're not moving in their own frame of reference. If you blow up the balloon fast enough, they separate faster than lightspeed.

"The expansion was driven by a dark energy field. That's the inflaton. In the Big Bang, it was isotopic. For FTL travel, you want one that's unidirectional."

"The energies involved must be enormous," said Leonard.

"Yeah...when they reach their destination, the inflaton decays. The inflated region is left behind as a sort of stretchmark in spacetime..."

Leonard snorted.

"...and they have a way of recovering the energy. That's where the waypoint comes in. Without recovery, it's ruinously expensive for routine use.

"Here the story gets a little weird. You can swap energy back and forth between matter and fields on the one hand—what they call stress-energy tensor in relativity—and potential energy stored in the gravitational field on the other."

"I bet our physicists don't have a clue about that!"

"*Our* physicists," said Marsha, "have known this for a hundred years. In the Big Bang, at the start of inflation, the mass equivalent of the entire visible universe started out at about a kilogram times c-squared."

"You mean you can dip into the gravitational energy and extract all the energy you need?"

"The gravitational energy gets more and more negative, but..."

"Wait! Isn't that what Daniels is trying to do with the Stoney Drive?"

"The Stoney drive violates local momentum conservation! Of matter fields! Not the same thing!" cried Marsha.

She could have reacted faster. Really should have...

It was said of Leonard Amber—by some—that the impedance mismatch between his skull and the universe was so astronomically high, it was next to impossible to get an idea into it, but once you did, it was next to impossible to get it out.

Amber Enterprises was structured as a dictatorship. It took no time for Amber to reorganize his company to focus on two crash projects: Establishment of a self-sustaining colony on Mars, and mastering the technologies required to manipulate dark energy.

The project lead for dark energy was Daniels. Amber gave him *carte blanche*. He also encouraged him to take an interest in the AE Mars Colony One initiative.

AE HQ, Two Weeks Later

As part of making his corporation come about, Leonard had issued an All-Hands ukase. This meant ordering lunch delivered in.

Marsha joined Fernando and Vincent. A glistening vat of commercial-grade pad thai graced the table in a disused canteen.

"Vanessa's been passing me intel on Daniels and dark energy," she said. "Leonard's decided he's a visionary instead of a lunatic. She tells me his ideas that aren't nonsense on stilts are barking mad and could I please help with her resume?"

She turned to Fernando. He looked subdued.

"Thought you'd be happy being off the Rossum project?"

"Yeah, but Leonard wants me to find a legal firm. He's not wild about our in-house shysters. Not gonna believe this…"

"Yes?"

"I put out a feeler to Big Bad Law Firm—Burrows, Baker, Larsson, and Faulkner. They said thanks but no thanks. They're representing the 'nKlommar."

"What."

"There was an internet kerfuffle, Terran chauvinists whining that the Moon is terrestrial territory and wanting n-thingy to bugger off because, claim jumping.

"The 'nKlommar hired BBLF, who issued a statement that parried by citing the Outer Space Treaty, and riposted by invoking the High Seas doctrine."

"And that would be, when it's at home?" asked Marsha.

"Something to the effect that a state can't claim sovereignty over anything in the high seas. Guess that applies to outer space?"

"Does the surface of a planet count?"

Marsha's phone made a funereal *gong*.

"Gotta run. Leonard wants me to hear some pitch from Daniels."

INTEROFFICE MEMORANDUM

TO: R. Daniels

FROM: M. Sparke
SUBJECT: Proposal for terraforming Hellas Planitia

I found your presentation on 1/Apr/2028 most enlightening. A few observations:

You propose to salt the atmosphere inside Hellas Planitia Crater, beneath the topographic datum, with a mixture of 50% oxygen and 50% a superheavy inert gas of atomic weight ca. 630. At the crater floor, 7 km below datum, the atmospheric pressure will be comparable to that of Earth sea level and the resulting partial pressure of oxygen will vary between 0.16 and 0.5…

"Lordy me," sighed Marsha. "Where to begin?"

1. I estimate the mass of the superheavy noble gas required to terraform the Hellas Planitia atmosphere exceeds eighty petagrams, or thirty times the mass of asteroid 1566 Icarus.

2. No noble gas of atomic mass 630 exists. The worldwide inventory of the sole artificially produced superheavy noble gas, of mass 360, is less than one picogram.

3. During a typical diurnal cycle the atmosphere will vary between -60 C and the freezing point of water at the crater floor. I question your description of these conditions as "shirtsleeve"…

She proofread her work. Minutes passed as she stared at her screen: No question who would read it right after Daniels.

"Oh, for fuck's sake, girl," she said. "D'ye want to live forever?" and pressed SEND.

She started the timer on her phone. Twenty minutes and change passed before the knock on her door.

"Miss Sparke, please accompany us."

Dr. Sparke, moron!

She rode the elevator down, down, down, flanked by security trolls outmassing her by a factor of two each. Her escorts led her to the front lobby door. One held it open for her.

She turned, dropped her cardboard box with its scant tawdry effects at his feet, and darted out before either goon could react.

Leonard had been busy. The sidewalk teemed with the formerly employed. "Hey, Marsha!" called Vincent. He stood next to Fernando.

"Leonard fired you, too?"

For the first time in weeks, Fernando smiled. "We *quit!*"

"What happens next?" she asked.

Vincent beamed. "Offworld is having a job fair!"

"Bring it on," said Marsha.

A consortium of UN member nations convened to address the challenge the 'nKlommar presented to Earth. No doubt it could be done—but should it?

Resources were a tetchy point. Observers outside of government noted that wealthy nation-states routinely expended their treasure on ruinous military adventures in quantities dwarfing the cost of a Martian colony. Their governments did not appreciate having this explained to them, any more than they appreciated being reminded of human needs left unaddressed on many a home front, for the same reason.

The 'nKlommar remained a perturbing element. They were in great demand on talk shows, gave standing-room-only lectures at universities and learned societies, and made countless visits to elementary schools.

They courteously but firmly declined to offer advice, or even express an opinion, on what Earth should do. "Entirely your affair," was their stock response.

Leonard Amber had no inhibitions when it came to giving advice.

"Humanity must accept and surmount this challenge, or stagnate and ultimately go extinct!" he declared. "I intend to establish a Martian colony myself!"

One month after he made his vow in a press conference, the United Nations Office for Outer Space Affairs in Vienna issued a Request for Proposals (Phase one).

The winning bid came from Offworld, Amber Enterprises declining to respond to the RFP. Amber meant to go solo.

The UNOOSA RFP contained a Contracts Data Requirements List item that raised eyebrows at Offworld for two reasons. First, it was classified.

Second, it had a list of personnel, weapons and ammunition for defending the colony.

Gaylord Agency, San Francisco

Winona Gaylord, licensed private investigator, was glad whenever a prospective client darkened her door. As a general rule…

The apparition opposite her was—probably—one of the 'nKlommar. Looked the part, anyway… and that *voice!*

"Why did you choose my agency?"

OUR ATTORNEYS BURROWS ET AL. RECOMMEND YOUR SERVICES HIGHLY.

That, at least, was reassuring. Before signing anything, however, she was damn well giving BBLF a call.

"How may I help you?"

The alien creature rattled off a list of tasks. Despite her professional instincts, Winona's pulse quickened.

We eat tonight!

Offworld, Inc., Boulder, Colorado, 2029. Sol Zero

Marsha stood in the middle of the canteen because there was nowhere left to sit. She couldn't even see Vincent or Ben or Fernando in the crowd. Not that she was looking…

No one in the room had eyes for anything but the arid landscape of Meridiani Planum appearing on a large screen.

Two figures in pressurized suits faced the camera. One carried a flag. With a bit of effort, they planted the flagpole, unfurled a banner bearing the United Nations logo, and proclaimed the founding of the UNOOSA Mars Colony.

"So, Marsha, how goes vacuum test?" asked Ben. He'd been right behind her.

"We're having difficulties maintaining peak thrust," said Marsha.

Project lead on the VASOMOTOR drive was the assignment of a lifetime. But…

She spent half her working hours keeping the project from coming apart at the seams. The other half she spent in meetings with upper management. Hand-holding, often enough.

Converting two hundred-million-degree xenon plasma into a

collimated jet was nothing like blowing down hot gas from a De Leval nozzle. And it felt strange reporting to Ben, who'd reported to Vincent at Amber Enterprises.

At least Ben was hard to spook.

Offworld, Inc., 2030. Sol 258.

"…Two week slip in shipping the flight article to the Cape."

"Daily updates!" said Ben. "Don't forget. It's hurricane season."

UNOOSA Mars Colony, 2031. Sol 397

It had been several sols, but Marsha still struggled with Martian gravity after six weeks transit from Earth, on the maiden flight of the VASOMOTOR drive Mars ferry *Petrel*.

Can't imagine how Vince and Fernando recovered from six months zero-g.

Anyhow, I'm on Mars! Actually on Mars!

It didn't quite feel real, yet.

Amidst the strangeness that surrounded her, one thing, one tiny thing, puzzled her. Food and shelter were provided to all in the colony, and everyone had an allowance of scrip for small purchases at an exchange. Their salaries, however, were paid into terrestrial bank accounts. One hundred percent: Personnel and equipment and risk all on Mars, but all the money on Earth.

According to Vienna, the same was true of Amber's colony.

Will we keep doing this when we're self-sufficient?

She got a call from Vincent.

"You're needed in the meeting hab ASAP."

Marsha's opportunity to visit Mars came with a *quid pro quo*. She'd been recalled to active duty and assigned to UNOOSA.

When she got there—winded, and having gotten lost on the way twice—the habitation unit was full to capacity.

All eyes fastened on her. Vincent nodded and began.

"Right. Here's what we know. Amber launched eighteen Starliner vehicles from LEO to Mars during the most recent conjunction launch opportunity, as the start of his colonization venture. The cargo payloads use direct entry at Mars, where your spacecraft just slams into the Martian atmosphere to decelerate, while crewed missions use the more civilized aerobraking entry.

"Cargo vessels just landed near Maedra Crater, about five hundred klicks from here."

Gasps and oaths filled the hab.

An Hour Later.

New Offworld Colony Administrator Ben Dowling began:
"Lieutenant Sparke…"
So, it's come to that
"…are we agreed that Amber situating his colony in close proximity to ours constitutes a threat?"

"I'm disinclined to put a benign interpretation on it. Like you, I've known the man for years. He's consistently pugnacious, and never subtle."

"So, yes?"

"Not clear. It's possible he located his colony here for much the same reasons we did. It's one of the easiest landing sites for mission planning. And it's now the only location on Mars visited by humanity."

"What are his intentions?"

"Haven't a clue. I'll ping Vienna."

Vienna sent:

1. Amber's operation relies on success-oriented project management with an ambitious schedule. UNOOSA assesses he proceeds at risk. He has deep pockets, but has taken out sizable loans to maintain schedule, and needs investors before those loans come due…

"*PUH-leeze!* Cashed my shares when he canned my ass! Gimme some dirt."

3. …Everything to do with Amber's venture is buried under non-disclosure agreements. UNOOSA lawyers consider AE contracts deceptive, based on the few we could obtain. Numerous terms and conditions in the fine print, which has applicants agreeing AE can

rescind provisions at will, and signing away any rights to seek remedies.

"Standard operating procedure for him...Hah, At last!"

6...regarding armaments, bills of lading we covertly obtained for AE cargo sent to Mars show small arms and ammo only, mostly pistols and shotguns. Apart from a small number of assault rifles, these seem intended for crowd control, vice combat.

7. Amber has stated publicly that the UN has no authority on Mars, and UNOOSA governance of the Offworld colony is therefore illegitimate.

"That's one take on high seas..."

8. ...secondhand account that Amber spoke of annexing the UNOOSA colony. We lack independent reporting, and the reliability of the original report cannot be determined.

"What the hell, Leonard?" said Marsha., "Is that why we brought all the guns and ammo, and I got called up? *Were you drunk?*"

Gaylord Agency, Mid-2032. Sol 615

SOMEONE HAS APPROACHED US CLAIMING TO HAVE USEFUL INFORMATION.
"Who is this person, and what have they got?" asked Winona.
BEST IF YOU MET. USE ONE OF OUR SAFEHOUSES.
The safehouse was an anonymous suite in the Financial District. A middle-aged Black woman waited for her.
"...Patti Slocum?"
"My work name. Joan Greene, on secondment from UK Secret Intelligence Service to the UN."
"Winona Gaylord, for the 'nKlommar." They shook hands. "Do you have something for me?"
"I do! My cover is secretary in Disbursements at Amber Enterprises. I have unrestricted admin access to most AE servers. Lucky for me, their password OPSEC is piss-poor. Child's play to set

up a backdoor and install my favorite rootkit."

Joan handed Winona a thumb drive.

"This drive contains several years of financial statements and internal audit findings…"

"Be still, my heart!"

Joan smiled.

"…It also contains intercepts of Mr. Daniel's messages from my keystroke logger. He and Mr. Amber exchange sensitive communications using a proprietary encrypted disappearing messaging service. Outstanding! Never seen anything like it, still haven't cracked it. I think you will find Daniel's side of the traffic rewarding, however. Happy hunting!"

Gaylord Agency, later that day

In Daniel's half of his dialog with Amber, Winona had treasures untold in her grasp.

Even if reading it made her eyes water.

…Soils ls*X*ab ug*X*nab,*X*,e*XX*le to meett*X* target forvo*XX* perchlorate removal fir ci*X*onversion of Martiab*X*n soil to arable polder for agri…

"You have to be one of the most ham-fisted jackasses ever to pummel a keyboard! Did you even learn typing in school? Thought that was mandatory."

…How arecwecto*XXXXXX* we going to attract new in *X*vestors? What do we have innMar*XXXXXX*oM*XX*on Mars that investors on Earth would have the slightest interest in?…

"I bet *Joan* reads this without having to edit it. Screw this for a game of soldiers. I'm writing a script to cut the crap."

…Got it, Message to sell: Successful colony pays off in trade with ET's once we're plugged into galactic commerce. Not sure about floating IPO with name like Alien Technology Futures.

How do we convince investors our colony is A, thriving and B. will soon be self-sufficient? Neither true. We have 400 colonists, if that, and recruitment is stagnant. Not much time left to pull ourselves out of the red.

Agreed. 1000 goes in prospectus. Only buys us time…

"Gotcha!" said Winona. "Conspiracy to commit fraud. And they weren't even clever."

Mars, Maedra Crater. AE Mars Colony One, September 1, 2033. Sol 1035

Raised voices, distorted in the Martian atmosphere. Automatic weapons fire.
Screams…

Gaylord Agency, September 12, 2033. Sol 1047

Winona scrolled through the latest tranche of Daniel's keyboard fumblings from Joan.
"Oh, my, Mr. Amber!" she said. "What have you gotten yourself into?"

…Bad news. IPO tanked big time. Headlines say, "Amber sees stars, markets see 'crypto'."
Burn rate unsustainable. Credit lines tapped out. Loan payments due…

"By the pricking of my thumb, he'll miss payroll in three, two, one…"

Mars Colony One, Sol 1051

Amber Enterprises exerted total control over communications between Earth and Mars. Text only; No video or audio: Conserve that precious bandwidth! Outbound messages censored: Make sure those NDA's aren't violated! Nothing inbound that might affect colonist morale!
To get an actual message through, you had to get tricksy.

Hector Delgado, indie security contractor, looked forward to the chatty text messages from home each month, filled with the doings of a rambling extended family.

On this occasion, however, he reread a single sentence, over and over.

In other news, Yolanda's nephew Diego found a new source of funding for his college tuition.

"Sasha? Take a look at this," he said.

"Good for kid," said Sasha. "Why show me?"

"Yolanda," said Hector, "is my sister."

Sasha's eyes narrowed. "Diego?" he asked.

"Middle name of my oldest."

Hector swiveled his chair to face Sasha.

"His tuition came out of my salary."

Sasha's eyes widened. He drew breath. Hector braced himself…

Nobody swears like a Russian merc who's not getting paid.

UNOOSA Mars Colony, Sol 1,068

For a full Martian year Marsha had the time of her life. Working on the Earth Return Vehicle let her get her hands dirty for the first time since grad school. More rewarding still, she stood up a machine shop for building equipment such as helicopter drones, with an eye towards replacing Martian assembly of Earth-built equipment with indigenous manufacture.

"*Sine qua non* for self-sufficiency!" she preached.

Her active-duty status barely interfered with her work. Some five dozen UNOOSA colonists had military training. A good number of those were combat veterans. They drilled together on Mars, led by Sergeant Sally Tutu, chief NCO for colony security, under Marsha's loose command. One weekend a month, in Earth terms.

All that changed in a heartbeat.

A quartet of Aresynchronous satellites juggled communication between locations on Mars, as well as between Mars and Earth.

Message traffic between the Amber Enterprises colony and its terrestrial parent was, without fail, encrypted. Traffic between AE and UNOOSA colonies varied between vanishing and nonexistent, its tone warm as a summer's day on Mars.

For many sols, a graffito adorned the ground station bulletin board: 'UNOOSA Mars Colony: Request permission to pay you a visit. Mars Colony One: Denied. Trespassers may be shot.

An *en clar* message from Mars Colony One was the last thing the watch expected. Dismay erased astonishment as they listened.

"UNOOSA, this is Mars One. Do not reply. Broadcasting at peril. Phones confiscated. Unauthorized comms forbidden. Desperate straits. Heavy food stock losses. No estimate first harvest. Widespread hunger. Amber loyalist security shot protesters. Warring factions Amber/loyalists against colonists/contract security mercs. We outnumber Amber/he outguns us. Remaining food sequestered/starve us into submission.

"Perimeter barriers disabled at…"

"We have to notify Vienna, soonest," said Vincent. "I'm buggered if I know what to tell them."

"The message itself is evidence Mars One is a basket case," said Marsha, "Send it. Bigger issue. If Amber's colony is having a civil war, what do we do?"

"There are colonists at risk of starving," said Fernando.

"How many?"

"As many as four hundred, last I heard."

"Many of those would be in poor health. Can we even feed them? We only have one hundred fifty."

"For some months," said Ben. "We have another shipment landing in four. I'll check the manifest, but it always has consumables. We can handle four hundred extra mouths for a while. Wish we had another return vehicle."

"So, we can. Should we?" asked Vincent.

"I have zero interest in walking in on someone else's gunfight," said Marsha, "But if we don't intervene and Amber puts down this revolt, what's stopping him from coming after us? He's wrapped a bit too tight on his calmest days, and he can't be having many of those now."

"What would the justification be for intervention?" asked Fernando. "Vienna won't sign off unless it complies with international law, even if we are in the Wild West."

"High seas," said Marsha.

Vienna replied instantly, by UN standards. Less than a sol.

1. Believe message genuine based on other intel.

2. Intervention authorized as necessary to prevent humanitarian disaster…

"Magic, that is," said Marsha. "What is this intel, and why aren't they sharing? Might's well be back in the Navy."

She now had fish to fry. As sole commissioned officer in the colony, the buck stopped on her desk. She summoned Sergeant Tutu, and they made their plans.

Weaponry was small arms and a few shoulder-mounted rocket-propelled grenades. Helicopter drones for recce; pressurized coaches for transport. It would have to do.

Another shoe dropped. Vienna ordered her to lead the expedition.

Mars Colony One, Sol 1076

The lead coach halted a kilometer short of a cluster of hab units.

Three drones flitted up and down the narrow lanes between units, collecting visible and thermal video from eye level. A fourth drone hovered a hundred meters over the cluster, collecting video of the settlement as a whole.

"Nobody home," said Jake, watching the thermal feed.

"Right," said Marsha. "Take us in, Jake. Squad B, Suit up!"

The squad approached the nearest unit. Marsha made a rapid circuit around it.

Mars One hab units came in a single configuration: A squat cylinder ten meters across and ten high. Units could be mated door-to-door, or connected by cylindrical passageways.

It was a good design, rugged and as close to dead simple as anything meant to keep humans alive on the surface of Mars would ever be. Marsha admired it; Vincent's design team had wrought well.

From what Masha saw of the ground level, it was unfurnished and had never been occupied.

A small power reactor sat a safe distance from the habs. Someone had run cables from it to the cluster, but hadn't connected them. Radiation levels were too low for it to have ever gone critical.

"Spread out and check the rest of the habs to be sure, but looks like we've got another Potemkin village," said Marsha.

Constructed at vast expense. That made five so far.

"Now *this* is interesting!" said Jake. Hab after hab had come up empty, until…

"What have you got?" asked Marsha.

"Comm gear!"

"This, I gotta see."

"Spotted the antenna outside, and found these," said Jake. He pointed. "Transmitter. Radioisotope thermoelectric generator for power. And a computer to run it. Nice autonomous broadcast setup, this."

"You thinking what I'm thinking?" said Marsha.

"*Funkspiel!*"

"What's that?" asked a squaddie.

"German term for deception using radio broadcasts. As the fake settlements are meant to delight the eye," said Marsha, "the radio gear is to delight the ear."

"What would they broadcast?"

"Anything, really. Encrypted white noise sounds like white noise. Wonder who's the intended audience?"

Someone on Earth, or I'll eat my helmet.

Sol 1078

"Lieutenant?" said Sally. "Nav says rendezvous's half-a-klick off."

"Launch drone," said Marsha.

Thermal imagery showed a warm hab unit. "Got a live one, Ma'am," said the pilot. "Single bogy."

"Let's get better acquainted," said Marsha.

The squad escorted a single colonist back to the convoy lead coach. He removed his helmet to reveal a gaunt bearded face.

"You got my message," said the man. "Sasha Andreevitch."

"Lieutenant Sparke, UNOOSA. How may we help you?"

"I could do with hot meal."

Marsha lobbed a softball question, one for which she already knew the answer.

"We passed several unfinished habitation clusters on the way in, like Potemkin villages."

Sasha laughed. "That's what they are, for sure!"

"Why?"

"Eye candy to fool stupid investors with images from low Mars orbit, by tarting up habs and power units that never went into service. Only problem, not enough stupid investors to go around. Mr. Daniels' idea, pretty sure."

"What went wrong with Mars One?"

"What didn't? Everything, from moment we set foot on Mars. Phones confiscated. We send dictated texts home.

"Not going home after two-year tour. We stay till Amber says we can go. Pretty sure he means feet first.

"Your hydrothermal spring. Does it give potable water as well as hydroelectricity?"

"It does," said Marsha.

"Only five hundred klicks away, should be same damn geological formation, and ours is corrosive brine. Don't even think of running that through turbines! Can't wring enough perchlorates out of soil to plant crops, and we lost three hundred metric tons rations. Half to entry vehicle making very large crater on meeting Mars--"

"*What?*"

"—you *missed* that?—and half to mold. Cryo failure during Trans Mars cruise.

"Amber ordered reduced rations until next shipment. Six months!"

"Why didn't he ask us for help?" asked Marsha. She kept her voice calm.

Sasha shrugged.

"Not sure. Bad optics for investors. Scared of being *failure.*

"Couple months go by, grim times. There was protest. S*iloviki*, his loyalist security from San Francisco, panicked and opened fire..."

"Panicked?" asked Marsha.

"Saw Amber's face," said Sasha. "Looked sick. Dozens killed.

"S*iloviki* cordoned off hab compound with rations. Amber ordered contract security—mercs like me—to keep order and get people back to work. Dunno how much labor Amber thought he could get from starving workforce.

"They stopped paying us. We switched sides and shared extra rations with colonists. Many already dead.

"We outnumber Amber and *siloviki*, but they got assault rifles, and we only got pistols and shotguns. We trade potshots, but nobody wants to waste ammo.

"Another thing. They're blind. We disabled their drones and surveillance feeds."

Marsha looked at Sally, then at Sasha.

"Please excuse us."

They left Sasha thoughtfully sipping a cup of hot chocolate.

"Sally,' said Marsha, "I know we planned for armed recce, but we're authorized to intervene. Can we take Amber?"

Amber's praetorians expected to overawe—or massacre—malnourished, all-but-unarmed civilians when they sallied forth, on seeing a number of figures in pressure suits approaching their compound.

They rushed into crossfire laid down by Sally and her squaddies, and froze at the muffled sound of gunfire in the Martian atmosphere. Even when some crumpled and fell, they failed to seek cover.

Sally had trained as a sniper. She marked her target and dropped him. Her opposite number, who passed for the leader, rolled on the ground in agony.

That spooked the goons into a stampede. It was a rout; not one of them hung back to give covering fire for his fellows. They left a scattering of bodies writhing in the dust behind them.

In the quiet that followed Marsha's voice sounded in her earpiece.

"Talk to me."

"Them's as could, scarpered, Ma'am."

"Good. Put one through the front door."

"*Grimes!* Fire one!"

Corporal Grimes shouldered his RPG launcher and shot an HE round through the compound wall. Even on Mars, it made one helluva noise.

Marsha yelled "Hold your fire!"

Silence.

"Leonard Amber. This is Lieutenant Sparkes, USN, for UNOOSA. Lay down your arms and surrender. You have my word you will not be harmed, and your wounded will receive medical treatment."

Longer silence.

Amber's voice: "We surrender."

Once it was certain the shooting was done, a crowd gathered at the compound of Amber's Last Stand.

First came his goons. Last came Amber. A cry went up.

"There's the bastard! Get him!"

Enraged colonists pushed past Marsha. She whirled around to see them rushing at him, and sprinted towards Amber, shoving and kicking bodies out of her way. Fury lent her strength.

Marsha Sparke, one and a half meters tall and fifty kilos soaking wet, stood between Amber and a mob, and screamed *"NO!"*

The mob fell back. She was the only one armed with a pistol.

Through visors, she saw shocked faces. Confused. Some looked ashamed. Heartbeats earlier, they'd blazed with bloodlust.

"Sergeant Tutu!" she barked, "Escort the prisoner to the lead coach and set a guard."

"Yes, Ma'am!"

Sally took Amber by the elbow and led him away. The crowd parted before them. Marsha stared after the pair until they vanished into the coach.

She turned to see Fernando and Vincent looking on her strangely.

UNOOSA Mars Colony, Sol 1079

"What are we going to do about Amber?" asked Vincent.

"Crimes Amber committed on Mars can't be prosecuted on Earth. High seas," said Marsha. "But he and Daniels conspired to defraud investors on Earth. He can try his chances there, or here, with no friends, no legal system, and no rights. High seas cuts both ways.

"Some choice."

"Sasha never said it out loud, but I believe Amber was a hostage of his own security goons. Sasha called them *siloviki*. That's the word Russians use for securocrats like ex-SVR or FSB who really wield power in society. My bet, Amber won't want to stay on Mars one sol longer."

"The one point of agreement between Amber and his former colonists, I expect," said Vincent. "What do you think the 'nKlommar make of all this?"

"Who can say? We're a long way from having a self-sustaining colony. I don't know, any more than you, when we'll pass their damned test.

"Ben's been interviewing the surviving Mars One colonists. Most of them want to join us."

"Really? That says something for their grit," said Vincent. "Or sanity."

"Bring it on," said Marsha. "My gut tells me humanity just stopped failing."

--

Frank Dumas lives in Southern California and has been writing for about ten years. His short stories Enter the Carnotvore, The Braneworm Returns, *and* Supernova Chasers *previously appeared in* Alien Dimensions, *and his alt-history/steampunk story* The Lunar Asylum *appeared in issue 295 of Interzone.*

The Great Deception

By Lawson Ray

Commander Kent grabbed onto the only nearby railing that wasn't hot enough to incinerate his skin. The ship shook and jerked, plummeting, failing. His heart twisted and his pores opened against the unbearable heat, but what troubled him even more than the face of death was the failure of Project Gentro.

The Commander watched as the decorated flight engineer, Brian Littler, swatted at the flames blazing from the electrical box with a towel like he'd overcooked his salmon. White smoke filled the ship's cabin and crept into Kent's lungs. He let out a hearty cough and tried to wave the smoke away, but it only seemed to get worse. Kent looked to his right toward the porthole window and saw it: flickering fires thrashing at the crackling glass like a thin, flaming veil between him and the endless red sands. In an unemotional tone, the ship repeated itself over and over again. "Total system failure. Total system failure. Crash imminent. Please brace for impact. Total system failure."

"We're going down!" said the engineer. He persisted swatting at the flames, but the fire was far too hot and the extra oxygen from the fanning towel only stoked it further. The edges of the white towel charred black and flickered and then a spark ignited the cloth.

"Brian!" Kent yelled. "The towel!"

The engineer didn't hear him, but it didn't matter. The flames wouldn't be Brian's demise.

"Total system failure. Crash imminent. Brace for impact," the ship continued, alarm bells whirring.

With another hard jerk, Kent's fingers flew from the metal pole and his body thwacked into the side of the ship. He fell to the ground with a bruised back and bloody elbows. He rubbed his head, and then his eyes and as his blurred vision returned, he saw where Brian had landed. Blood spurted, then dripped from his lips, oozing down to soak his shirt and waistband. Incinerated. Impaled. Dead.

Kent gasped and grabbed at his chest. "Brian, no!" he screamed.

"Relax, man." Brian knelt down and placed the back of his hand on Kent's forehead. "Still running a fever, huh?"

"What?" Kent said. He shot up straight in bed and his eyes darted around. The ship was fine. Everything appeared normal. "But…" he trailed off. He reached out with both hands and grabbed at the engineer's face. His skin was still there, soft but not without its valleys of pockmarks. He then ran his fingers over Brian's scraggly beard. It was more unkempt than Kent remembered, but it was still there.

"Woah, Commander," Brian laughed. He softly took Kent's hands and set them down. "Settle down. Looks like you had a bad dream."

"No," Kent said. "There was a fire and sparks and smoke, and the ship was crashing! I was coughing and you were fanning the flames, and the windows were cracking, and we were crashing on Mars! There was this total system failure, and the alarms were going off and I…" Kent stared at Brian, his eyes wide, bewildered. "I watched you die, Brian."

"Wow. Quite the dream."

"It wasn't a dream," the Commander said, exasperated by his own fear. His voice was hollow, and then unsure. "It couldn't have been. It was all so real."

Brian stood and spun around twice. "Well, it must have been, right? Here I am, in the flesh. Alive and well."

Kent didn't respond. He knew what he saw then and there. He had felt Brian's face with his own two hands, but he'd never before had a dream that seemed so real.

"There is one thing your dream did get right though," the engineer clicked his tongue. "We did crash."

"Crash?" Kent whispered. His face grew hot again. Hot like it was burning up against fire and smoke and he could even feel it scratching his lungs. He grabbed at his chest, then coughed. "Have you been outside? Have you gotten to explore at all?"

Brian shrugged. "Not sure there's much to explore. We're not on Mars."

"What? Well, then…where *are* we?"

"That's what I've been trying to figure out for the last few days.

Got the ship mostly up and running. That is if you discount the communications relay and the navigation system."

Kent adjusted in the bed just enough so he could see out the porthole window. It was fully intact, not a crack to be seen. Outside the window were plains and valleys of sand further than he could see. "This isn't Mars?"

"Not a chance."

"How can you be so sure?"

"Well for one, the sand isn't red. But I confirmed via air sampling. I even went outside without a helmet. It's fine. Brimming with oxygen."

"Without a helmet?" said Kent. "You could have died!"

"No, of course not," Brian chuckled. "I didn't start off that way, at least. I got the gas chromatographer up and running and took that thing out there for some readings."

"And?"

"78.08 percent nitrogen, 20.95 percent oxygen, and just under one percent of argon."

Kent shook his head and bit his tongue. "Earth."

"Yep. Earth. Totally breathable."

"How is that possible? How could we still be on Earth?"

"Well, we were in cryostasis of course for the journey to Mars, so I'm not quite sure. But when the ship started to fail, it broke cryostasis and woke us up. Well, it woke me up at least. I honestly wasn't sure if you'd made it. But from what I got out of the system logs, there was some sort of vague electrical failure. It gave me code 43900x, which is something equivalent to a 'total system failure'. I'd bet it was caused by prolonged overheating. And based on that, I'd also bet we never even broke the mesosphere. They just don't make engineers the same anymore, do they?"

"But Brian, *you're* an engineer."

Brian looked down to his shoes, then back up as if it were the first time he'd ever examined his own body. Commander Kent watched Brian's eyes closely, studied every movement, every mannerism. Something seemed off. "Right, I am," he said. "But I meant…in general."

Kent nodded slowly. "Right. So, you're saying…we're on Earth. Just in some random desert with no communications. No Navs. And nobody has found us."

"That's right."

Kent's nodding continued, his eyebrows taut and gaze trained on Brian. Kent had had his fair share of benders in his wayward youth, but he couldn't remember a single one where he'd blacked out. He'd always had a strong memory. All the teachers and professors had commended him for it when he was growing up. They all called it 'photographic'. So even in a night drowned in booze, Kent had never lost a memory. Never had a chunk of his life go missing. That is until now. He couldn't remember the crash at all, just the wanderings of a dream. A vibrant, terrifying dream.

"Right," said Kent. "We better get moving then. We don't have enough food to stay out here and wait for someone to find us." He unclipped his bag and pulled it out from storage. He reached inside and grabbed his Walther PPQ, checked the ammo, and pulled the slide to see a round readied in the chamber.

"What's that for?" the engineer asked nervously.

"We're in the desert," Kent said. "And depending on what desert, it might be dangerous. Can't be too careful, right?"

Brian nodded, but with a strained, unconvinced stare. He'd survived days without knowing the Commander had brought a gun aboard.

The Commander and engineer left the shuttle and stepped out into the vast desert. The sun shone strongly that day, relentlessly beating down on them, blinding them. Kent spun around, trying to figure the time of day by where the sun was. He looked down to his watch which was surprisingly still working. He then checked back behind them to see the lander. It was clearly patched and dented, but it appeared Brian had mostly fixed it up and remarkably so. There were a few screws missing, some damage to the hull, but otherwise nothing seemed broken. The lander was even standing on its four legs, perfectly upright upon the undisturbed sand. "It doesn't look like we crashed," Kent mumbled. He turned to confront Brian.

Brian itched at his neck and then his hair. "I've had a few days to work on it. Couple of the legs were missing when we hit the ground, but I was able to find them close by and weld them back on. Once I got that sorted, I used the momentum and suspension in the legs to stand it upright. It was tough, but I managed."

"Tough?" Kent scoffed. "The lander is about twelve hundred

pounds. What, did you find a forklift out here?"

"No. You know, I thought you needed to pass physics to become an astronaut."

Kent didn't find it funny and shook his head. "This all just seems strange, don't you think?"

"What about it?"

Kent looked down to the sand, then above. He couldn't see anything but sand, and couldn't fathom for how long it went on. "I had a dream about crash-landing on Mars and about a total system failure. We did crash, and there was a total system failure."

"You didn't get it all right," Brian reminded him. "We're still on Earth. Not to mention the fact that I'm still alive."

Kent put his hands on his hips. "It's hot as shit out here. We won't have much – " The Commander stopped. His face grew numb and he rubbed at his eyes. There was a long streak of burnt sand behind the lander, stretching at least a half mile. In it were charred bits of foil and metals, scraps that had broken off the ship on impact. "How…"

"What is it?"

Kent pointed to the streak. "That? That trail of junk. How did that get there? The black sand? The trail of parts?"

"That?" said Brian. "Well, I don't know if you've ever seen a movie, but crashing isn't the prettiest thing, you know. Bits and pieces and oil everywhere."

"But it wasn't there before," whined the Commander. "Just a moment ago, there was nothing there. The sand was fine. Yellow. Undisturbed."

Brian patted Kent on the shoulder. "Sounds like you're still half awake."

"Yeah," Kent said. He squinted and stared at the streak. The crash landing. The sea of red sand. Total system failure. The taste of copper as a crimson drip rolled off Brian's lips and stained his shirt. His lifeless, black eyes. "Must be."

The two then set out to find anything they could to survive: wires, gadgets, missing parts, the radio battery that was conveniently dislodged and misplaced. Commander Kent kicked at the soot and watched the sand bunch up in dusty clumps, then fall slowly back to the ground. He kicked over metal bits which clanged against his boot. He turned over everything he could. He drew his hand over his mouth as the coughing continued, just as it had in his dream. Only this time, he thought it was probably from the constant smell of burned rubber and sheet metal and gasoline polluting the sand.

Kent even stopped a few arbitrary times to dig in the sand with his fingers. He kicked the sand again, then watched it again. It rose in a clump, then dispersed. The fine grains spread and twinkled to the ground as slow as a snowflake on Christmas morning. "Brian," Kent called out.

The engineer came rushing over. "What is it? Did you find something?"

Kent shook his head, still watching the last grains fall in place. "Maybe. You said we're on Earth, right?"

"Of course." Brian searched the horizon with wide gestures. "Can't you tell?"

"Did you test the gravity?"

"Didn't feel the need. Why?"

Kent pointed to the ground. "Watch this." The Commander arched his foot downward so his shoe's toe hovered over the sand. He then kicked at it once more and waited for gravity to take over. Again, the sand burst upward in a clump, then spread and fell back to the ground. Kent let out an incredulous groan. "Wait. No. It was faster that time." He kicked again, and again the sand rose and fell just as it would on Earth: quickly, no hesitation.

"What about it?"

"No," Kent said, growing impatient. "I'm not seeing things. I swear. I kicked the sand earlier and it fluttered to the ground like a bunch of snowflakes. It was slow, much slower than it is on Earth. About thirty percent slower, roughly equaling the difference in Martian gravity. And I've felt lighter here too. Haven't you? Haven't you noticed you have more stamina? We've been out here for hours even though its blazing hot and I don't feel the least bit fatigued."

Brian shook his head. "We did some training before the mission. Maybe that's what you're feeling."

"Then how do you explain the sand?" Kent yelled.

"I think you need some rest, Commander. Let's get you back to the ship."

And so they returned.

On the journey back, the engineer made some passing comments regarding the weather, what they might have for dinner, and life back home. He pondered the search and rescue operation, what their families might think, the media frenzy that plastered every TV screen in every household twenty-four hours a day. He imagined aloud the warm welcome they'd receive when they got home. Perhaps there'd be a ticker-tape parade, or an invitation to Saturday Night Live to tell the late-night audience about their comedy-sketch of a disappearance in the deep dark space of planet Nevada or wherever they happened to land. But all the while, Commander Kent didn't say a word. None of it made sense. None of it.

Kent suggested they sleep in the ship together side-by-side for shelter from any wildlife of which they were yet to see. Not a snake, not a bird, not even a bug. But Brian insisted on sleeping under the stars. He explained his reasoning by rambling on about a camping trip he'd been on with his father. "There was one time where Pops and I went camping out in the Sonoran deserts when I was just a boy," he said. "It was so beautiful laying beneath the stars and sleeping out in the open. I've never seen the sky so vibrant. It was like you could look out into the universe, tug it apart and see straight to the other side. Won't you do that with me? Won't you lay beneath the stars? Oh, come on, Kent. It's just so beautiful."

Kent was almost repulsed by the idea. "No, I'm alright. It's unwise. We don't know where we are or what's out there, not to mention how cold a desert gets at night. You could wake up freezing out there if you're lucky enough to not get bit by something venomous. We're not here to go sightseeing, Littler."

But for some reason, the engineer was set on sleeping in the wilderness, and the two agreed after much debate that they'd sleep apart. Kent retired to the ship while Brian roamed the desert, searching for the perfect spot to lay, as if watching the stars from one angle was an entirely different experience from another fifty meters away.

At first, the Commander slept soundly. The unbearable heat of the day coupled with his own distress tired him endlessly. He slept without dream this time, but suddenly awoke with a sharp pain shooting up his back and into his shoulders.

Kent winced and howled. He tried to sit upright, but it only got worse. He rolled his shoulder in circles and pressed hard into the muscle, trying to massage away the pain. It was no use. Kent looked out the port window to see it was still dark. Nothing but the darkness of space and empty red sand for farther than he could see. He laid back down on his back, careful to not further disturb his muscles.

"Wait!" he exclaimed. Kent ignored the pain and shot up to his feet and scampered toward the window. "Red sand!" *Red* sand. Despite the darkness, he could see the sand was clearly not the yellows and whites he recognized from earlier that day. It was red now, red as rust. Kent pressed his face against the porthole, then rubbed the condensation he'd breathed onto it away. "We made it," he whispered. His lip quivered and a smile shot up his cheeks. He'd done it. Him and Brian were the first men to land on Mars. Project Gentro wasn't over.

And then he remembered his dream: the way he'd lost his grip on the metal pole and catapulted against the ship's wall, badly bruising his back. Kent fumbled for his pocket mirror in his bag and pulled it out, then contorted so he could see a small bit of his back in its reflection. It was almost entirely black and blue. But the bruise hadn't been there before. Or had it? He realized he'd never checked.

Then came a static from the communications array. "Hello? Hello? This is Houston. Commander Kent Giles. First Class Engineer Brian Littler. If you can hear us, please answer. Do you copy? This is Houston. Commander Giles, do you copy? Day four of no contact. Do you copy? Mission critical. Over."

Kent wheezed and broke into hysterical laughter. He tugged at his hair and began to sob. He lunged for the radio and pressed the button on its side. "Hello? Hello, Houston? Hello, do you copy? This is Commander Giles. We're safe. We're safe…over."

"Commander Giles?" the radio crackled. "Boy, are we glad to hear from you. What's your status? Over."

Kent sniffled, tried to compose himself. "We've been stranded out here for days. Communications were down…navigation too. Littler did a handy job at fixing some of it up, but he didn't tell me he got the radio working again. I thought we'd crashed in some desert on Earth, but…well, we don't know where we are. Cannot provide coordinates. Experienced a total system failure. Over."

A long silence hung on the radio. The Commander couldn't stand it longer than a few seconds. "Hello? Houston? Do you copy?"

Another long pause. "We copy, Commander Giles. We copy. Building a status report now to narrow search efforts. You said you crash landed. Is the ship operable? Over."

"Mostly. Just navigation is off now."

"Supplies?"

"We have a decent amount of dehydrated MREs. Could maybe last us another week together."

"And the Project Gentro cargo?"

"Destroyed. Gone…over."

A heavy sigh came over the radio. "Figures. You know, between you and me, Commander, I don't think that planet wants us. Four missions to colonize Mars. Four catastrophic failures. It's like something doesn't want us there."

"Yeah," said Kent. "I kind of know what you mean."

"And Littler? Where is he?"

"He's…" Kent laughed. "He's out there stargazing somewhere. I'll go find him. If I'm not back in an hour, you'll know something happened. Over."

The radio hissed and crackled again. A laugh echoed in static over the line. "Right. Best of luck, Commander. Nice to hear from you. It's a damn miracle you two made it. Over."

"Over and out." Kent grabbed his pistol, jumped into a pair of pants and yanked a shirt over his head. On his way out the ship door, he tugged on his boots and patted his crazed oily hair down. "Brian!" he called out. Kent stopped on the ship's ramp, dead still. There were still miles and miles of red sand, but it wasn't uninhabited. Not in the slightest.

In the distance were large, geometric structures like colossal, thin hourglasses. Smokestacks climbed over the horizon and artificial lights shone back so bright Kent had to cover his eyes. "What the…" He could hear rumbling engines and the muffled noise of dissonant orchestral tones from afar, something like haunting music. There were shining shades cloaking some of the lower buildings, like an umbrella fitted with string lights. There were vehicles and mud homes, glass statues, and even a few purple-leaved trees wrapping like boa constrictors around the buildings. "Brian!" Kent yelled, louder this time. He saw a shadowy dot up on the red hill above the lander and ran toward it. The red sand kicked up and lingered in the air just as it had earlier that day. Even though the path was uphill and sandy, Kent ran faster than he ever had before. He was nimbler than a cat, faster than an Olympian.

He reached the top of the hill without a bit of energy exerted, not a droplet of sweat hanging on his brow. "Brian," he said softer now. He stopped, and bent down. A blanket covered a gray mass, skinny, bony, emaciated. Kent was quiet now, cautious.

It wasn't Brian.

The thing was tucked beneath a blanket and had jagged, insect-like limbs that curled up into the creature's torso. Kent wrapped his fingers around the blanket slowly, so as not to disturb the thing. He lifted the blanket as horror paled his face, as his gut fell to his toes. As the blanket rose, Kent shrunk in revulsion at the sight of the creature. It was built like a leopard-sized cricket without wings. Its antennae flickered in its sleep, and its legs were tucked under its slimy, sweating thorax. Its ribbed abdomen rose and rattled with each breath. And its large beady eyes were a cloudy white as if it were blind.

The Commander released the blanket and let it fall back onto the creature. He stumbled back from it and fell on his back. He winced and yelped against the pain snapping up into his shoulders and suddenly, the creature's eyes weren't so cloudy anymore. They flickered and changed to black and shone in a series of intertwined hexagons. The giant cricket twirled over, and its legs planted into the sand. It shook its head and rattled its abdomen in a panic. It then dipped its antennae toward the Commander. Kent thrusted an arm over his face to block the attack, but nothing came.

"Kent!" he heard. "Couldn't resist the view, could you?"

Kent dropped his arm from his face and searched for the voice. Beside the blanket on the ground was Brian, sitting upright with his hands planted against the yellow-white sand. "But…" he looked out to the horizon. No more hour-glass skyscrapers. No more smokestacks. No more lights. No more music. "No." He drew the gun from his waistband on the engineer who shot to his feet and raised his hands.

"Woah, wait now! What's gotten into you? Watch where you point that thing, Commander. Please! Be reasonable."

"Reasonable?" Kent shouted. Spit flew from his clenched teeth. "What are you? Where are we?"

"I told you; I don't know. Some desert. The navigation system is busted, and we haven't had communications for days. Don't you remember? We were just talking about this today."

"Bull shit!" Kent said. "You can't do this to me anymore. Whatever you are, what are you doing to me?"

"Doing to you?"

"I wake up and the communications array is working just fine. I talk to Houston and they answer. I look outside and there's red sand as far as the eye can see. And then there's a whole damn city with smokestacks and skyscrapers and hovering vehicles and some kind of music I've never heard. Then I come up here and see a Goddamned bug sleeping under this blanket. What are you?" Kent flicked his wrist so the gun was inches closer to Brian. "Answer me!"

"Maybe you were dreaming again. What was it? You had a dream about some city in the desert and –"

Kent was sweating with anger now. He tightened his arm and his index finger twitched, hovering over the trigger. "Don't lie to me! What are you?"

Brian backed up some more. He waved his hands in the air and pleaded. "Kent, please! Don't...alright. Fine. I'll tell you. Just put that thing down."

"I'll put the gun down when you tell me what the hell is going on!"

Brian lowered his arms and sighed. "Alright, you win. Okay? This whole thing has been fake. One giant deception."

"Deception? What do you mean? Explain!"

"I've been fooling your mind, projecting images onto it so you see what I want you to see, not what's really out here."

Kent flicked the gun toward the creature posing as Brian again. "Why? What's out there that you don't want me to see? Is it that city in the valley?"

"Because..." Brian's body pulsated, and his skin turned back to the creature's gray. He then shrunk to the ground before Kent and was a giant cricket again: six legs, two antennae, and an oily, gigantic thorax and abdomen. But it still spoke to Kent all the same. The sand slowly turned back to red, but the city in the distance was still nowhere to be seen. "Because we're afraid."

Kent stared, unblinking at the creature. He couldn't believe its ability to manipulate his mind so easily. "Afraid?" the Commander asked. "Afraid of what?"

"Afraid of you. And from the way you wave that gun around, rightfully so."

Kent looked down to his hands, saw the muscles tight and bulging beside his thumb. He kept the gun on the creature. He wouldn't fall for some cheap extraterrestrial guilt-trip. "You've been lying to me this whole time. You lied about the communications being down. You lied about being my friend. You lied about *what* you are. You even changed my whole world so I saw things that weren't true. And if I hadn't caught on, what were you going to do? Set me in an endless loop looking for parts we already have until I starved to death out here?"

"I didn't have much of a plan," the creature said. "And besides, I'm not sure I would have made it that long."

"Why's that?"

"Us Junksoins, or 'Martians', as you call it…we have a fantastic immune system." The creature jittered and convulsed, then continued. "But you've infected me with something with which I am not familiar. Luckily, I was the only one out here. I was on a hike into the wilderness. I like to come out here to clear my mind. And then I found you…and your friend."

"Where is he?" Kent snapped. "Where's the real Brian?"

The creature's antennae curled outward. "Your dream was not a dream," it explained. "He died in the crash. I found him impaled by some sort of metal fragment that broke off your ship. He was severely burnt, covered in blood. He'd been long dead by the time I arrived. I buried him about two cubits beneath the ground behind that hill over there," the cricket pointed down toward the other side of the lander where a shallow hill stood.

Kent covered his mouth with one hand and shuddered. "Dead," he croaked.

"My condolences," the creature said, its hexagon eyes twirling. "I figured, if you woke up and found me beside the body, you would have thought it was me who killed him. Then it would only be a matter of time before you killed me. I guess it didn't matter either way," the creature rubbed its hindlegs together and chittered.

The Commander grunted and holstered the pistol. "I won't kill you," he said, then paused. "Not yet at least. How do you explain the oxygen composition here?"

"We are also oxygen-based lifeforms. This planet has always had a high-level of oxygen, just like yours."

"But the readings from the rover missions…"

"Faked."

"How?"

"The same way I've been deceiving you," said the creature. "Well not exactly the same, we Junksoins just have a knack for that sort of thing. We can't exactly infiltrate the mind of a robot. It has none." The creature's thorax jolted again, and it chirped loudly. Kent watched these foreign movements with a sense of disgust mixed with fascination. "We would usually figure out where the device was going to land, and then trap it in a box that looks like the planet it is expecting to find: barren, desolate, lifeless. Eventually, we would lure the machine into town by giving it rocks, and sometimes a little push." The Martian's antennae vibrated. Kent wondered if that meant it was laughing. "But eventually we would get the machine into a large building where we could leave it to roam around and collect samples of real rock and dust to report back, but it would never be able to report that it found us."

"And you'd fill the building with a falsified laboratory atmosphere."

"That's right," said the cricket. "It's not the most advanced tactic ever, but it's worked so far."

"Well, you've fooled the best minds we've got," the Commander nodded. "I'm impressed. Sounds like you're quite the species. Technologically advanced enough to deceive us like this."

"No, I wouldn't say so," it said. "We have our deception, that is all. No grand weapons or vast trade systems or anything to the level of your planet."

Kent huffed. "You're afraid because you don't have advanced capitalism yet?"

"We're afraid because of what you do with all your power. We have observed from here on Junkso for a long while now. We have seen horrors from your planet we could not have concocted in our greatest deception. We've seen your skirmishes for petty control, your killing, conquering without remorse. On more than one occasion we have witnessed concentrated fires the size of small moons through our telescopes that were created for no notable reason at all.

"We Junksoins are not without our wars, no sentient species can be. It's in our nature to want more, to explore, to wonder. That's what makes us sentient after all, isn't it? A quest for something greater than survival. The reason we are afraid is because, if you do such terrible things to each other, there is no telling what you would do to a species that looks like me from a planet far away. Your lust for conquest will undoubtedly be insatiable."

Commander Kent's chest deflated. His rage was gone, even that for his deceased engineer. He no longer cared for the days' worth of deception, the lies, nor even the intent to starve him to death. He glanced to the gun in his holster and stoically locked his jaw.

The creature didn't speak for a long moment. The wiry hairs on its front legs stood, and its hindlegs dug into the sand. It leaned backward, throwing its weight into its abdomen, and then jolted forward with another noisy chitter. "What is that?" Kent asked. "Why do you keep doing that?"

"The infection," it said. "I told you: I'm dying."

"Dying? I thought you said you had a strong immune system. You can fight it, can't you?"

"I could have," the creature lamented. "But not anymore. You see, if I rested properly, I could have fought it off without a problem. But I have spent my time working hard to deceive you, staying up long hours in the heat, using all my body's energy on mind tricks over healing."

"Because you were afraid?"

"Because I didn't want you to find the other Junksoins."

Kent shook his head. "Well now, you know it was for nothing. Once I bring back real samples of the atmosphere here and tell my planet that this place is perfectly habitable and there was just an advanced species fooling us this whole time, you know what the reaction will be? It'll be a shift in science not seen in hundreds of years! I'll be famous, they'll name towns and cities after me here. The name Commander Kent Giles will be one of the most recognized in human history. I'll be the founding father of the Martian colonies. Not a single member of my family will ever work again!"

"I know. And you know, as well as I do, they will kill us all." An especially chilled breeze caught the hill and kicked up small tornadoes of wind and the creature shivered. It stepped crabwise toward the blanket, then nestled its abdomen atop it and tucked its hindlegs in.

"I'm not sure of that."

"I can read your mind, Commander. You cannot lie to me," the Martian's voice was rapidly weakening. "You don't have to tell them, do you?"

"It's my job," the Commander protested. "I *have to* tell them. It'll be the greatest find of the century, maybe ever. It could change the whole trajectory of humanity."

The creature's antennae bowed. "And in turn, it would change ours." It paused for a moment during which Kent said nothing. "I am begging you, Commander. Examine your inner thoughts. I have been in them. I know you understand what I am saying. Please save my people. Tell yours that there is nothing here."

Commander Kent nodded in acknowledgement, but made no such promise. He tucked the blanket over the Martian's thorax, and eventually its antennae fell limp and its abdomen no longer jolted. The vibrant city reappeared in the distance with its purple-leaved trees wrapping around thin skyscrapers. Roaring incongruent tones, the buzzing engines, the sounds of Mars. The unsuspecting people living on. And when the city fully reappeared, clear as it was when the creature slept, the Commander wiped his eye.

The Martian city wasn't quite like anything Kent had seen on Earth. He stayed sat atop the hill beside the deceased creature for a moment, watching the mud structures and wondering what their cities looked like from up close. He wondered how he'd handle it. He wondered if seeing a city of gargantuan crickets would make his skin crawl. He wondered if they'd accept him or murder him. He wondered if they stomped on little humanoid pests in their homes.

Kent headed back down the hillside and returned to the ship. The radio still crackled without words from the other end. Kent picked it up and pressed the button, then raised it to his mouth. "Hello? Houston? Do you copy?"

A long moment of silence. "Yes, sir. We copy. We were starting to get worried about you. You said it'd be an hour. It's been close to four on our end."

"Yeah. Sorry."

"So?" said the radio's voice. "Did you find Littler?"

The Commander looked at the cross hatches in the radio's speaker and pictured the cricket's hexagonal eyes clearly. He thought of great fires and war and death and famine and sadness and atomic bombs and conquest and space exploration and even his own children. And when he finally pressed the button again, he said, "No. Littler is dead. This place is a death trap. There's nothing out here."

A pause, and then the radio hummed again. "Ugh, that's a shame," it said. "Sorry about the engineer. But I can't say I'm surprised. What did I tell you? Four catastrophic mission failures under Project Gentro. I get the feeling we're just not meant to live on Mars."

Kent looked out the porthole to see the smoke rising over the Martian morning horizon. The virgin red dust glistened beautifully and the blanket at the top of the hill flapped just enough that he saw a limp hind leg hanging from it. The Commander nodded. "Yeah," he said. "We're not. Returning to base. Over."

--

Lawson Ray is a data analyst living in the Washington DC area who writes horror and science fiction short stories. You can find more of his stories on www.lawsonray.com, or find him on Twitter @RealLawsonRay.

Guardian Friendship
By Geoffrey Hugh Lindop

Amanda checked her results yet again. She was sure she had detected an artifact, but she couldn't risk being made a laughingstock. Her reputation on Mars Colony had deteriorated by claiming to have detected a fossil within the Gediz Valley three times, and each time after extensive, and expensive, investigations by the rest of the team, no fossil was detected.

Each time her research was checked by other team members. Most of them agreed with her, and were happy to carry out the investigation. The exception being Philip Harding. Several incidents, when they were both at university together, drove them apart. They hated one another. At least when they were at university, they had the freedom to avoid each other. Fate took them both to the colony around the Moon's South Pole. Although they lived in separate habitats, joint meetings brought them together at least once a week.

It was a hard decision to apply to join the Gediz Colony on Mars. It meant leaving Graham, her beloved husband, on the Moon. He was a geologist involved in an important investigation on Moon rock around Copernicus Crater. She didn't see him every day. Catching transport from the Lunar South Pole to Copernicus was not as easy as catching a Number 7 Bus in London, but they managed to have a day together at least once a week. Going to Mars seemed the perfect solution to get away from Philip. It was only when she was traveling in the close confines of the spacecraft that she discovered her fellow passenger was Philip. He too had decided to go to Mars to get away from Amanda on the Moon. If only they had talked to one another, but enemies seldom chat casually. Now they were in the close confines of the Moon to Mars spacecraft for six and a half months. Each day the signal to talk to her husband took longer and longer.

It was Graham's enthusiasm for geology that focused Amanda on looking for fossil evidence for life on Mars. Now she had found it.

"So, what do you think Graham?" It was wonderful to see her husband's face on the screen. The time delay on the signal emphasized their temporary separation, yet to see his face brought them together.

"You have definitely found something. Looks too artificial to be a fossil, though."

"That's what I thought. What do you reckon it is?"

"Only one way to find out, and that's to dig it up."

It took a few days to organize the dig. Now it was the big day, and Amanda was joined by Thomas and Melissa as they walked the corridor around the circumference of the colony. All three were dressed in their space agency uniforms. They passed through the horticultural zone whose green leaves, and colorful flowers were in stark contrast to the bleak sand covered landscape that could be seen through its large south facing windows. Each of the six habitat modules had large south facing windows that captured the sunlight necessary for photosynthesis in the six horticultural zones.

"Good luck." Ruth looked up from her task of tending a tomato plant that gained additional photosynthesis energy from a bright artificial light above it.

"Thank you." Amanda smiled at her friend.

They opened the airlock door, and walked down the passageway and into their buggy. It had three double wheels on each side which were made of a material able to withstand the knife-like shards of rock embedded in the Martian surface.

"Buggie Three to Control." Amanda sat in the driver's seat, her two colleagues either side of her.

"Control to Buggie Three. We are receiving you loud and clear and confirm your video signal is good."

"Permission to leave."

"Granted. Good Luck Amanda."

They headed east. The Sun shone fairly high in the red sky so didn't dazzle them as they made their half hour journey. The distant hills were misted grey. Although there was less atmosphere than on the Earth, it was sufficient to create the familiar illusion of distance that is lacking on the Moon.

A flashing light on top of the base camp beckoned them. The large cylinder held all the supplies needed on their expedition. It sat on top of a massive six-wheeled AI controlled boogie that had delivered the base camp a day earlier.

Once inside the base camp they helped each other dress into their space suits. They emerged from the door opposite where the buggy was parked.

The incline before them was too great for ARCHIE, the AI generated robotic excavator, to contemplate. Amanda, safety rope in hand, hopped backwards down the slope as she followed the instructions of Melissa, who was holding the other end of the rope.

Once safely at the base of the incline, Thomas sent a motorized trolley downhill. He held it in check with his rope. Amanda removed the ARCHIE from the trolley and set it in the correct location.

"Okay Tom. It's all yours," radioed Amanda.

"That's confirmed. I am getting a good signal, and all systems are go."

"Present coordinates confirmed. Activate ARCHIE," said Amanda.

ARCHIE moved slowly forward digging a straight trench as it did so. Two meters further on it stopped, retraced its path and dug a ditch another millimeter deeper.

"Second coordinates confirmed. Well, I guess we'll leave ARCHIE to get on with it," said Amanda.

Seventy hours later the artifact was on the table in the laboratory. It was made of gold, a cylinder four inches in diameter and four feet long. Tests confirmed that there were no organic compounds on it, and it was safe and scientifically acceptable to be touched. Amanda was given the privilege of being the first person to do so. Her speech was beamed to the Earth and Moon in 3D virtual reality.

"Well. What do we make of this? Obviously artificial."

Philip was furious. For the last three months he had enjoyed being the center of attention. His colleagues looked up to him as the first person to discover a fossil on Mars. However, it was only a piece of coral, insignificant to Amanda's discovery.

"There is just one line of something etched into the surface. It could be simply a graphic design, or a greeting, a number, who knows? That must be the subject of our next investigation." Amanda stroked the characters as if pouring her love into the artifact. The fingers on her right hand reached towards the end of the cylinder and rotated within small cup-shaped depression. 'And what is the significance of this inverted dome?'

The next instant she was no longer in the laboratory. She was in a tall conical room. There were no windows, but the walls glowed with a cream white light. A creature sat looking into an array of six cubes displaying scenes, and information, in three dimensions. The creature's four arms, each with six fingers, danced across the cubes, tweaking something as they did so. It made minor changes to some cubes, but completely changed the display on others.

Its hair, if you could call it that, was of two-inch straight strands that were florescent. They continually moved, and changed color. Possibly, they made it sensitive to brainwaves, and other energy sources. Suddenly the hairs stopped moving, turned brown, and went straight upright. The creature looked shocked, aware that someone was in the same room.

"Yeg ra me soo trool greg." It stood up and moved towards Amanda.

"I … I … I … I'm sorry I … I … I … mean you no harm." Amanda, alarm in her voice, faced the creature, and slowly walked backwards.

"Ze frit kety junt." The voice sounded slightly calmer. There was a pause of about two seconds.

"Hello Amanda," said the creature. "You took me by surprise. Please relax. I want to be your friend."

"Who … Who are you? How do you know my name?"

"My name is Zebrisky, but you can call me Zeb. Thank you for rescuing Yargsup's Stanzlick. It's been missing for billions of years, you know. I have the honor of being its guardian."

"And you've been its guardian for billions of years?"

"No. No. No. I'm not that old. We have a life span similar to your race, but the title of its Guardian is passed down the generations."

"Wow." Amanda could hardly take in a civilization lasting that long.

"It took us about a million years to get ourselves sorted out. Initially, we were like beings on your planet with civilizations coming and going. Here on our planet," it waved some of its arms in the air, "we live closer to the center of the galaxy. Our stars are closer together. Once we mastered space travel all the peace-loving people moved to other worlds, and united with other civilizations."

"You know about our civilizations, but you live so far away."

"When you touched the hollow button, you were automatically taken through the Fifth Dimension and brought here. You are about two of your seconds in the past, so our conversation may be a little slow. A bit like the time it took Neil Armstrong to tell ground control that 'The Eagle has landed'."

"You know about Neil Armstrong? You speak English. That's crazy."

"No, I don't speak English. Your ears can tell you that, and until a few moments ago I never knew Neil Armstrong. What I do know is how to read your mind. At the moment your mind is full of your association with your ancestor. He was the first man to step foot on your Moon, and you are the first woman to step foot on an extra-solar planet. Congratulations."

She found it had read her mind to such an extent that it knew Amanda, married to Graham Braithwaite, was the daughter of William and Janet Armstrong. She had been fascinated that her surname was the same as the first man to walk on the Moon and it had stimulated her interest in astronomy and space exploration. Amanda's and Neil's common ancestor lived in the fifteenth century, but that didn't bother Amanda.

"For my part," said Zeb, "I am the first Guardian in billions of years to meet the person to have rescued it. I am honored to meet you."

Amanda was in the laboratory standing behind the artifact. It was as if she had never left. "Well, I think this inverted dome is their equivalent of a button, and when pressed it would take the user back to his home planet."

"It's nothing like a button," said Philip, "Amanda. You can't make this up. What do you mean it would take him back to his home planet? It's an artifact not a spacecraft. It offers no protection from the vacuum of space."

"But a spacecraft is old fashioned. This will take the user to the center of the Milky Way instantly."

"Rubbish." Philip pressed the so-called button. He did not appear before Zeb. He moved away from the artifact. "See. I didn't travel anywhere." He pointed at Amanda. "Its pure luck that this woman has found this artifact. She has no scientific background, and makes things up as she goes along."

Amanda knew she was right. She had seen Zeb. She had traveled to the center of the Galaxy. She expected Philip to do the same. She found comfort in caressing the 'button' with her fingers, gently rubbing them around the inverted dome. Instantly she was back in front of Zeb.

"Well, he got a bit upset, didn't he?" said Zeb.

"But I don't understand," said Amanda. "He pressed the button. He should have come to you."

"It doesn't work if you press the button. You need to gently stroke it like you do. Besides he has the wrong mental characteristics. He has a hostile mind. We need to communicate with friendly people, like you. What you have just found is what is called a stanzlick. It's the device we use to take us through time and space."

"Time and space. Wow. How far back in time can you go?"

"Would you like to see how the stanzlick you found got lost?"

"Could I." Amanda was overwhelmed with excitement.

"We need to make flesh contact." He moved behind her. "Do you mind if I put my hands on your waist?"

"Go ahead." She pulled up her top to allow him to do so, then replaced it over his hands. She found the experience quite pleasant.

"That leaves your hands free, and my other pair of hands can hold, and control my stanzlick."

"Is that your stanzlick." Amanda looked at the batten he carried as if he was about to conduct a symphony orchestra. Or perhaps it was a wizard's wand.

"Yes. This is the modern equivalent of the device you dug up," said Zeb.

Amanda watched as the four space-suited explorers walked across the Martian beach. Each one dragged their equivalent of an inflatable dingy across the sand. Health and Safety regulations demanded that each one carry a stanzlick so in an emergency they could immediately return home.

The beach was lined with primitive plant life - like tufts of grass. It was early days, and the plant life was insufficient to put much oxygen into the atmosphere of carbon dioxide and nitrogen.

Griedma, one of the team, simply touched the grass. The next day Griedma would go into the Fifth Dimension, and go back in time to that moment. Then, in the Fifth Dimension, she would go inside the plant. She would be so small that she could watch as the atoms and molecules move beside her. The atoms and molecules in her body would be in the present on her home world, but in the Fifth Dimension her body could be as big or as small as she wanted. She didn't need to do a chemical analysis or take a sample to the laboratory. She simply watched the atomic physics play out in front of her. She knew molecules, like astronomers knew constellations or vets instantly knew the sub breed of dog in front of them.

Job done.

The task now was to sail across the channel to the crater, whose walls emerged above sea level. The channel was 15 miles wide and nearly two thousand feet deep, but the crater was in the middle of the channel and only a mile away.

It was a fine day. Perfect for a trip across the calm waters— fractocumulus clouds breaking up the blue sky. How different to today's cloudless Martian red sky. The team were unaware that the clouds were a remnant of a heavy rainstorm the day before. The team were half a mile from the crater when the storm waters from the upstream tributaries hit their dinghies. Three of them successfully sailed their craft through the rough sea. Yargsup was taken by surprise. His dingy sank; punctured by a sharp stone carried in the flood water. His stanzlick fell to the bottom of the channel. They rescued him, and pulled him into one of their dinghies.

The team managed to reach the crater, and after a short period of rest, carried out the planned survey of the meteor crater. Its central peak rising above the waters that covered the crater floor. They took their measurements, and touched rocks of interest as a marker for when they returned via the Fifth Dimension. They had achieved all the goals of their mission. Now they had to organize getting Yargsup home without his stanzlick. In theory it was easy. Two or more people could use the same stanzlick providing they were in flesh contact, like simply holding hands. Flesh to flesh, not glove to glove.

Although they were wearing spacesuits, the environment was not as hostile as the Moon, or present-day Mars. The atmospheric pressure was about half what would be expected on Earth, but lacked breathable oxygen. The other two members helped Griedma and Yargsup seal their sleeves at the wrists. They removed their gloves and Griedma and Yargsup held each other's hands. Three of their hands were in flesh contact. Griedma used her free hand to operate her stanzlick. Instantly they were back home. Minutes later the other two returned with the equipment.

Amanda let go of Zeb's hand. She was back in front of her stanzlick. She started talking to the others in the laboratory.

"As I was saying before I was so rudely interrupted." Amanda gave Philip a hostile glare. "This device belonged to a man exploring Mars when the planet was covered in a vast ocean in its northern hemisphere. When he was sailing down a major channel in what was his equivalent of a rubber dingy, a Martian storm suddenly sent a rush of water downstream. The dingy sank. He escaped but this artifact fell to the riverbed and became covered in silt."

"What happened to the man?" asked one of the onlookers. The story had caught everyone's attention, except Philip's. The number of people watching remotely was increasing.

"Oh, he wasn't alone. His colleagues were in separate vessels. They rescued him. One of them shared her device and got him home."

"You are a good storyteller, Amanda," said Philip. "But you can't know that. Where is the proof?"

"I'm only repeating what Zeb told me. The story is a legend on her planet."

"What are you talking about? You were just as mystified as we were when it came out of the ground. You have been with us all this time. You have not been talking to Zeb or anyone else. So, you are talking utter rubbish. Go away woman and let a real scientist examine it." He pushed her aside.

"No. It makes sense what she says." Madeline moved forward and touched the artifact. "Amanda has picked up some psychic signal."

"Oh, you are going to tell me next that it's the ghost speaking through her. Well, I'm sorry I don't believe in ghost stories." Philip touched his head with one finger and made a gesture implying that Madeline was mad. Meanwhile, the number of remote viewers continued to increase.

Amanda was back in the conical room. "Let me take you back to the formation of Mars." Zeb moved behind Amanda and made flesh contact again. Instantly they were on its molten surface.

"But we are not wearing spacesuits." There was alarm in Amanda's voice.

"No. Don't worry. Time does not exist in the Fifth Dimension. External forces cannot affect you, because that would need time. You don't need to breath, because that takes time. Your physical body is still in the laboratory on Mars."

They watched as a giant comet struck Hellas Planitia. The comet's ice particles liberated by the impact were forced into a ring. They were static, defying gravity, as Zeb froze their passage through time.

"Now I have stopped time."

"I don't understand."

"Let me take you to the next time-universe." Each ice droplet moved slightly higher. "The Fifth Dimension is a multiverse of time. Before we were moving through a number of time-universes, very, very quickly. Now we are in just one. I have frozen time throughout the whole of Mars." He moved them away from the impact. Amanda saw the ripples on the ocean frozen in time.

"Time is frozen not only on Mars, but throughout the universe," he said. "Let's have a look at your planet Earth at this precise moment." The Earth was not a blue planet but a red-hot molten world with the proto-moon clearly discerned escaping from it.

"Because Mars was smaller than the Earth, and also did not have a major impact like the one that created the Earth-Moon system, Mars became habitable slightly earlier than on Earth."

When Zeb moved through the other universes towards the present, Amanda could see primitive plant life taking hold on Mars at a period when the Earth was still barren. Zeb also described the basics of how the stanzlick worked. When Zeb let go of Amanda, she appeared in the Mars laboratory as if she had been there all the time.

Amanda stood behind the gold cylinder, and in front of a group of colleagues. It seemed to her that she had spent an hour in the company of Zeb, but no time elapsed in the present.

"Inside this device is a laser, which is focused on a pebble of dark matter," said Amanda. "The idea is that if you change the frequency of the laser, you can travel through space, and if you change the pulse repetition rate you can travel through time."

"What are you talking about?" Philip paced in front of her. "Dark matter is a theoretic concept. Nobody has ever detected it."

"The civilization that left this device was far more advanced than we are. One day we will learn how to mine it, like they did."

"And what makes you an expert on dark matter?" He waved his hands in the air as he paced the room.

"All I am saying is what I have been told."

"Hmm."

"You can't follow the path of an atom. One moment it's here, the next moment it's there. Where did it go? I'll tell you. It went into the Fifth Dimension."

"Where?"

"It interweaves between our four dimensions of height, length breadth and time then builds a replica of the present."

"Rubbish!"

"The way it was explained to me is that the Fifth Dimension is like a pack of playing cards. Ten seconds ago the Two of Diamonds was made. It was a perfect replica of the world ten seconds ago. Nine seconds ago, the Three of Diamonds was made, and so on. Now I don't know the thickness of these cards, certainly less than a second, probably milliseconds - I don't know. But do you get the idea."

"I get the idea that you are crazy. So where is this matter in the Fifth Dimension? There must be more of it in the so called Fifth Dimension than is possible to create here."

"The dark matter of the Fifth Dimension has a gravitational effect on normal matter," said Amanda. "Only its gravitational effect is not inversely proportional to the square of the distance, but of time. The matter created in the last few minutes has a far greater gravitational effect than the matter created a year ago."

Philip was speechless and stood still taking in what she had just said.

"In the first millisecond after the Big Bang," said Amanda, "there was hardly any dark matter and the universe expanded rapidly - very rapidly."

"Yes. That's a nice hypothesis but where is the proof?" Philip stood defiantly with his hands on his hips.

Amanda was frustrated. What more could she say? What more could she do to make the group understand. Not only the group in front of her but those watching on the Moon, on the space stations, on the Earth and at other Martian colonies. The number of viewers was expanding exponentially. She played her hands on the button without thinking.

Instantly she was back in the conical room. Zeb was absent, but she materialized a few seconds later.

"Well that got their attention. Well Done." Zeb walked to be closer to Amanda, her hair flashing all the colors of the rainbow and moving in sympathy with Zeb's footsteps.

"Oh Zeb. Were you there?"

"Of course I wouldn't have missed it for the galaxy. I was two seconds in the past, so nobody saw me."

"But Philip's right. I have no proof for what I said. How can I convince them it's not just hearsay?"

"Your people's understanding of temporal physics is nonexistent. How would you explain that the Earth is a sphere to Mr. Neanderthal?"

They hatched a plan.

Amanda took her hands off the artifact. "It's a lot to take in. Any questions? Oh, I can see my husband on the Moon colony." She pointed to the screen on which he appeared. "Graham darling. You have dug up more artifacts than I have. What do you think? Oh, silly me. I forgot Mars, in its orbit around the Sun, is quite a long way from the Moon at the moment. It will take about seven minutes for Graham to get my question. He will think about it then take another seven minutes to send his reply. What shall we do for the next quarter hour? I know, I will ask my friend Zeb to speed things up."

BANG!

Everyone looked shocked to see the source of the explosion.

"Darling! Welcome to Mars!" Amanada ran across the room to kiss her husband who suddenly appeared. "I'm sorry about the bang. Graham displaced a large amount of our air when he appeared. You really must lose more weight darling."

Laughter broke the tension of the situation.

"Ladies and Gentlemen, my husband travelled from the Moon to Mars instantly through the Fifth Dimension, which is what I was trying to explain earlier. He didn't use the artifact that we just dug up, but the modern equivalent in the capable hands of my friend Zeb. Now when I was stroking the button on the artifact, I too travelled instantly from here to Zeb's home planet. She told me all the things I tried to tell you, that Philip, and others, didn't believe. You can't see Zeb because she is in the Fifth Dimension about two seconds in our past. Zeb! Can you hear me? Will you join us in the present?"

Another bang and Zeb appeared. "Hello Earth people. My name is Zebrisky Nanologan, but everyone calls me Zeb. I have the honorary title of Guardian of Yargsup's Stanzlick - I am the Guardian of this artifact that Amanda and her team have just dug up."

The number of remote viewers increased again.

"This artifact is an important part of our history, and should be displayed in a museum on our planet, but we are prepared to have it exhibited in one of your museums, providing we can help you fix your climate change problem on Earth."

"Wait a minute," said Philip. "An offer like that is too good to be true. What are you getting out of the deal?"

"Nothing. Oh, I expect many people of our civilization will want to visit your museum, but we can come to a separate agreement about admission charges if you like."

"And will you tell us how we can make the devices?" said Philip.

"I don't think so."

"See you have a hidden agenda. You have to be honest with us."

"Shut up, Philip!" Madeline crossed the room. "We have an opportunity to save the Earth from the evil of climate change. We should welcome Zeb with open arms."

"Don't you see, we will be under their control. We don't have the technology to fight them off. It will be like a modern version of the Roman Empire. We will lose our independence."

"It's not your decision to make, Philip," said Amanda. "This should be brought before the United Nations."

"Excellent idea," said Zeb, telepathically, to Amanda. "I hereby appoint you our Ambassador."

"And I will be the Trilorgie Ambassador to the United Nations," said Amanda.

"Trilorgie?" said Madeline.

"That is the name of their home planet," said Amanda.

It was about seven minutes after the appearance of Graham that Philip's phone rang. It was a text from his friend Norma. 'The most remarkable thing. I was with Graham Braithwaite when an alien suddenly appeared, and took him away.'

Norma had been with Graham watching the telecast from Mars.

She was out of view of Graham's camera so was never seen on the monitor on Mars. She had messaged Philip, and was now in a stunned silence in Graham's empty room trying to comprehend what had just happened, and what she should do.

Zeb entered the Fifth Dimension. She read Norma's mind. She wanted the comfort of being with her friend Philip. Zeb sent a telepathic message to Norma, 'Hold tight. Don't worry. I'll take you to Philip.' Another bang, and Norma was on Mars holding Zeb's hand.

Everybody was a television presenter. Some just as a one-to-one with their friend, others having a following of hundreds or thousands. Professional news channels were still popular. They provided 24/7 coverage of major events and highlighted smaller interesting things. They also checked the facts, and were trusted by their viewers.

"Looks like they are not ready to start at the UN." Jeremy, the News Director, surveyed the array of screens in front of him and spoke into the microphone that linked into the presenter's earpiece. "We'll re-run that interview you did with Philip Harding."

It would have taken about seven minutes to ask a question, and a further seven to get a reply. Fortunately, Jeremy worked for a professional organization. Susan, the News Anchor, dictated her five questions to Norma. Philip's friend sat out of camera shot. The piece was edited with Susan in vision asking the questions.

While it was playing, Jeremy kept half an eye on the pictures from the United Nations. It was an important debate and he wanted to catch the chair's opening speech.

"Cut to UN!" Jeremy shouted. He had seen Zeb, the alien, and Amanda suddenly appear.

"Please excuse this unannounced intrusion." Amanda stood next to Zeb, her blond hair turning to green and swishing gently on her head.

The chair was shocked and pressed his concealed security button.

Amanda continued, "This is my friend Zebrisky Nanologan. He has the honorary title of Guardian of Yargsup's Stanzlick. Following my discovery of this artifact on Mars today he asks, on behalf of the people of Trilorgie, his home planet, that they be allowed to join the Earth's United Nations and to this end he has appointed me his ambassador. Furthermore ...."

She was interrupted as ten security officers were about to grab hold of Zeb and Amanda but fell on the floor when the two moved back into the Fifth Dimension. The room was in chaos.

Jeremy was distracted by a bang in the control room. Amanda and Zeb appeared behind him. Startled, Jeremy looked to see what had happened.

"I never got to say anything at the UN. Can I give you an exclusive interview instead." Amanda looked him in the face.

"Err ... wow ... yes ... yes by all means yes."

"Thank you."

"You were in New York ten minutes ago. How the hell did you get here?"

"My friend. I was on Mars a couple of hours ago. I need to tell the general public about my discovery, of how the people of Trilorgie can travel instantly through time and space. More importantly I need to tell the World that they want to be our friends and solve our climatic crisis. It's important that your viewers know the truth, and not generate false speculations."

"Bob, take Amanda to Make-up and fit her with a microphone."

"Sandra. You are not going to believe this." The News Director spoke into the microphone before him to give talk back to the presenter through her earpiece. "You have an exclusive with Amanda Braithwaite."

"OK. Is she with the United Nations crew?"

"No. She's in Make-up at the moment and will be in the studio with you in a few moments."

"What? How is that possible?"

"That my dear is one of the questions you must ask her. Apparently, she was on Mars a few hours ago. Oh. And she will be with her alien friend, but he doesn't speak English."

Sandra could hardly believe what was happening, but she was professional, and took it all in her stride. She gave a voice-over commentary of the live scene at the United Nations, then a voice-over of the replay of incident. Then she was in vision.

"The extra-terrestrial being at the UN doesn't speak English, or any other language of Earth. Her spokesperson is Amanda Braithwaite, the lady who today discovered a strange artifact on Mars. It takes over six months to travel from Mars to Earth, so don't ask me how she can be on Earth today. Instead let's ask her."

"Cut to Camera Two." The Vision Mixer followed his command.

"With me now is Amanda, and we are joined by Zeb, the first extraterrestrial to appear on live TV. Amanda. We saw you a few moments ago in the UN building. How can you be in our studio so soon?"

"Yes, amazing isn't it, but, as you say, I was on Mars just a few hours ago as well."

"You certainly get about."

"The device that I dug up was a tool that the people of Trilorgie use to travel through time and space."

"Trilorgie; where is that?"

"Oh, it's a planet fairly near the center of the Milky Way. The stars there are fairly close together and, in the past, it was easy for them to share their knowledge with their neighbors. Now, they have this device that can take them through time and space instantly."

"But it's just a pole, not a spaceship."

"This is a device that has been developed over millions of years. The one I found was lost about 4.5 billion years ago. My friend Zeb, here, has a modern version.' The camera showed Zeb waving her batten as if conducting an orchestra. 'And as long as I can hold one of her hands, she can take me instantly from Mars to Earth, from New York to London. I couldn't get a spaceship in the studio, but with Zeb's baton I can travel anywhere."

"So why did you go to the United Nations?"

"What I have found is part of the history of Trilorgie. It's an ancient monument. They want to put it in a museum. So, if I found the telescope used by Christopher Columbus, should that go in a museum in America ,or Europe? Likewise, should the artifact I found go into a museum on Mars, the Earth or Trilorgie?"

"And I suppose your friend Zeb wants to take it back to Trilorgie."

"Not necessarily. He would like to have it on Earth, but there is a condition, well two conditions."

"Which are?"

"It is part of their culture, so he wants his people to be able to come to Earth, and see it for themselves."

"That's understandable, and the second condition?"

"He wants to reduce global warming on Earth, and bring it back to pre-industrial levels."

"Surely that's not a condition. We all want that."

"Ah, but you see, when I discussed it with my colleagues on Mars, some of them said it was too good to be true and that it was a way of taking over our culture through the back door, so to speak."

"And what do you think?"

"It's not my decision. It has to be decided by the United Nations as the decision of the Earth as a whole."

"And that is why you were there today."

"Yes. But I am a scientist. I know nothing of the protocol of that organization. All I wanted today was to say, "here we are talk to us" but instead of that we were treated as terrorists."

"So, what happens now?"

"I have been appointed as the Trilorgie Ambassador. If the world as a whole wants to keep the artifact, they must contact me, and I will discuss it at the UN."

"And if they don't contact you?"

"Zeb will take it home with him."

"If the UN doesn't agree with you, would that lead to an interplanetary war."

"Definitely not. The Trilorgie are a peaceful race, and would never hurt anybody."

"But if the military protected the artifact?"

"The Trilorgie science has over 4 billion years more experience than experts on Earth. There is no way the military can stop them taking back their rightful possession."

It was a few weeks later that Amanda was due to give her first official address to the United Nations. In the meantime, delegates had prepared questions that they needed to ask, and administrative procedures were put in place. A lot of preparation was required by Zeb and Amanda. They often went their separate ways, Zeb to develop support from experts on Trilorgie, his home planet. Amanda needed to get used to the geography of the building, and to understand the procedures involved.

It was all very new, and confusing to Amanda who was taking a few minutes to relax over a cup of coffee in the refreshment lounge in the UN Building.

"Excuse me but are you the person that discovered that artifact on Mars?" A lady about Amanda's age was passing the table, her long brunette hair gathered in a band at the back reached down her back almost as far as her waist. Amanda looked up and was fascinated by the way the stranger had shaved her hair about half an inch above the ears, leaving just an island of hair on the top of her head.

"Yes, I'm Amanda, would you like to join me?"

"Thank you. My name is Aishah Bianka I provide admin support to whoever wants me."

"Really? How long have you been doing that?"

"Oh, about ten years, but my ambition is to become part of delegate team, but I think I have messed up my chances by being a freelance, and tagging onto any country that needs me at the time."

"Well, I need you. I'm an astronomer. Just because I was the first person to contact the Trilorgie civilization doesn't make me qualified to be their ambassador."

"Yes, I can understand that. There is so much paperwork to get through. But aside from that what was it like to make first contact?"

Zeb was, at the present, on Trilorgie, but he frequently entered the Fifth Dimension for a few seconds to make sure Amanda was alright. He was a minute or so in the past when he checked out Aishah's history. He found her really talented, and experienced in matters of procedures in the United Nations. He sent a telepathic message to Amanda.

"It was unbelievable," said Amanda. "The sort of discovery that you never even dream of making. I was looking for fossil evidence of grass seed or something. Then this thing showed up that was obviously artificial. It had been buried for over 4 billion years. Nobody expected it to still be working."

"When did you realize that it was?"

"Almost straight away. I was just feeling it, getting the sensation of actually touching something that old, when I accidentally activated it. I was sent half-way across the Milky Way."

"Did you feel anything?"

"No. One moment I was on Mars, the next instant I was near the center of the Galaxy. Can you imagine that? About forty years ago, science fiction addicts imagined traveling at a top speed of ten times the speed of light - what did they call it?" Amanda looked at the ceiling as if the light bulbs would give her tell her the answer. "Warp Ten. Well at Warp Ten it would take them nearly three thousand years to do what I did instantly."

"Wow! I wish I knew as much about the universe as you do."

"And I wish I knew as much about working in the UN as you do. Tell me will you be my assistant?"

"Your assistant?"

"Well no. More than an assistant. I need you to do my job for me. As their Ambassador, I have to be upfront, and make all the speeches, and that, but I need you to support me."

"Oh Amanda. I would be honored. It's just what I have always wanted to do, but you don't know me. I only stopped for a coffee with you, so how do you know I am capable of doing the job?"

"I know all about you."

"But I have not told you anything about myself. How do you know me?"

Amanda laughed, reached out and put her hand on Aishah's. "The artifact that I discovered can take me through time and space. The artifact is on Mars, so I don't have access to it at the moment. My friend Zeb, the alien I met when I first appeared on Trilorgie, uses a smaller more modern version. At some point he was here, and eavesdropped our conversation."

"I didn't see him."

"That is because he was a minute or so in our past. But he went even further back into your past and discovered your life history. You don't need to write out your CV for me, Zeb has told me all about you. He agrees with me that, you and I will be a great team."

The team was more than the three of them. Zeb had approached many experts on Trilorgie. There were more members on Zeb's team than delegates at the United Nations. One Trilorgien was assigned to each UN delegate. Through the Fifth Dimension the life history of each delegate was observed, and their minds monitored. Zeb knew what was on the minds of every delegate. He saw the situation from their points of view. He knew the arguments they would put forward against his plan. He also knew that he had more support than opposition throughout the assembly. Zeb's team brought their minds together to produce the script for Amanda.

Amanda mounted the platform and bowed to the applause. She didn't have a written script in front of her. She switched the teleprompt off. She just started speaking. She repeated the thoughts fed to her by Zeb, so didn't need to remember anything. She started with warm words for their most ardent critics, answered the questions they were about to pose, and offered a solution they couldn't refuse. She described how the Trilorgiens had modified the climate on a number of planets. Using their expertise, they could terraform Mars and restore the Earth's climate to its pre-industrial parameters. She received a standing ovation. The debate that followed was not what most delegates had anticipated, as Amanda had taken the wind out of their sails. Instead, it centered on which museum would exhibit the artifact initially, and in which order other museums would participate.

--

Geoffrey Hugh Lindop, interested in astronomy and space travel for over 60 years, is now developing his writing of non-fiction into science fiction and has just completed his first novel. His freelance astronomical and astronautical newspaper features were syndicated to over 200 newspapers across the globe. His work has been published by the British Interplanetary Society, in which he was a fellow for a number of years. He has also edited a national astronomy magazine when he worked closely with Sir Patrick Moore, Britain's most famous amateur astronomer. Now living in the South of Scotland, he has just published a book promoting the dark skies of that area.
He has been influenced by the work of Arthur C. Clarke, and attended the premiere of 2001 - A Space Odyssey. Back in 1968 the film was set in the future.

Limbo on Elysium Mons

By Mary Jo Rabe

Chuck Davis tried to blink. None of his muscles seemed to move even though his senses functioned better than ever before. That couldn't be good. His gaze caught the dark-black sky, which, unsurprisingly, overwhelmed him with awe.

He felt pleasantly insignificant, considering the billions of stars in the Milky Way and the billions of galaxies in the universe. That feeling was liberating. Whatever his personal situation, this was a magnificent universe.

He stared and felt a sudden contentment. He was part of something huge, long lasting, and incredibly stunning. He was tempted to lose himself in the depths of that sky as he contemplated the distances those lights represented. Then Phobos moved into view and dragged him back into the real world.

Strange. He knew that he was somewhere in the summit caldera at the top of Elysium Mons. The astrophysicist in him should demand further reliable data, but he felt no such need. For all practical purposes, considering the minimal atmosphere at this altitude, he was in outer space. What he was doing on top of the fourth highest mountain on Mars wasn't so clear to him.

He was perplexed that he could see the dusty Utopia Planitia, the largest impact basin on Mars, down on the ground over to the left. It should be too far away for him to recognize. Somehow, though, distances didn't seem to make the same sense that they used to.

His body also didn't make any sense. He looked at his arms and legs. He had the same chunky shape, the same clumsy body parts, and seemed to be wearing the same clothes as before, whatever before meant. Somehow, he wasn't entirely sure.

His entire body was translucent. He could see his body, and he could see through it. Somehow, he could also see his body from a distance, and he could see things behind his body. Yet, he couldn't see any structures inside his body, no bones, no inner organs, no blood vessels. All he saw was a chubby, middle-aged man with thinning brown hair and bloodshot blue eyes.

His legs didn't move, but he did. Suddenly his location was two meters to the left of where he had just been and actually several centimeters above the rocky ground. He tried to clap his hands. They met but didn't exactly touch. However, they also didn't push through each other.

His brain wasn't functioning quite right. His memory seemed fuzzy, but maybe it was clearing up, though slowly. His wife always said he was the typical absent-minded professor who could never remember important things. What on Earth was going on, or rather what on Mars?

Right. He did know one thing. There had been an accident. He should be dead. No human body wearing indoor habitat attire survived being blown out onto the surface of Mars. Was he hallucinating, or dying? How did he suddenly get on top of a Martian mountain? Why didn't he feel cold? Why didn't he have trouble breathing? Was he even breathing?

A solid-looking, pinkish-gray boulder, more or less as tall as he was — Chuck being of average human height — rolled over in his direction. "I'm here to answer any questions," it somehow broadcast into Chuck's consciousness.

"And who or what are you?" Chuck asked. It occurred to him to wonder why it seemed natural and normal to talk to a rock. How could he talk in a vacuum anyway? How could he do anything in a vacuum? Or maybe he hadn't actually vocalized anything; maybe he had just thought his question.

"For your information, I supply knowledge. I give honest answers, though they are often not all that satisfying," the boulder answered. "I don't know who or what I am, possibly an AI or a robot or a life form from another universe or something completely different. It doesn't matter. I can tell you that you are a dead Martian colonist formerly from Earth, what you creatures in your ignorance usually call a ghost."

Chuck gradually remembered a few things and tried to organize his thoughts. He had been a former high school science teacher whose wife helped him go back and get his doctorate. He was a respected professor who joined a settlement on Mars. He didn't believe in ghosts or any kind of afterlife. However, as a scientist, he had to analyze the available data. And here he was.

He remembered helping out in the habitat gardens on the surface. Barbara Lou More, a somewhat clueless colonist, was also working there. She had pressed an unfortunate combination of buttons on the console that then suddenly rolled up one wall of the vegetable tent. They were both blown out onto the surface and died.

And now here he was, completely mobile and more and more conscious of his surroundings, surroundings completely hostile to human life. "Okay," he thought, somewhat consciously sending his thoughts in the direction of the boulder. "What am I exactly? I never believed in ghosts. If I still exist somehow, why am I here?"

The boulder rolled back and forth. "Some, but not all, of the Martian colonists show up here after their physical demise. They discover that there is some task they want to accomplish before they move on. The universe is in favor of this."

"Move on?" Chuck asked.

"There seem to be different designations for what you creatures call your next stage, your afterlife. Some call it heaven, Valhalla, or nirvana. Some refer to the spirit in the sky, reincarnation, or merely returning one's essence to the dust of the universe, in order to wait for transformation into a star," the rock explained.

"And those who don't believe in any kind of afterlife?" Chuck asked.

"After a while, when they think their previously unfinished task has been completed, they also leave. Unfortunately, I can't explain it any better than that. You wouldn't understand the more complicated calculations the universe provides."

Chuck looked around again. Suddenly he saw the translucent figure of Monsignor Horton Beck appear some meters behind the boulder. The old cleric no longer looked frail or sickly as he had when he was alive. He was the same short and obese figure in a dark suit wearing a Roman collar. His thinning, white hair was neatly combed as always.

Before Chuck could try to talk to him, the boulder turned and rolled back toward the old man. A short time later, the boulder rolled off in another direction and Monsignor Beck floated over toward Chuck and stood in front of him.

"Well," Chuck began. "Now I can ask the expert. If we are dead, what is this place? This seems like a pretty poor excuse for what you people call heaven. Is it maybe purgatory?"

Monsignor Beck laughed, and Chuck heard it in his mind as a loud, enthusiastic guffaw, even though, of course, under these vacuum conditions, there could be no sound.

"No," the monsignor said. "That I'm sure of. Purgatory is a place for people to purify themselves, a place for those who aren't good enough for heaven but are too good for hell. There's nothing like that here.

"If you ask me, this seems more like what medieval theologians called limbo, a neutral place, neither good nor bad, and yet a place of uncertainty. Limbo, as a theological concept, has long since been deliberately forgotten. But maybe there was something to it. Unfortunately, our loquacious boulder doesn't seem all that knowledgeable."

Just as Chuck was thinking about what to say to this, the figure of a short little boy, Mikey Lemkeel, appeared. He looked exactly as he had in the habitat with his somewhat flat face, slanted eyes, and small head on a short neck. The child talked to the boulder and then hopped over to Chuck and the monsignor.

"Why are we on Elysium Mons?" he asked. Chuck and the monsignor stared at each other. In the habitat, Mikey had always been cheerful and outgoing, though completely nonverbal, which everyone assumed was due to his Down syndrome.

Mikey chuckled. "You know, back in the habitat I always understood things, just more slowly than the rest of you. It took me a while to process new ideas, to listen, to comprehend, and to talk. The way my brain was wired, the signals flowed very slowly through the neurons. Now my physical brain structure no longer slows me down."

"Have you given any thought to the name of this place?" Mikey continued. "It's Elysium, the name for paradise in Greek mythology, where souls live in complete happiness. So, it would be a perfect place for ghosts to soak up some strength and then go about their remaining tasks."

"So, is this a kind of resort for ghosts?" Chuck asked.

"More like a transit area," Mikey said. "This is where we get the chance to fix any unfinished business with the living so that we can move on."

Chuck still couldn't imagine just how the process should work.

Never having believed in ghosts, he didn't know the protocols.

The boulder rolled up to the three of them. "It looks like there will only be three of you here today," it said. "It takes different lengths of time before a dead person transitions to what you might as well call a ghost and then sometimes comes here."

"To complete the transfer of information at my disposal: Ghosts have the capacity to go wherever they choose. Creatures still among the living don't detect the presence of ghosts directly, that is, non-ghosts don't consciously see, hear, or feel ghosts. Ghosts tend to communicate with the living by interfering with their sleep cycles, appearing to them in dreams."

"So, first we have to realize what our unfinished business is," Monsignor Beck said. "And then we can help the living or persuade them to do something?"

"My unfinished business is obvious," Mikey said. "I was murdered, but my father believes it was an avoidable accident, and he blames himself. I have to bring my murderers to justice and show Dad that nothing was his fault."

"Hmm," Monsignor Beck said. "I was certain that I died a natural death. After all, I was old and not that healthy when I came to Mars. However, as my memories come back to me here, and I see things here that I didn't notice back in the habitat, I'm afraid I was also murdered."

"What do you want to do?" Mikey asked.

"I made a terrible mistake, and I have to save the soul of my murderer," Monsignor Beck said automatically. "I thought I was so concerned with the welfare of all those I came into contact with as judge, but I ignored the sufferings of my own employee. She is a good person. Her guilt will overpower her, and she may try to kill herself, something I have to prevent."

Chuck shook his head; he felt his memories loading, though still slowly. His mind was functioning a little better. "My death was an accident," he said. "The person to blame also died. So, offhand I don't see anything I need to fix."

Chuck looked at the other two and wished he knew what he should do. His wife often said he was oblivious, and probably she was right. He had a feeling he was missing something important.

The boulder bounced a few times and then said, "I can only say that so far every ghost who showed up here had something he felt he

still had to do."
Then Mikey Lemkeel disappeared.

Sheriff Curtis Long yawned contentedly and stretched his massive legs under the sturdy table in his residence. Things were good in the Bradbury habitat. He and Emma the cafeteria lady had finally gotten rid of the evil mayor, and no one would miss him.

Old Ned, Emma's brother back on Earth who was still paying for the whole Mars project, had promised that in the future every mayor of the habitat could be elected from candidates living in the habitat and not appointed from some committee on Earth. Emma said she would start organizing the election of a habitat council.

Emma was a genuinely good person. She appreciated Curtis, understood that his background as an enforcer for the family business back on Earth made him the perfect sheriff on Mars. The good people in the habitat were his family, and he protected his family from the bad guys.

This was usually no problem because Curtis was able to intimidate evildoers with his two-meter height and hundred-twenty muscle-packed kilos, as well as his enthusiastic willingness to use force.

The funeral for the judge, Monsignor Beck, this morning had been dignified and genuinely spiritual, just like the old gentleman himself. Curtis wasn't religious himself, but he decided he wanted to praise Father Greeley for doing a good job, and so he tapped a reminder into his communication device.

So now, the habitat wouldn't have a judge for a while, at least until Ned sent another one from Earth or appointed one from the habitat. Curtis hoped the habitat wouldn't need one in the immediate future. He certainly hadn't always agreed with the good monsignor's mild judgments and sentences.

Sheriff Long reached for another cookie from the stack on his plate. Emma had created an unusually tasty brunch for the habitat after Monsignor Beck's funeral, had really outdone herself with the desserts this time. Still, nothing was quite as good as her chocolate chip cookies. Emma had nodded conspiratorially when he stuffed two stacks into his pockets as he left.

It was time to sleep. Curtis needed a full eight hours to be in good shape when he got up. He accomplished his efficient hygienic routines and was asleep five minutes after he got into his well-built stand-alone bed. These foldout beds were way too flimsy for his bulk, and so he had insisted on a real bed for his living quarters.

Curtis sat up in bed. Mikey, the kid with Down syndrome who had wandered out of the habitat and died, sat on a kitchen chair in front of his bed.

"Don't worry, Sheriff," Mikey said. "You're just dreaming. I found out that us ghosts can appear to people in their dreams."

Curtis took a minute to think. Okay, possible. He often had dreams but usually about things that had happened on Earth. This Mikey looked a little like what a ghost should look like, sort of invisible, but Curtis could still see him.

And Mikey was dead. Curtis had found his corpse, out on the surface. Mikey's father had been so upset that he had refused any kind of funeral or memorial. They had just buried Mikey's remains under a brick gazebo out on the surface that his father built.

"You're probably wondering why I'm here," Mikey continued.

Actually, Curtis was beginning to wonder how Mikey could talk. The kid looked just like he had before he died, but the old Mikey couldn't talk and had a definite learning disability.

"Ghosts don't have the same limitations that their human forms had when they were alive," Mikey said. "Actually, we have more abilities. For example, we can read minds, which is quite useful."

Curtis was relieved that he hadn't used insulting words in his thoughts about Mikey.

"Don't worry," Mikey said. "Your thoughts aren't anything to be ashamed of. I've always liked and respected you. That's why I'm here. I need your help."

Now Curtis was all ears and ready to go. He helped good people; that's what he did. And this kid Mikey was a good person. Curtis would help him if he could.

"How can I help you, kid?" Curtis asked, no longer giving any thought to Mikey being a ghost.

"My death wasn't an accident," Mikey said. "Richie and Reggie murdered me. They came dressed in surface suits, opened their helmets and told me they had seen a dog outside. I missed dogs here on Mars. They closed their helmets, led me through the exit area, and pushed me out onto the surface. Then they watched me die. I shouldn't have gone with them, of course, but I couldn't think that fast, back then. I just trusted people."

Curtis was enraged but, the more he thought it over, not surprised. Richie and Reggie were scum. Their parents had bribed the selection people to get their criminal kids sent off to Mars when they became too much of a nuisance on Earth.

Curtis had had his eye on the two of them for a long time now, but hadn't been able to dig up any evidence to support any of his suspicions. As sheriff, he did feel an obligation to search for proof of what he suspected before he arrested anyone.

"So," Mikey continued. "I need you to review what the cameras at Exit 5a must have recorded the day I died and then show the recordings to my Dad. He still thinks I wandered out onto the surface by myself because he left me alone for a few minutes. I never could have managed the exit protocols, all the complicated combinations of buttons you have to push. Dad should have realized that. Somehow he still just blamed himself."

Curtis nodded. "Don't worry, kid. I'll see to it that everyone finds out what really happened. Thanks for letting me know."

Mikey smiled. "Once you have taken care of things, I'll enter my Dad's dreams. I might be able to console him before I go. Thanks for whatever you can do."

And Curtis woke up, mad as hell. Why hadn't he thought of foul play in Mikey's case? He sent off a message to the habitat tech people demanding a copy of what camera 5a had recorded. Apparently, the tech department never slept. A few minutes later, he had the video, complete with sound, showing how the two adolescent murderers had shoved Mikey out onto the surface.

Curtis was never one for bureaucratic niceties. He ordered up four enforcement robots and proceeded to drag both of those creeps out of their beds, confiscate their communicators, and throw them into his temporary jail facilities next to his office.

His first instinct was to execute them immediately, but then he remembered how Emma asked him to always talk to her before he killed anyone. This had been good advice with respect to the evil mayor. After talking to Emma, they found a much better way to kill the man.

So, Curtis just went back to bed but slept very well.

The next morning, he went to see Emma in her cafeteria. She was busy making more cookies, but she reminded him that the settlement's charter required criminals to have their day in court before they were punished in any way. The situation with the mayor had been an exception. Unfortunately, the settlement didn't have a new judge yet, but maybe the court clerk would know what to do in such circumstances.

Curtis didn't feel like wasting any more time talking or listening to anyone. However, remembering that Emma always gave good advice, he made his way to the courtroom office in the hopes of meeting Maria Sergeant, the court clerk. It was possible that she would know what he was allowed to do in this case. There was no need for him to get himself into unnecessary trouble.

The courtroom clerk's office was one of the smaller rooms in the habitat, sparsely furnished with a small, red, plastic desk and two plastic chairs and no personal touches, no pictures, posters, nothing that would reveal anything about the person who worked there.

Maria Sergeant was a slim and trim, young woman, petite in height, with long, dark curly hair. She dressed in the newest and most becoming habitat wear and wore a minimal but highly effective amount of make-up. And yet, Curtis couldn't see her as attractive, maybe because her thin lips produced such a grim facial expression.

As it turned out, this expression was an accurate portrayal of her pessimistic outlook.

Curtis explained his dilemma and showed her the video of the murderers at work. "Vicious, guilty murderers," she spat out. "I wish you could throw them out onto the surface just like they did to that poor kid."

"Fine with me," Curtis said. "Am I allowed to decide what to do with the prisoners since there is no judge available for a trial?" He hoped he was hiding his eagerness well enough, although maybe it wasn't even necessary. He and Ms. Sergeant seemed to be on the same wavelength.

"Let me check what you're allowed to do," she said as she tapped the communicator on her desk. After only a few moments, she looked up and said sadly, "No, every possible situation is strictly regulated. In the case of serious crimes when no judge is available, you have to send the accused back to Earth and beam down copies of the evidence."

"What a waste of time and money," Curtis said. "Too bad the good monsignor is no longer with us."

Ms. Sergeant sighed. "You don't know that he would have found them guilty," she said. "He always found mitigating circumstances and excuses for people. I think he was too good for this world."

Curtis had to agree. In his opinion, the judge had always been far too lenient in his decisions.

"But vicious murder is something else," Curtis said. "Anyone who murders a helpless person doesn't deserve to live." That hadn't been the case, of course, when he and Emma offed the mayor. That was for the good of the habitat, and the mayor hadn't been a good person.

Ms. Sergeant stared at him and then looked away. Probably he had shocked her. "I'll follow the rules, of course," he said. "But I don't like them."

"We all do what we have to do," she said while she continued to stare at her communicator. Curtis took the hint, processed the information behind it, and left.

He took care of the formalities, informed the authorities on Earth, sent them the video, and promised to transfer the accused young men to the spaceport jail so that they could leave on the next spaceship heading to Earth. They didn't have a new mayor or a habitat council yet, so Curtis didn't think there was anyone else on Mars he needed to inform, though, of course, he told Emma everything. She agreed with his decision.

The temporary jail facilities at the spaceport for the transport of criminals back to Earth had never been used before. Nonetheless, Curtis summoned his deputy robots and transferred the felons from the habitat jail to the surface transport vehicle.

The young men were unwilling to cooperate, but miscalculated the mass of the robots and injured themselves trying to punch and kick Curtis's mechanical deputies. The robots placed the two felons in the prisoner segment at the back of the vehicle and joined them there.

Curtis had deliberately chosen the larger surface transport vehicle so that the robots could ride along in the back. Curtis knew there was a suitable crevice halfway between the Bradbury habitat and the spaceport. He stopped the vehicle there and tapped his communicator. Obediently, the robots opened the back door, took out the murderers clad only in their indoor habitat suits and threw them into the crevice.

Curtis estimated that the criminals needed five to ten minutes for their miserable deaths. He waited fifteen and then told the robots to get back into the vehicle. He then wiped their memories.

Once he was back in his office, he sent a report to Earth. Sadly, the accused young men had chosen to escape on the way to the spaceport jail. He hadn't been able to stop them or apprehend them.

Curtis didn't expect any trouble from the authorities on Earth or the relatives of the young murderers, as he had also sent them copies of the video recordings with commentary that he would consider releasing the video to the mass media.

Then he loaded a separate communicator with the video of Mikey's murder and went to talk to Marvin Lemkeel. Marvin was a broken man, barely middle-aged, thin and bald.

Marvin and Mikey had built glass-brick, enclosed gazebos for flower and herb gardens all around the habitats. Mikey had been an expert bricklayer, and their custom-made constructions were popular and far better than the ones put together by robots.

"I thought it was my fault," Marvin said. "I mean, usually it took Mikey a long time to learn anything new, but I thought he might have seen what you had to do to get out the habitat exit. I hardly ever left him alone, but this time I was discussing a gazebo design with a new customer and didn't notice that Mikey had wandered off. I looked for him, but never thought that he could be out on the surface."

"He was killed by murderous scum," Curtis said. "We can't undo what they did, but they will never hurt anyone else."

Marvin sighed. "Thank you," he said.

That night Marvin slept well for the first time since Mikey's death. After one hour of deep sleep, he found himself sitting on the edge of his bed. Mikey floated next to the bed. "How are you holding up, Dad?" Mikey asked.

Marvin shook his head. "Mikey," he said. "You can talk, but you, you're …"

"Yes," Mikey said. "For all practical purposes, I'm a ghost, and I am no longer affected by body issues. You don't have to worry about me. I had a wonderful life with you up until the day I was murdered. We created wonderful buildings for the settlers here on Mars. We gave people a beautiful place where they could grow herbs and flowers on their own. So, you mustn't stop building these gazebos. The settlers on Mars still need you."

"But I miss you so much, Mikey," Marvin said.

"I understand," Mikey said. "Unfortunately, I sense that ghosts can't stick around forever. I know you'll always miss me, but I want you to be happy again, just like I was always happy together with you. Promise me that you'll give other people a chance, that you will go and make friends. That's what will comfort me on my journey." With that, Mikey disappeared.

He didn't want to, but Marvin slept better than he had since Mikey's death.

Mikey appeared again on Elysium Mons. "Go for it, guys," he said. "Finish your unfinished business and move on to the next segment of your existence. It's possible, and it's good." Mikey's ghost arose and floated out toward Pluto.

"I still don't know what to do, though," Chuck said as Monsignor Beck disappeared.

Maria Sergeant stared at the yet unopened bottle of Ascraeus wine on the dusty kitchen counter of her efficiency apartment in the Bradbury habitat. She wanted to get a full night's sleep this time, something that hadn't been possible ever since she poisoned the judge.

Every night this week she had taken a shower and washed her long, dark, curly hair, knowing that the use of this much water was a luxury that would have serious financial consequences sooner or later. But when she tucked her trim, petite body into her fold-down bed, the nightmares began. She saw monsignor and his kind eyes.

So, she was afraid to sleep. Since she needed sleep, she started taking some of the sleep-inducing medication she had been hoarding for years. Knocked out chemically, she didn't have any nightmares.

She didn't want to take any more pills; she was starting to worry about addiction. She just wanted to lie down, shut down her thoughts, and not regain consciousness until morning. Maybe she wouldn't have to be drunk, but surely a certain stage of inebriation would also take the edge off things, prevent thoughts and nightmares, and let her relax and sleep.

She didn't understand why it was so hard. Back on Earth after she had sabotaged her unfaithful husband's favorite flying unicycle, she had had no trouble sleeping. On the contrary, no longer having to put up with his lies and constant theft of her hard-earned money made her feel great.

It was all she could do at the funeral to stop herself from dancing around his grave and — according to family lore, like her great-great-grandmother had done before her — chanting, "You're down there, you lying bastard, and I'm still up here, ha, ha, ha!" Maybe she had inherited her homicidal instincts from great-great-granny.

She had fled to Mars, not because there was any suspicion about the reasons for her husband's demise, but because she couldn't stand running into all the women he had cheated on her with. She thought a new start would do her good.

Life in the Bradbury habitat was good, as was her job as a court clerk. She actually liked the judge when she first met him. He was an elderly priest who had only been willing to take on the job because old Ned, who was paying for the Mars project, promised him there would be no crime on Mars and he would have nothing to do.

Unfortunately, the judge, Monsignor Beck, turned out to be gullible and naïve. He refused to recognize evil when he saw it. Old Ned should have known better. He had selected many of the colonists himself. Many good people came to Mars as did a number of bad people. Monsignor Beck refused to recognize the difference—insisted on seeing some good in everyone.

After a few months, Maria couldn't stand to watch any longer. Evil people fooled the judge over and over again. He insisted on giving everyone a second, third, or even more chances.

People lied to him, and he chose to believe them. He let people take advantage of him. She looked into Monsignor Beck's eyes and saw her old, stupid self, the one who had believed her lying, larcenous husband for so many years.

She couldn't stand the view, which is why she poisoned him with the substances she had accumulated when she considered poisoning her husband. After he was dead, the nightmares began. As soon as she closed her eyes, she saw the reproach in the monsignor's kind, childlike eyes.

She twisted the plastic cap off the Ascraeus wine and chugged half the bottle. She considered drinking the rest but stumbled over to her foldout bed instead. She didn't even pull off her habitat coverall before she collapsed onto the bed. She wasn't sure if she felt the alcoholic influence. Maybe she was just exhausted. She closed her eyes.

She must have fallen asleep, but then suddenly she felt like she was wide awake and sitting on the edge of her bed. Judge Monsignor Beck sat in her office chair just a few feet away from her bed. "Maria, I forgive you," he said and looked at her with nothing but acceptance in his sympathetic eyes.

This was different. In her previous nightmares, the judge had floated in the room and stared at her reproachfully. He had never talked. She didn't feel the same anxiety she did with the nightmares, and this time she didn't want to wake up.

"How much do you know?" she asked him.

The monsignor chuckled. "Sorry," he said. "This is all new and unexpected for me. I expected a conversation with St. Peter at the Pearly Gate, not a temporary life as an omniscient ghost."

Maria stared at him. She hadn't known this wry side of the judge. He had always been kindly but no comedian.

He then looked at her more seriously. "It seems that I know everything. You were very much in love with your husband. When you discovered that he was a thieving, serial philanderer, your love for him turned to hate and you killed him. Then you came to Mars and killed me because I disappointed you, too, though in a different way."

"It's a little more complicated than that," Maria interrupted him.

"The details aren't that important now," Monsignor Beck said. "You are. You are a good person, but you have let yourself give in to temptation to do wrong. You have let yourself be overwhelmed with bitterness and anger. But because you are a good person, your helpless remorse is destroying you. You realize that you can't live with yourself."

Maria nodded. "I can't sleep. I have had nightmares of you every night since you died. I can't live like this anymore. I've even thought of telling the sheriff that I poisoned you. Murder is a crime; he's the law here in the Bradbury Habitat. He would probably tell me to take a long hike with a short supply of oxygen, and I think now I would take his advice."

Monsignor Beck shook his head. "No," he said. "Remember, I'm the judge, not Sheriff Long, and I don't sentence you to death. I want you to regain the good that is in you and live. You have so much to offer; you can be of assistance to so many people."

"No," Maria said. "Maybe I was like that once, but not now."

"Remember that I am presently an omniscient ghost," Monsignor Beck said. "I know you have a capacity for empathy and kindness. I believe in you. You are a fighter. Now you have to fight to let the good in you overcome the evil. Otherwise, you will indeed eventually find yourself in the back of the sheriff's vehicle on the way to a cold, lonely crevice."

"I don't know if I can," Maria said, but the monsignor was gone. "But I guess I have nothing to lose by trying."

Monsignor Beck appeared again in the caldera. "My job is done," he said to Chuck. "I feel myself being drawn to my creator. All I need to do now is encourage you to finish your work on Mars. Think of your wife left alone on a planet she never wanted to move to." And he was gone.

Chuck wanted to kick himself, but that didn't seem possible with his ghostly structure. He cursed his slow memory.

How could he have forgotten how much Angie must be suffering? As usual, he had only thought of himself. Angie hadn't wanted to go to Mars. He had been the high school science teacher who wanted to explore the universe. She supported him while he went back to college and was looking forward to a quiet life at the small university where he got his first job.

When he wanted to join the Mars settlement, Angie only came along because she loved him and because he promised that their children would be genuine Martians. Now she was alone in a place she never wanted to be. He had to help her.

Angie was physically, completely exhausted. She let her somewhat emaciated body drop into bed. Ever since Chuck died, she helped out everywhere on Mars where people were needed to supply arduous physical labor, in the fields, in the factories, in the robot testing areas. She never had a real job on Mars; she had just accompanied Chuck and then helped out in the settlement occasionally.

She had always been slim, but after Chuck's death, she only ate enough to keep working. After a while, she stopped looking in the mirror. Her stringy, short, blonde hair framing her increasingly wrinkled, fallen face depressed her.

Chuck was dead, and she was completely alone. People tried to help her, tried to befriend her. Yet she only wanted to work herself into a mindless fatigue and then fall asleep completely worn out before she could think or remember.

What else could she do? The trip to Mars was free in exchange for your work in the settlement. If you wanted to return to Earth, it was prohibitively expensive. She refused to think about hopeless things; that's why she worked hard enough to sleep without thinking first.

She fell asleep immediately, but then she was sitting up, and Chuck sat in his reclining chair, a luxury she had insisted that they buy for him. She started to say something, but Chuck beat her to it, as always. He was the extrovert of the two of them, the one who enthusiastically started up each conversation.

"You're dreaming, Angie," Chuck said. "And it seems that I'm a ghost who has the power to come and talk to you in your dreams. You're not crazy or engaging in wishful thinking. I'm really here, just not exactly corporeal."

Angie stared at him. "Chuck," she said. Then she started to cry.

"I know," he said. "I'm so sorry. I didn't want to leave you, especially since you only came to Mars because of me."

"It's so unfair," Angie said. "That stupid woman got you killed. I will never stop hating her."

"She's dead, too," Chuck said.

"Her own fault," Angie said. "She was being silly, playing around with the console. That stupid woman pressed the wrong combinations of buttons, and opened the crop tent, leaving both of you unprotected on the surface of Mars. No one understands how she could have been so stupid."

"Barbara wasn't the brightest bulb in anyone's lamp," Chuck said. "I think she couldn't help it. She was just spontaneous and probably more than a little hyperactive. She never should have been in a situation where she could endanger others."

"I can't forgive her," Angie said.

"You don't have to," Chuck said. "That's not why I'm here. I'm not certain, but I think I'm here to help you find happiness on Mars without me."

"How am I supposed to do that?" Angie asked and started to cry again. "What can I do here without you?"

"I don't know that much about this ghost business," Chuck said. "But I'm pretty sure that I can't stay very long. All I can do is remind you why I fell in love with you. You are strong, intelligent, and kind. You encourage people to excel, to go beyond their perceived limitations. You have a huge capacity for empathy. You automatically sense what people need, and then you build them up."

"Look at me," he continued. "I started off as a mediocre high school science teacher and you encouraged me to get my doctorate in physics. You gave me the feeling I could accomplish anything. Now you need to do that for yourself."

"Don't leave me again," Angie said.

"I think I have to leave," Chuck said. "Trust in yourself and look around. Give yourself the same encouragement and help to do new things that you gave me. Find people who will help you. Discover what the planet Mars can offer you. I have every confidence in you." And he faded away.

Angie returned to a deep sleep and woke up hungry. She decided she wouldn't volunteer for the field work today. She would go to the lecture she saw on her communicator. A Dr. Paul Power was going to talk about archaeology. "Well," she thought. "If an archaeologist can find something to do on Mars, a certifiably dead planet that never had any civilizations, then I can, too."

Chuck found himself back on Elysium Mons, alone with the boulder. "Now what?" Chuck asked the boulder.

"I think you'll figure that out for yourself," the boulder answered, and Chuck felt his own ghostly shape slowly dissipate into dust. It felt good and right to be yet one more piece of the universe.

--

Mary Jo Rabe writes science fiction, modern fantasy, historical fiction, and crime or mystery stories, generally displaying a preference for what she defines as happy endings. Ideas for her fiction come from the magnificent, expanding universe, the rural environment of eastern Iowa where she grew up, the beautiful Michigan State University campus where she got her first degree, and the Black Forest area of Germany with its center in Freiburg where she worked as a librarian for 41 years before retiring to Titisee-Neustadt. Mary Jo Rabe's stories have appeared in Alien Dimensions Issue 20/21, 4StarStories, Starry Eyed Press's ONE-WAY TICKET, and other magazines and anthologies.

You can find out more about her published stories at Mary Jo Rabe's blog: maryjorabe.wordpress.com/

It's a Lot Simpler from Orbit

By Siv Art

(Crew of Explorer Vessel- Kiemea- Mars 2033- Orbital Approach over Orcus Patera)

"You have got to be kidding me!" Commander of the Kiemea, Samantha Reyson, was not impressed. Her face, tone, and body language all spoke annoyance with the man before her.

The man turned to her, his face lacking any emotion. "I wish I wasn't, but the facts speak for themselves." He folded his arms, as if to say that it was the end of the matter.

"We just left the surface, John. You're telling me that the signal we came looking for, the same signal we couldn't find for two weeks while we were on Mars, has now reactivated? No, no, no! It can't be! Check the instruments again. There's not enough fuel to go back!"

"Like I said, Sam," he stopped, realizing that informality was inappropriate. "Like I said, Commander. These are the facts."

"These are the facts!" she exclaimed, annoyed by her second in Command, Pilot John Azurro's, matter-of-fact stance. How could he be so calm? "The facts are that three other countries' vessels are just behind us and about to reach orbit. And they still have enough fuel to land and find the source of the signal. For us, it is over. We get nothing out of this. We go home empty-handed, unlike the competition. These are the facts." She angrily slammed her open hand against the wall.

But it wasn't that they couldn't find the source of the signal that frustrated her. It was what she had to do next. She began pacing back and forth, feeling like a caged animal, trying to figure a way around it. Back and forth she went, back and forth.

She turned back to John. "Still broadcasting?"

"Yes, Commander."

It didn't matter. Nothing mattered now. She had already reached that painful conclusion. She let out a small cry of frustration, then turned to her mission specialist, Lin Adams, a young, intelligent, motivated, highly praised but impressionable woman who would do anything to impress her Commander, anyone in charge for that matter. Sam had believed Lin was at the beginning of a long and successful career. But now, she had to give her the order and had no idea what the consequences for Lin would be.

"Adams."

"Yes, Commander."

"You know what to do." It wasn't framed as a question. It was an order any of them should have been able to interpret.

"You can't be serious!" John exclaimed. "The repercussions. It could lead to war back home."

Sam raised her hand indicating to John that she wanted silence. "Thank you, John, as always for your unsolicited consultation, but we have no choice. Now, while Lin is calculating our new course, I am going to get 'home' on the line, and I will inform them of our next steps."

John did not look happy. His face couldn't conceal his frustration. "You are actually going to do it? Nuke the landing site from orbit so that nothing will be left when the others arrive. Humanity's first and possibly only chance of detecting alien life, and you want to destroy that so that our magnificent God-fearing country can save face. How primitive of you! How dare you!"

"I have my orders, John," she paused. "And you will help follow them. Or do I need to remind you of the consequences for disobeying a direct order?"

"Is that a threat?" John knew the directive very well. Disobey and Sam, as Commander, had the right to terminate his contract immediately. And also terminate him, if need be.

She smiled, though it was apparent to him that it wasn't sincere. "No, John. I am simply stating what it is that both you and I know, that is clearly stated in your contract. That is what you signed up for, and failure to comply... let's just say it wouldn't end well for you. I am just trying to remind you of this and nothing else."

The Commander was right, as always. They knew what they signed up for. However, no one ever honestly contemplated the consequences of a worst-case scenario. They always looked and dreamed of the positives of the mission. The positives were a lot simpler. They were in space; they had landed on Mars and were supposed to be the first humans to detect an alien signal.

They were supposed to be the first humans to land on Mars.' And now that they weren't, John knew that alternatives had to be considered. None of them would end well. And now this mission, a potential rebirth of space exploration could end before it even began. And instead of unifying humanity, it could send Earth once more into the dangerous abyss called War.

That is, after all, why they were sent here. Enough robotic missions, time, and money had been invested, and the public had lost faith in reaching the red planet. It didn't make economic sense anymore. Humanity was focused once more on spaceship Earth, caring for the environment, and creating a green future for all. There was no need to go off-world anymore because, finally, the planet was being restored to its former glory. Previously on the brink of global war, nations now worked for a common good.

And then the signal came, and with that, the old rivalries started up once more. Another in a long line of space races had started. It was a no-brainer for Sam and her team. They had to be first to the signal. And they arrived, ready to make waves for their country and humankind. The whole mission was being broadcast live. They did it; they were first.

Then came the landing and something they did not expect. The signal stopped. They were at the position where the signal had come from, but there was nothing. They searched tirelessly across the terrain. Scoured night and day until her crew of four was exhausted and all resources had been depleted. The scientists back home couldn't figure it out either and the broadcast was cut off.

'Were they too late?' they wondered, *'or maybe the more likely off possibilities, the signal turned itself off upon their arrival.'*

To the Commander, none of this made sense but it was just one of the potential scenarios she had trained for. The signal itself had been detected over three years ago. Just enough time to get ready for a launch window and scrap whatever technology and resources remained from the twenty-twenties when wealthy billionaires, now trillionaires, dreamed of colonizing the solar system and immortalizing themselves in history. It was a big risk to begin with and now 'home' had to protect their reputation and any potential undiscovered technology. Sam knew the order should they not be able to secure the site and the source of the alien signal; to destroy the site before anyone else could get to it. She didn't question the Command's merit. After all, an 'order was order.'

She didn't want a mutiny. All she had to do now was convince John that the course of action was necessary. Better that he agreed rather than having to terminate his contract. Lin would fall in as she always does. And then there was Communication/ Payload Specialist Thomas-Jayne Smith, who seemed to be going along for the ride. He would need no convincing; she doubted if he even cared. She believed she could convince them to fall in line with the wishes of 'home'.

She had to.

The Commander decided it best to meet at the comms room of the Kiemea at the personnel switch rotation planned for 1400 Hours. She would take over the shift with Thomas-Jayne and inform John and Lin that the launch is scheduled for 1200 Earth Time, the next day.

"So, it's a done deal?" John didn't need an answer. He was the team's oldest and with the most experience. He was their North Star and their guiding compass in the darkness that was space. He was the only one who could hold the team together for such a long trip. And now he was breaking, and there was still a long way back home.

Without him coming along for the journey, there would be no mission. There was no one else available except for John. Those with knowledge from the last decade had gotten along in years and were not up to a trip of six months to Mars and then another six months back. John, however, lived and breathed every day as an astronaut. He was fit and ready to go. Age meant nothing to him. Discovery was in his blood, and he lived every day as though it was his last.

It was clear to Sam that John, who had devoted his life to science and discovery, would be against this decision. But she also knew when it came to it, he would fall in line. She worried though about what would happen afterward. It could break him, her, and the crew. How would they make it back to Earth? How could they survive another six months, stuck in this metallic cylinder they called home?

She decided better in the end to leave it up to historians to decide who was right. After all, she had a family and a life back home and knew full well that if she disobeyed that order, then there would be consequences for her and them.

What the Commander needed now was a distraction. And as luck would have it, one came. Well, there were three of them.

"Smith, show the others what you just showed me."

Thomas-Jayne, or just Thomas, was the communications and payload specialist and the last of the four-member crew. His reasons for being on the mission were multi-faceted in nature. It was half for the adrenaline and half the science, but he had no place for allegiances to God, country, and service. He was the rogue in the group, an oddball of sorts, and the least trusted.

"Pulling up the feed now," he replied, projecting onto the displays showing the locations of three other crews now in orbit and slowly preparing for their descent.

'They are already here,' Reyson acknowledged once more. Seeing it for the second time now made it real.' All four crews were now in orbit around Mars at the same time.' Sam realized that this was not the distraction she had hoped for and that she had misjudged the situation. 'Things are going from bad to worse.'

"What do you want us to do, Commander?" Lin was eager, if not a little afraid, to see how her role model would react to this situation.

Sam ignored Lin. She hated being asked directly for orders by her subordinates. It always seemed to her too critical, as though they were looking for some weakness under her skin. She felt it was as though they were antagonizing her. Maybe it was just her, but it didn't change the fact that she hated the direct approach. As a commander, she knew that this trait was probably the most unbefitting of her role.

Sam knew she had to give her crew an answer. She thought about the predicament knowing that she couldn't launch a strike on the landing site now. The vessel had to fly directly over the site to launch and that wouldn't be before 1200 Hours the next day. That was another twenty-two hours from now. "How long until you think they are ready Thomas, the other crews I mean?" she asked.

"Hard to say. All three crews have simultaneously arrived in orbit and should be doing preparations for landing. Normally, I would give them at least 32-48 hours for the prep. However, we have the unusual situation of three crews arriving at once, so they might want to push that clock forward."

"How fast?" She needed the data.

"I don't know. As soon as their orbits allow them to do so. Or they might want to burn up some extra fuel and get there before the others.

Maybe a couple of hours?"

It was the first time an event like this had occurred in the history of human exploration. While Samantha and her crew came from one of the wealthier nations on Earth with a history of space vehicle development and the resources and expertise that allowed it, three other countries decided to do something entirely unique. They pulled their resources together, distributed their responsibilities, expertise, and costs, and developed three modules.

These 'underdogs' even went one better, agreeing to share the transport module to Mars. That meant all three crews would rendezvous in Earth orbit and then assemble with the transport module before a slingshot around the moon to save energy while attempting to reach Mars. The idea was once in Mars orbit, they could then detach separately and individually attempt to reach the surface. It also allowed the possibility that if one module failed, then the other two modules could pick up the slack. To ensure that everyone could take credit for the discovery, every module had a mixture of crew members from the three countries. They weren't playing poker like Sam's crew, they were 'stacking the deck', making sure that they could increase their chances. Nothing like it had been seen before. On Earth, they were the 'underdogs', but they were also the popular favorites.

The 'Longshots' had arrived. They had made the six-month journey and had a chance to make history. In Sam's mind, this made Mars a little too overcrowded for her liking. And now she had possibly only a couple of hours to stop them from reaching their goal.

"Understood." The Commander acknowledged Smith's assessment. There were too many variables now. She couldn't nuke the surface while the new crews were enroute to the landing site or even when they were on the surface. They would perish and their actions would most certainly ignite a new war back on Earth. It was cold-blooded murder, and even if 'home' gave her the order she didn't think she could pull the trigger.

"Ahh, Commander." It was Thomas again. He kept his head, face focused on one of the screens pointing at it. "We got a problem. Object launched from one of the teams. It appears to be a lander."

"You just said a couple of hours, Smith!" Lin was the first to express her shock. They were going to lose this race. *'No pages in the history books for us'.* She thought.

"Yes, I assumed," Thomas retorted. "If I were to assume again then

I would say it looks like they are ignoring their protocols and safety checks and rushing to get down there. I guess with the competition, they decided being first was worth the risk."

John turned to Sam, staring her down. It wasn't the dread of not being the first to discover alien intelligence that she saw on his face. It was the dread of what she was going to do next. John shook his head at her.

"Get me command on the line, now!" She ordered Thomas, then rushed out of the room.

"You know this is insanity," John commented.

Sam walked faster now. "Now, Smith!" she shouted, and with that, she was gone.

Lin went to follow her out. "I will go and see how she is."

John stopped her with a hand on her shoulder. "Stay here!"

"Who put you in charge?" It was a low and smug comment designed to elicit a response. John knew it but cared not to play.

"Trust me, stay here. The Commander has got a lot to think about. Even I can't interfere."

"And that's why I have to go and talk to her," she demanded, and brushed John's hand away. Lin turned to the entrance to find Thomas now standing in the way. He had seen what was transpiring and decided it was time to intervene.

"No chance, Lin." He said in a careful tone. "This one's above your pay grade. It's above all our pay grades. It's for the Commander alone to decide."

She tried to ram herself past Thomas but failed and fell comically onto the floor, landing on her bottom.

"Let me pass!" she demanded still on the floor. "I know what she is going through."

No," John said. "You don't." He put out his hand to help her up which she ignored. He backed off and let her get up on her own. "Now sit down." His tone had deepened and the volume in his voice had increased. "You want to do something, then help us to monitor the situation from here."

"Besides," Thomas interjected. "The Commander will need a status report when she has made her decision. Don't you want to be the one that gives it to her?"

The Contact Clock Begins- T-Minus 30 Hours.

Commander Samantha Reyson disappeared for some time. Almost two hours had passed since she stormed out to speak with 'home'. It was worrying for the crew but understandable given the predicament they found themselves in.

Sam called her for a meeting. The crew assembled into what Thomas would call the 'recreational' part of the ship, but that was just his 'joking' term for the science and research part of the vessel, and it was one of the only areas without artificial gravity. Sam chose it for that very reason. She knew it was a lot more difficult for one to get angry and shake about when you were forced to hold onto something or risk floating off in some other direction.

"Status report!" the Commander ordered Thomas.

"Lander has reached the site," Lin interjected. "And their team is now on the surface searching for the signal,"

"And Communication Officer Smith?" She wanted more information and was confused as to why her mission specialist, Lin Adams, was answering questions that were not meant for her.

"That's just it," Lin once again interrupted, which annoyed the Commander. "The signal stopped again. As soon as they landed. Just like us, it stopped. The other crews remain in orbit. They show no intention of landing on the surface. Maybe they are just reevaluating the situation?"

The Commander thanked Lin but nodded her head acknowledging her. Lin was happy but the Commander's face said otherwise. Her face seemed concerned.

"I think I might know why," Sam took a deep breath. "I've spoken to 'home'; we've got bigger problems."

The crew was confused by this statement. *How much worse could things be?* They wondered.

"Bigger Problems than this," Thomas smirked. "What could be bigger than this?"

Sam pulled a display from the wall and punched a few buttons. On the screen was a media file currently in pause.

"Before I play this, please be aware that what you are about to see is classified as top secret."

"Don't worry," Lin wanted to be heard. "We won't tell anybody."

"Good," Sam answered. "Because as of five minutes ago, all

communications except that with 'home' have been deactivated."

The group fell into shock.

"Is that wise, Commander?" John was well aware of the dangers of going silent. "Given the current trajectory, having open comms might not be a bad idea. Don't you think?"

"Not my call, John," she replied. "Command did it remotely."

"What!" John was no longer calm and collected. "How? Why did they do that?"

Sam pointed to the display. "Watch." She said, pressing play.

T-Minus 29 Hours 30 Minutes.

Thomas processed this new information the quickest. "So, they are telling us that there are two signals, one which we thought only appeared on Mars three years ago, which is much older. Like possibly thousands of years older."

"Maybe, maybe millions, Tom," Samantha stated. "I know just as much as you."

"And our government has known about it since the beginning of the early twentieth century. And they never said a thing." The communications specialist smiled as he appreciated an excellent secret successfully kept by a government for so long. "Talk about your conspiracies. I must say 'kudos' to them for keeping it hidden for so long."

"And so, if I understand this right." Lin sounded more intrigued than shocked by the development. "The signal has always been there, but it was just ignored? No one would discuss it. It was dismissed as interference, and anyone looking into it was either brought into the conspiracy or otherwise."

"Correct," Sam answered. "I am just as shocked as you are. It has always been there, directly in plain sight. But sometimes, having access to knowledge that something is there isn't necessarily a conspiracy, although Thomas-Jayne here might say otherwise. You just possess the technology and the knowledge to know something is there. Gravity was always there, but we were too stupid or didn't care to recognize it before Newton. Electro-magnetism and the speed of light have always been constants and facts that have been with us the whole time, right underneath our feet. We have always had these things and never knew they were there. How easy it must have been for the governments to dismiss this signal when it was first discovered as interference or nothing of value. A signal bouncing back from Earth, for example."

John agreed. "Indeed. The signal wasn't blocked. They probably weren't even sure what it was in the first place. And when they did discover its source here on Mars, it was already relatively easy enough for them to dismiss this as something else."

The Commander sighed. "And the signal never stopped, not once during the fly buys in the 1960s or the Viking missions in 1975 with the smaller or larger landers in the 2000s. Or the failed remote landing shuttles of the 2020s. "

Thomas continued processing the information. "And they are now saying that this entire mission, this rush to get here, was because three years ago, they detected a similar signal outside our solar system. And obviously, it didn't take long for our enemies to recognize this fact and try to pursue the signal here on Mars."

"Yes," Samantha answered. "It wasn't like we could visit the other signal at the solar system's edge."

"So, we did detect the signal three years ago," Lin laughed. "Just not this one on Mars. Do you think the two signals are communicating with each other?"

"That's what 'home' believes." Sam answered. "And here is what you don't know. So, the signal stopped when the first humans placed our feet on the ground. And then, as soon as we left, the signal started again. 'Home' figured out there was, however, something different this time. The other signal just outside the solar system, that stationary signal, is no longer stationary. Its position is changing and accelerating, heading towards the inner solar system at a tremendous speed, most likely towards us."

"What are our new orders?" John wasn't playing coy. He knew Command had already decided. That was the real reason behind the communications blackout.

"Our orders are to wait and analyze the threat. If the source of the signal, most likely a vessel, reaches the planet, we are to observe and document. If it proceeds to the surface and contacts one of the other crews, we have been authorized to use all means necessary."

"You mean force?" Lin asked.

"All and any means necessary," Sam answered.

"Oh Geeze," Thomas wasn't going to hold back. "So now, instead of starting a global war back on Earth, we want to try and start an interstellar one as well? Well, why the hell not." He laughed, slapping John on the back.

John did not find it funny, and neither did the others. Thomas's smile soon disappeared.

"How long do we have, Commander?" Lin asked, "Until they get here?"

"Twenty, maybe twenty-five hours," she answered. "

"Hmm, what a coincidence," John remarked. "That puts us directly within range of a launch."

"Strange times indeed," Sam said. "Now no time to muck around. We have to prepare."

"This is a very bad idea, Commander," John stated.

"I agree," she said. "But it isn't our call."

T-Minus 3 Hours 15 Minutes.

The object was nothing like they had ever seen before. It didn't look like a typical spaceship. It resembled a polished stone, the type you would throw into the water to see if it could skip. There were no lights notifying anyone of its presence and no natural way of detecting it until it got close enough to the planet.

"Commander, the signal from the object has now stopped and the object itself has come to a halt," Thomas informed them.

"What? How?" Sam asked.

Thomas just shrugged his shoulders. "No idea. This thing travelled who knows what type of speed to get here and then just suddenly stopped. I see no signs of heat dissipation or anything that indicated some sort of propulsion." Sam could see that Tom was intrigued. "This thing could have been out there for centuries, millennia, eons, and we would have never seen it or found it with technology like that"

"There you have it," John smirked.

"What?" Smith didn't understand John's remark.

"Against these guys, with this technology. We don't have a chance."

"What do you think, Lin?" The Commander wondered why her mission specialist had been quiet for so long. She always wanted to convey her point, her 'two cents' worth.' This was uncharacteristically not like her.

"It doesn't make sense. Why now?" The mission specialist was unsure. It was a rather unusual position for Lin to have.

"You might want to elaborate," said John, who also found her answer to be quite vague.

She pointed to the display screen showing the object's trajectory, from where it had initially been heading towards the source of the signal on Mars, and indicated its original location. "This thing is probably millennia or millions of years old and alien. It has sat hidden, most likely at the solar system's outer edge, and has done nothing in this time. Humanity has evolved, sent out radio signals, sent exploration vehicles throughout the solar system, landed on the moon, and it's continued to do nothing. The signal suddenly stopped only when humans, not robots, landed on Mars. Robot explorers have landed here in the past and there was no change. Now finally, a biological species has landed and in turn, this object decided to come in and investigate. Why do you think that is?"

The question was rhetorical as it was puzzling, but everyone agreed it was a valid point worthy of discussion.

"Continue, Lin," Sam said.

"What do we know?" Lin asked. "We know this object activated only when a biological entity landed below. The signal stopped on Mars, triggering a response from the outer object."

"And don't forget the signal itself," Thomas interrupted, "That signal is deliberate and has a purpose. It had been projected out into the solar system for who knows how long. Wouldn't it make more sense to activate a signal when we landed and not before? It would save a lot more energy. Unless its purpose was to attract biologicals to it in the first place."

"Like a fly into a spider's web," John answered. There was an ominous tone in his answer.

"Exactly," Thomas replied. "The signal is designed for any biological space fairing entities to come and find it. And so, we know one thing already. We know it is no rescue signal."

"What else do we know?" the Commander started collating the information running through her head.

"There are probably no aliens on that thing out there," Lin replied. "Nothing biological that we know would be awake or alive for that long, ready to answer immediately as soon as the signal on Mars stopped. It had to be automated, most likely a machine."

"That's based on what we know," John wasn't convinced. "Who is to say that the creatures behind this object don't live very long lives or have some sort of cryogenic sleep technology available to them? We would just be guessing here. But okay, maybe a machine intelligence."

"What else do we know?" Sam needed more information.

"The technology is old and very advanced. Whoever they are, they can accelerate here so quickly." Lin replied.

Thomas jumped in. "They cloaked themselves from being detected and hid amongst the extreme cold temperatures of the solar system for hundreds, maybe thousands, possibly millions of years. We are out of our league here. "

"We have little chance of understanding their intentions as much as a bacteria would have of our own," John added.

Thomas sighed. "But what if it was less about them and more about us? Specifically, what if it was about our reactions?"

The Commander recognized the point immediately. "You mean the fact that we all raced here and are prepared to destroy each other and this object along with it because that's who we are?"

Her crew looked to their Commander. They didn't expect that response from her. Not after she had been supporting the status quo, constantly telling them to prepare for what needed to be done. She told them that terrible things would be done to them if they disobeyed. It was strange to them that she would even entertain such a thought.

"So, you are now saying we should stop the launch?" John was curious. "Stop this potential planetary and interplanetary war from ever starting?"

Sam looked around, looking them all in the eyes, gauging their emotions. "I am not saying anything. I am simply looking at the facts. We either let the object land and do whatever it is about to do and let the other crews take the credit. They go home as the proud heroes of Earth and their country immortalized forever, or…" she sighed. "We use force, and we stop it all from happening. 'Home' comes up with some sort of tragic propaganda story saying that there was an accident or maybe that it was all just an attempt from a 'bad actor,' or a rival nation designed to bring us to this point, this edge of war. And we all go back to those repercussions and unknowns."

"Except there is one very big unknown," Smith pointed to his display and the object. "That unknown."

"These are the facts," John sounded disappointed. "But it is what it is."

Thomas's mind always ticked a little differently, and alternative options bouncing off each other ran through his head. He thought about the scenarios and looked at them from every one of their possible sides and then he found something. "I mentioned before that maybe it was more about us and our reactions. What if it is all a test? To reveal to the universe what we are like as a species."

"Why would they do that?" Lin processed what Tom was saying and tried to follow his course of thinking. "Unless you wanted to 'weed out,' to remove those species who might be a threat to them?"

Tom wasn't convinced of this statement "Maybe they want to remove any competition? It would help explain a reason why, among thousands of stars, the universe is so quiet. Maybe there is a peaceful galactic federation out there ensuring we are ready to join it. And that we are safe to join it and they are safe from us. Although I am not a fan of this option."

"Why not?" Lin asked. "I like it."

Sam agreed. "I like it too. At least I hope…"

Tom interrupted." Hope, exactly. That is the problem. Because it is more fantasy and wishful thinking than anything else. "

"He is right you know," John had seen enough of the world to know better. He had developed a healthy dose of cynicism after many rotations around the sun. "The world is cruel, Lin. Life is about survival, the fight to live another day."

"But the things that created this are so far advanced. They must have moved beyond all this. They must have morals?" Being the youngest, Lin felt confused. Her elders were hostile to the idea of peace and a better world. Was she in the wrong for her lack of cynicism, she thought. Or were they? They seemed to have lost all hope here and couldn't see this event happening before them as to what she saw it as, something positive.

"That is if they have the same morals as us, Lin." The Commander had listened enough to the conversation, she had made her decision and now she was going to steer towards it. "We don't even know if these beings, these creatures have emotions. Do they feel things like us? Or maybe they feel nothing at all? They could have grown up somewhere in the galaxy where every waking moment was a fight to survive, adversaries around every corner. They could be a species that does not trust others but fears others." Sam breathed. "I have decided. I thought I was torn as to what to do. But I know now."

"Commander," John looked Sam directly in the eyes. "Your orders."

Sam sighed, smiled, then reclined back, head against the room's wall. Then, she pushed herself off and just floated in peace. "We do nothing! As you have given me all the facts, and there is one important fact in all of this. They are too advanced for us. There is nothing we can do."

"And what about 'home'?" Lin asked.

"We tell them the truth. There is nothing we can do except start wars. This would not only endanger us, but it would also endanger all of humanity. So, sit back, relax and we will see what happens next."

T-Minus 30 Minutes

"So it's confirmed," Sam asked Thomas. "It has begun."

The crew moved into the observational lounge and took their seats. Sam preferred to stand while Lin preferred the comfort of sitting on the floor. Thomas-Jayne had seen minutes before that the object had begun its approach to the crew at the landing site and informed his crew of the change. Watching from the viewing window, the crew of the Kiemea marveled at the object heading down to the planet. It flew through the atmosphere without resistance as though matter was nothing but a fluid it could pass through. No supercharged particles hit its hull as it passed through. None of the heated ionized orange particles, typical of a landing craft could be seen. It was as though it wasn't even there. The crew were both fascinated and terrified about what might happen next.

John turned to Sam. "We do know one thing about them. I realized it just then. They were never after our resources. That limits our suspicions a little. We know that they aren't here to conquer us and take what is ours.

Sam smiled once more. "They might still want to conquer us. Maybe *we* are the resource. Think about that."

John hadn't. *'What if we were the resources? Soon to be slaves to an advanced species.'*

Sam moved toward the comm station in the room. "I will inform the other crews that we offer no threat, and hopefully they should do the same. Let the crew on the ground have the glory and be damned with the consequences back on Earth. Besides, this moment was always too important for politics and rivalries. And our 'knee-jerk' violent reactions would amount to nothing in the grand scheme of things."

It was at that moment that John finally respected Sam for who she was as a person. He did respect her before, but he respected her position and respected those in power in choosing her for Command. However, not once did he truly appreciate the individual that was Samantha Reyson. That was until now.

She sent her message then came over and sat beside John and smiled. "Besides," she said, "do we think that something this advanced will be affected by one of our primitive weapons? If we did nuke it, I suspect all we will do is give the thing a little scratch."

T-Minus Zero.

"What's it doing?" Lin asked.

Tom was baffled. "Nothing, it is just hovering over the landing site. Maybe twenty meters above the crew. Nothing more." Smith was watching the object from the display while the others watched out from the window.

"And the crew?" John asked.

The display connected directly with the surface observational satellites in orbit. He could see everything in the clearest of details. "They look confused," Smith replied. "They are using open communication and requesting help from home. I am picking up their signal. Their Command tells them to get off the open line, but the crew says they are on a secure line. Something's not right."

"Explanation, Smith," John demanded.

"If I had to guess, the object was doing it? Maybe it's opening communication for everybody?"

"Is this contact?" John wondered. "Is this its way of communication?"

Thomas pondered the question. It took him a couple of minutes to come up with a possible solution and explanation. "It couldn't be that simple," he muttered.

"What did you say? Don't mumble Smith." The Commander hated people whispering under their breath and gave Thomas a face to express her disaffection at his articulation.

"What if they *have* been communicating with us?" Thomas pulled up the display again, showing the object on the solar system's outskirts and the signal coming from Mars. He tried to explain. "Let's pretend you are on a scouting mission millions of years ago, looking for life. And not just any life, intelligent life, but you don't find anything. Instead, you find primitive life, maybe dinosaurs, but nothing you can communicate with. Do you give up, or do you keep looking?"

"Well, keep looking, of course," Sam answered intrigued to see where this was going. "But you move on."

"No," Thomas answered. "You don't".

Thomas-Jayne Smith had now the attention of the entire crew. "You don't leave. You have found life, and you know how scarce it is. To leave the solar system and look further reduces the probability of finding intelligent life even further. What if..." Thomas tried to gather his thoughts.

"What if?" John prompted.

"What if you wait?" Thomas responded. "You wait until a species evolves which usually is millions of years. And then you communicate. But how? We don't share the same language."

"There's mathematics." Lin jumped in.

"True," Thomas replied. "But you are assuming they understand mathematics from a human point of view."

"But mathematics has laws; it's universal and understandable." Lin countered.

"I don't think that to be true," Tom looked around to find something to demonstrate his point, but couldn't. "This object out there is not us. We have no common frame of reference. Maybe we missed some things in our evolution, steps in our knowledge that it has, and we do not. No, we need to find common ground on a more fundamental level, non-threatening."

"We could just say hello," John laughed.

"No, that wouldn't work either." Thomas sniggered. "How would you do that? Your words, your expressions might come across as aggressive."

"Well, hell, Tom, anything will appear aggressive when you think about it. Flashing light in someone's face will come across as aggressive. You can't avoid it." John paused. "Unless you used something that no one would notice, that was hidden in the background, passive in nature."

"Exactly. Background noise is constant and on a spectrum that you would only pick up once you have developed a certain amount of technology and understanding. And yet remain somewhat unobtrusive in nature," Tom pointed to the display. "The signal."

"But how is that communication?" John couldn't quite fathom.

"Two signals, constant between two objects," Sam felt she had the answer now. She knew what Tom was getting at. "We land, and the signal goes off. We leave, and the signal goes on again. The other crew lands and the signal goes off. On, off, on.... Off."

"Zero and One," Tom said. "A simple version of nothing, then something. No one is here, and then someone is there. And now that object hovers above the crew on the planet's surface, and they have no idea what to do, but we do."

"Play the signal, "Sam realized. "Play it back to them, it, or whatever. Do it now!" she ordered.

"Already on it, Commander." Smith tapped a few buttons. I am informing the crew on the surface.

"Why not us?" Lin was confused. "Why shouldn't we get the credit?"

"This being is down there waiting for centuries and then comes to the planet's surface to investigate what may be intelligence. Let's not confuse the thing with our politics and the need in wanting to be first with everything." Smith turned to the Commander, who nodded in agreement.

"They are relaying the signal," Smith informed them.

"Maybe this object is simply exploring like we are." Sam wondered openly. "And perhaps it was alone until now, waiting in the dark and the cold for so very long; waiting for someone else in the universe to come along and say hello."

The Commander opened her arms up, waving her hands as she told her crew to come in closer. "And now, after such a long wait," she began embracing them. "These beings will finally get an answer back."

She thought to herself. *'It all seemed so much simpler from orbit.*

--

Siv Art was born in Australia and lives in Germany, and has been writing for over 20 years. He writes under the pseudonym Siv Art purely for fun and has done this to express his creative outlet. Slowly he has progressed to his own self-publishing but would naturally love to have others publish his work. You can find out more at sivart.eu's Siv Art SF – The Verse is simply how you see it.

sivart-sf.blog

Sustained Life on Mars
By Jon Cox

Sometime in the not-too-distant future, many of earth's leading minds and entrepreneurs will come together in an effort to stave off the extinction of the species. It became ever more apparent that humanity was trying to destroy itself via a nuclear holocaust, as governments grew ever more corrupt and dangerous to their own citizens. The call was sent out to entrepreneurs worldwide; build a sustainable colony on the north pole of Mars and save the human race.

Ten years into Mars Colony 2 on the north pole of Mars, the colony was finally becoming self-sustained, albeit for some deliveries they were still tethered to the earth for - mainly ships and landers that were currently generations away from being produced on Mars. Black water from the colony's sewer treatment was being refined and used to introduce bacteria and fertilizer into the Martian soil. This made production of crops in the above-ground greenhouse domes possible, and using military style rations was no longer necessary, but they were kept as a precautionary measure just in case some unforeseen blight attacked the greenhouses. Backup plan after backup plan was made prior to and during the actual colonization period of Mars Colony 2, the failure and deaths of the first colony almost ended interest in colonizing Mars at all.

Luckily, the effort to leave earth and colonize the red planet was not left to the corrupt politicians, who would lose popularity and / or votes, if the colonies failed. Instead, brave, insightful entrepreneurs from around the world, seeing the deadly path that the governments of the earth were heading down, drove them to colonize Mars even more enthusiastically.

Min was a 32-year-old Martian Botanist who arrived at the colony from China; she was extremely punctual and put effort into improving her fellow Martians' lives. When she worked, she did not do so in a lethargic manner; she planned everything meticulously, and prepared for every possible incident that could arise. She was now sitting in a self-contained solar battery powered rover, impatiently tapping the steering wheel with the tips of her fingers. John, who was a colony mechanical engineer, was supposed to join her in this expedition. He was already late and had not yet contacted her via their colony's wrist communicators. Min suspected John, who had arrived at the colony from the US, was probably hungover and still asleep.

She contacted rover control and asked them to open the blast doors at the entry to the motor pool, so she could be on her way and begin the expedition.

Petrov, who had come to the colony from Russia, came over the communicator. "No one is allowed to go out alone, you know the protocols."

Min was annoyed but held her tongue, remembering that one of the downfalls of the previous colony was the slow descent into unprofessional and careless conduct. If they were to make this work, she had to be civil at all times. Though, with John, it was a challenge.

John finally arrived and climbed up the rover's side ladder, opened the door, secured it behind him and immediately apologized for being late.

Min gave John a resigned look. "Fine. Just don't do it again. Strap yourself into the navigator's chair. It will take us two hours without incident to reach sector five on time in full sunlight." John smirked, but said nothing. After strapping himself in he began checking the rover's systems. Min then called rover control again and requested permission to depart.

"Permission granted," said Petrov. "Blast doors opening now, please proceed with caution and have a safe and *uneventful* journey!"

Min drove the rover down a short tunnel and shot out through the open hatch onto a dusty track that led around the colony. The hatch closed behind them.

The rover headed Southwest, past one of the solar farms and multiple wind generators, and finally into the open wasteland of sand and rocky outcroppings. Min liked going this way because she could see her pride and joy, both of the large above-ground domed greenhouses. They were spaced about three kilometers apart, just in case a rogue meteor or comet strike inadvertently took one of them out. Again, backup plan after backup plan had been created, endless contingency measures. Even the large Martian polar ice glaciers, that provided the colony with drinking water and air, were filtered multiple times and scanned for unknown pathogens. Everything was being done to ensure Mars Colony 2 would be a stunning success and shining example of human ingenuity.

For the next few hours, John was busy monitoring the feed from one of the Martian orbital satellites. He reported to Min that he didn't see any evidence of current storms, but it appeared they might have a small front of weather developing by evening. "If nothing goes wrong, we should be able to beat it on our way back."

"I plan on not taking long," replied Min. "Just a few soil samples, evidence of any metal deposits during scans." Barring any mechanical breakdowns, she didn't foresee any issues that would interfere with the scheduled expedition. She checked her wrist communicator. "Radio check time."

John acted immediately. "Rover control this is rover 3 for a radio check, over?" He waited a few moments. "Rover control this is rover 3 for a radio check over?"

Petrov's voice crackled over the speakers. "This is rover control, we read you lima charlie."

"We are green, and we just passed phase line alpha. We have about one hour to go until we reach the sample site. Currently there are no issues with the rover, battery level is still around 98%, mechanicals are green, weather is green as well."

Petrov could be heard typing this information into his keyboard as he responded. "Good copy rover 3 and God speed to you! Please call again when you arrive and when you depart."

"That's a good copy rover control, wilco!"

"By the way," added Petrov, "The idiots back on earth are threatening each other again with nuclear war. If anything happens, I will call you and relay it, along with the colony's follow-up. Rover control, out."

"Good, copy that!" Then he turned to Min. "Check-ins completed; everything appears green with our trip. You heard what he said about Earth right?"

Min nodded, a concerned look on her face, while continuing to focus on driving the eight-wheeled rover around and over the dunes.

About an hour later, a GPS tone began sounding over Min's steering console.

"We have arrived in the sampling area," she stated. "I'll find a good position for the rover." She noticed a small outcropping of rock in the area, and decided to take a sample near there. The outcropping appeared wind worn due to centuries of exposure. As Min drove closer, they noticed what appeared to be a small cave opening. "That wasn't on the drone footage."

John grinned, excitedly. "We have to check that out!"

Min frowned. "As long as it's safe to do so, and only after the samples are taken and secured in the rover."

"You and your work ethic," he smiled. Then he looked serious. "Of course, I have no issues with completing the mission first."

The rover pulled up near the outcropping of rocks and slowed to a stop. Min set the brake locks on the rover, unbuckled her seat belts, then tapped the controls on her steering console to align the rover's solar panel to its best angle to the sun. The whine of an electric motor sounded, and the angle of the solar panel pitched to catch the best sunlight possible.

"Not too bad," said John, checking the stats for the panel. "We only went down to 78% on that trip, charging along the way. Estimated recharge time of the batteries in direct sun, about 2.55 hours."

Min did a final check of all systems, while John checked the weather again via satellite connection, reporting that they have about five hours before the front moves in.

"Let's say two hours for sample gathering," said Min. "Maybe an hour to check out the cave, then return to base. We should remain ahead of the weather until we get back."

"Sounds good."

"Suit up, grab the hammer probe, hammer and a bucket, and let's take at least five samples and secure them."

Once both John and Min had suited up, both said "pressurize", and read-outs appeared on the visors of both helmets. A computerized voice in John's helmet said, "Pressurization complete, safe travels!" Min's suit, on the other hand, said "Pressurization stopped, leak detected in left hand glove! Do not proceed!"

Both parties could then hear a slight air leak from the suspected glove.

"Hold on just a second, I have an idea!" said John. He then went to the back of the rover, into one of the storage shelves, and grabbed a roll of silver duct tape. He then returned to Mia and wrapped the tape around the suspected leaky glove.

"You're kidding me, right?" said Min, staring at him through her helmet, incredulously. "A piece of tape isn't going to hold back a vacuum."

"1% atmosphere isn't a vacuum. Just trust me, and attempt to pressurize. The glue on this tape is pretty strong."

Min knew she had to complete the mission, but this was entirely unorthodox and against protocols. Why wasn't the hole picked up in checks earlier? Or were her suits degrading already. Pushing the thoughts out of her head about failing equipment, failing colonies and possible death, she angrily said to her suit computer, "Pressurize, damnit!"

"Command not recognized."

Min forcefully calmed herself. "Pressurize."

"Pressurization complete, safe travels!"

Min turned to John and looked him seriously in the eyes. "If I lose pressure and suffocate, I will come back as a ghost and haunt your dumb ass!"

John laughed. "I will bring the tape with us, just in case!"

"That is extremely reassuring, thank you!"

Both exited the rover and, after securing the door, they climbed down the ladder and proceeded to the rear of the rover. Once there they opened a storage compartment and obtained a hammer probe, a hammer and several sample containers placed into a bucket. Min screwed the hammer probe "T' onto the long portion of the probe. Once the probe was assembled, they walked around looking for odd colorations in the soil. They hammered the probe into the ground, which didn't take much since the ground was pretty soft. They took several samples in different areas, some in dark soil, some in light. After taking each sample, they took the core sample from the probe, and emptied it into a sample container, which resembled a silver Nalgene bottle. They marked each bottle with time and date stamps, along with a GPS location from where the sample was taken.

After Min was satisfied that she had enough samples, they returned the samples and equipment to the rear storage compartment of the rover.

John, almost like a little child, had started bouncing with excitement in the low gravity. "Can we finally explore the cave?"

Min frowned at him. "It's probably just a small hole in the rock, anyway! If it turns out to be large, we'll have to come back as we don't have the time. We'll be out of coms range, and we have limited air in our suits! If our suits get anywhere near 60%, we return no matter what we find! I don't care if we find a city or a ship, or someplace an alien took a crap, is that understood?"

John stared at Min for a second and said, "I don't have a death wish, so that is totally understandable. Agreed!"

Both walked over to the outcropping of rock. As they approached the cave, they could see it wasn't just a hole in the rock, it almost looked like a tunnel. The entrance was over two meters tall, and just over a meter wide.

Min checked her comms. "No signal. I'll leave a message updating them on where we're going." She tapped in a few words and sent the text to the rover. When the signal returned, the rover would transmit the message back to Petrov.

They headed inside. The tunnel went into the rock face for a way and then made an abrupt right turn, which turned into a downward slope.

"Turning helmet light on 40%," said their suits, which illuminated the darkening tunnel. As they continued further, the tunnel changed from being weather worn and rough to smoother and more manufactured. John looked at Min. "You know, I was hoping to find maybe bones or some artifacts. This looks a little bit more advanced than I'm trained for."

Min grabbed his arm. "Oxygen at 70%. Stay close.

"There must have been a reason this has suddenly appeared after all these years," said John, as they walked. "Not even detected from ground scans?"

They slowed their steps and carefully scanned the whole area in front. Even the floor had smoothed out.

Then they saw it. A door. And on its left side was a small obelisk. They both approached it, after looking at it for several moments, then at each other.

"Doorbell?" asked Min.

"Self-destruct actuator?" responded John. "Who the hell knows?"

Min reached her hand towards the obelisk, but John grabbed her hand and said, "What do you say we just mark this with GPS, and go back and report it? We can let the eggheads come in and do this properly!"

Min pulled her hand free of John's grip and slowly touched the top of the obelisk. "This could be the discovery of the century, and you want to walk away?"

A low whine vibrated through their suits, along with what felt like a large lock moving. The door slowly slid to the left.

"Well, I hope we don't need weapons, because all I have is a roll of duct tape!"

"Whatever this is, it hasn't been opened in centuries," said Min. "If there is anything in there, it's long since dead!" She walked slowly through the door; it was hard to see inside because of the dust stirred by the doors opening. Expecting to step on a floor the same height as the entrance, she stretched her right foot forwards and fell face first about a half meter down to the hard floor.

Even the lower gravity wasn't enough to save her suit. The visor of her helmet cracked. Air immediately began pouring out of her suit into a near-empty atmosphere within the chamber.

Her suit chimed in. "Suit is compromised and will not seal, shutting down air flow. Please correct immediately."

Min panicked and began gasping for air, wildly throwing her arms and legs. John jumped down from the door and ran to her.

He tackled Min onto the floor and placed his knees over her arms to keep her from flailing around. He could tell she was trying to scream, but didn't have enough air to do so. Then, to his dismay, she stopped moving. He grabbed the roll of duct tape and quickly patched Min's visor, but she was not responsive. He placed his helmet near hers and said in a loud but steady voice "pressurize!" Min's suit complied and responded, "Pressurization complete, safe travels!"

There was still no movement or coughing from Min. Then John attempted cardiopulmonary resuscitation through Min's suit. He knew there was no limit to how many chest compressions he could give, and he'd do it for hours if he had to. "Come on, Min. You can do this. Breathe, damn you."

But, after about 45 minutes, John couldn't do anymore. "I'm so sorry, Min," he said, as exhaustion took him, and he passed out beside her. As the blackness took him, he hoped that her message had finally been sent, and Mars Colony 2 were already sending help. Though, with a five-hour trip and not much oxygen left…

While both were unconscious, a small alien orb flew over both bodies and landed on each, releasing a blue gel-like substance onto both John and Min's suits. The gel appeared to be passing through the sealed suits, and into each occupants' bodies. The orb appeared to be some type of metal, which even though was extremely old, its flight was very precise and with an intent which was unknown.

Several hours later John woke up. He immediately sat up and said, "oxygen remaining?" the suit responded 10% remaining, please refill air immediately for your own safety." John, in a panic, moved over to Min. He put his helmet close to hers and said out loud, "status of occupant Min?" Min's suit responded. "Sleeping. Oxygen content of Min's suit: 10% remaining. Please refill air immediately for your own safety."

John shook Min's shoulders and yelled, "Min! Wake up! We have to go now! We are almost out of air!"

Much to John's relief, her eyes suddenly opened, and she yelled, "What the hell happened? I couldn't breathe!"

"We can discuss that in the rover. We have to go. Now!" John helped Min up, and they ran out of the dark room, then squatted and jumped up and out of the door, grateful for the lower Mars gravity. Once they did so the door slid closed and locked itself again.

They made their way up the tunnel and out into the storm. Both suits chimed, "5% oxygen remaining, please refill immediately."

The sandstorm had been going for a while. John yelled to his suit. "Provide path to rover entrance!"

His suit responded. "Follow green course to rover door." Immediately, there was a green path showing on his visor. He could see the path but little else due to the sandstorm. Both made it to the rover, and struggled to climb the ladder, before finally being able to open the sealed door, and close it behind them. Once inside the rover, both removed their helmets and strapped themselves into their seats. Min touched the steering control panel and said to the rover, "Emergency return, reverse path via GPS to Martian Colony 2, rover control." A computer voice responded, "Course set, rover 3 in full control. Fastest safest speed applied." The rover unlocked its own brakes and lurched forward into the storm. On the front viewport, the rover now displayed path information, including distance and time estimated to return."

"I guess Pavlov couldn't send anyone out to rescue us in this storm," said John.

Min nodded.

Two days later John and Min woke up inside Martian Colony 2's quarantined sick bay. They were watching news feeds from earth, both wearing hospital gowns. Min had a bandage taped over stitches in her forehead. As they watched, the reporters explained that the reigning corrupt government's economies were failing. Worse, the way the governments attempted to rectify this was through worldwide war. Reporters on the scene were horrified to stream exploding nuclear bombs, knowing they had seconds left. Reporters and cameramen dropping their equipment and running. Signals failing. The screen flashed scenes of mutual destruction, a nuclear war that all sides thought they could win, before all the feeds finally cut out.

Min and John couldn't believe what they had just seen.

"It looks like the monsters finally did it!" said Min. "Mars will have to take care of itself now."

John looked downcast.

Suddenly, they heard a voice. "Now that we are with you, we will make sure this never happens to your race again."

John looked at Mia. "Did you hear that, too?"

Mia's mouth was wide open. All she could do was nod her head in response.

"Who is this speaking?" asked John.

The voice responded. "You don't have to speak out loud, you will scare others around you. We are symbionts. We are speaking to you both telepathically, so both of you can hear and respond in your minds. Min died when she fell. We helped her back with your assistance, John. Very kind of you to try and save her."

John answered back in his mind. "So, are you some type of alien monsters?"

"No," said the voice, seriously. "We just watched the real monsters destroy themselves. We are here to help and to elevate the remaining humans. Through knowledge and assistance, and restraint, your race will go to the stars."

--

Jon Cox was born in Flint Michigan, after dropping out of high school, he lived on the streets for a short time, later to be housed by his grandmother and aunt. After turning 17 he enlisted and later retired from the US Army, during this time he obtained his GED, associate degree in arts, and later a Bachelor of Science in Criminal Justice. Jon enjoys writing stories, and tolerates running, mountain biking and going to the gym. Jon also has two rescue dogs and an uber fantastic wife he met in Germany.

Mars Orbit 2033
By Neil A. Hogan

With the crew of the lander wearing gogs, the image of Phobos was crystal clear and could be seen from any angle, thanks to the lander's multiple cameras and AI enhancement.

"Touch down in 5…" began the AI. The volunteers braced for impact. Of course, there wasn't one.

"Touchdown successful," said the AI.

The crew in the control center, almost weightless, began to push themselves out of their chairs, their pass-through gog cameras and perimeter alerts making sure they didn't bump into each other in the confined space. They'd been told that the landing would be uneventful, but with the vision of reddish hues on the otherwise dark land before them, the full impact, so to speak, was disappointing.

"We weigh mere milligrams," said Rishi.

"My wife would be pleased," said Bruce, finally extricating his bulk out of the tight seat. He pointed a pudgy finger in the air. "When I signed up, I thought landing on Mars was guaranteed. Not Phobos."

Wei floated over. "First flight," she said. "Orbital maneuver. Make sure everything is fine."

Bruce tapped his gog, and saw the underside of their lander. "One small step for a moon lander. One giant leap for conscious entities."

"Glad you're not being broadcast," said Aiysha, straightening her suit and tie, and wiping some shine off her bald head. "I've already got my script. Remember, investors are watching."

Bruce grunted. "Not into the whole media farce, thanks. I'll keep my distance."

Strawberry had been checking that all instruments were still functioning. They unclipped their belt and floated into the discourse. "First woman was on the moon in 2029," they said. "How about a non-binary this time?"

Bruce couldn't help but laugh. "Dudit, unless you're going to arm-wrestle Aiysha to get out of this lander, we're not going anywhere. If anything, the AI gets the credit."

Strawberry gave a wry smile. "Like buying a house. Born at the wrong time."

"Wrong reality," said Rishi. "You'd need the space race to have continued through the 70s to be able to be the first on a planet, though it would probably have been Europa."

"Alright, everyone, gogs off," said Aiysha. "I need your eyes."

Reluctantly, everyone unstrapped the goggles from their faces and blinked.

"Don't forget to squeeze your eyes shut a few times," said Wei. "Get those oil glands working. Too much screen time equals oil gland death."

The tiny room that greeted Bruce caused him to sigh. Everyone looked at him and he shrugged, his protruding stomach bouncing humorously. "Sorry, it's just that, reality isn't what I want it to be most of the time. Prefer to have my gogs on."

Aiysha nodded. "How's everyone's mental health?"

Rishi smiled ruefully. "Like we're going to tell you. And, even if we do, what can you do about it?"

Aiysha pointed at the lifeless land outside their tiny window. "This lander has an airlock. Just working out who to throw out first." She paused for effect. "Well?"

"Peachy!" said Bruce.

"We're all going to die!" said Wei.

"Just seeing your beautiful face has me jumping for joy," said Strawberry.

"You know me," said Rishi. "Cynical as always. No change there."

Aiysha sighed. "Alright, you lot. Don't overdo it." She looked down at her monitor, squinting. "Transmission begins in five minutes. Ready?"

Bruce was about to say ready, when the lander lurched slightly. "What?"

"How did we even feel that?" asked Wei. She looked out the window, but couldn't see anything.

"Gravity can't suddenly increase, can it?" asked Strawberry. Bruce looked at her in alarm as his body suddenly began to drift slightly faster to the floor. "You're on to something there, Strawbs." His shoes touched the floor of the lander, and he looked closely out the window. "Our own mass isn't going to affect the gravity of Phobos that much." The window continued to show the endless pockmarks of multiple impacts.

Then he blinked and looked again. "Uh, oh."

Aiysha floated over to him and landed on the balls of her feet. "Don't uh oh me. Transmission is soon."

"Guys," said Bruce. "Should Stickney Crater have a night?" He pointed at the rapidly moving shadows stretching across the crater.

"Oh My God," said Wei.

Strawberry was quick to come over, while Rishi sighed and put his hands behind his head.

"No doubt some disaster has befallen us," said Rishi. He closed his eyes. "Wake me when it's over."

Bruce, Wei and Strawberry looked briefly at him then back to each other. Aiysha was getting ready for the transmission.

"Phobos is gravity locked," said Wei, her face ashen. "Our landing must have triggered an orbital shift."

Bruce was already bouncing back to his gogs. He put them on, then swiped his hands a few times in the air, accessing trajectory, vector, route, distance, time and more. He pulled them off and yelled, "Fire the thrusters. We have to get off."

"What?" yelled Aiysha. "What is it?"

Bruce was already at one of the control consoles. "Phobos has been drawing closer to Mars' surface for ages, you know, tidal deceleration, though it was supposed to be about 50 million years before it hits." He tapped a screen, then threw it up on the display. "Our landing has pushed its orbit off course!"

"Surely by a miniscule amount," said Wei. "It's only 22kms in diameter. Hardly enough for Mars' gravity to attract it quickly."

"Yeah," said Bruce. "But how much does the lander weigh?"

"One metric ton," said Rishi, getting interested. "But we're 6000km away from Mars. Not worth rushing about for. Besides, it's velocity and position, not mass. We haven't done anything."

"He's right," said Wei. "Phobos is almost 10.7 trillion kilograms. We're just a tiny bug."

Bruce waved his hand agitatedly. "I'm thinking aloud. Why the increase in gravity? Get us off and give me time to work this out!"

Strawberry was at one of the consoles. "Uh, oh," they began. "Brucie is right." They made a grabbing motion with their hand and threw the data into the center. Everyone put their gogs back on, and entered a slightly different digital environment. A blank workspace. Strawberry grinned a generated grin in the VR. Like everyone else they had shaved off their hair in the Mother Ship before getting into the Lander, and they reflected that in their avatar.

Strawberry created Mars and Phobos in the air in front of them.

"No Deimos?" asked Bruce.

"Behave," said Strawberry. They pulled an image of the lander and placed it above the system, then pointed at a timeline above it. "This is when we raised our magnetic shields. Solar burst headed our way, probably influenced by Earth, Mars and Venus in conjunction. Protected us, but when we landed..." They swiped the image, jumping further along the timeline, then zoomed in on Phobos, showing the slowly turning moon.

"...it affected Phobos," said Wei. "Creating a magnetosphere!"

"Can't be," said Rishi. "Our magnetic shields aren't powerful enough to surround almost 11 thousand cubed kms."

"Estimated time for impact?" asked Wei.

Strawberry looked at the data, flicked a few more screens in front of their avatars.

"Well?" asked Rishi.

"I'm calculating!" said Strawberry, annoyed.

"Yeah," said Bruce. "All our calculations, fuel and oxygen are based on a gravity-locked moon. We've got to contact Earth to get new vectors. They need to run their servers to get us off."

"Can we turn the magnets off?" asked Wei.

"Still high levels of solar particles," said Strawberry. "We'd be fried."

Bruce called up another Phobos and spun it about. "Now that we're this close, we should do a scan. Find out what's inside. Maybe that's what's causing this magnetosphere."

"Estimated time to impact," began Strawberry. "A year."

"Scan authorized," said Aiysha.

"Rightio," said Bruce, his voice sounding relieved. "No urgent need to get off. Got it." He called up a few icons and flicked through them. Then pinched one that began a scan. A laser line appeared across his Phobos model scanning from left to right, then stopped. A new screen popped up showing the results.

"Bloody hell," said Bruce. "Sorry. You'll never guess what's inside Phobos."

"An alien spaceship?" asked Rishi.

Bruce sighed. "Alright. You guessed it."

"What?"   yelled   Strawberry.

"You're joking, right?" asked Aiysha. She threw her own screen into the center. "We're out of range of the laser signal to the MS. No transmission. We need to deal with this before we can contact Earth again."

Bruce's generated face shook his head. "Here we are, wanting to go to Mars to investigate possible alien life, and it's right here on Phobos." He pulled from the data image and threw the new screen into the center, replacing Aiysha's. "Saucer shaped, but tapered at the bottom. The actual size is unclear. Made of a highly magnetic mineral that can't be identified."

"A UMO," said Rishi.

"Haha," said Wei politely, struggling to deal with the information. "Occupants?"

Bruce's avatar shrugged. "It's near the center so, allowing for space debris build up, I'd say it crashed there during the age of the dinosaurs. The most we'd find is a well-preserved 66-million-year-old corpse, if they hadn't left in time."

"Find?" said Strawberry, horrified. "We're going out?"

Bruce's avatar grinned. "First contact situation is my jurisdiction, and I say we're going out. Looks like you will have your day, Strawbs. And I couldn't be prouder."

Strawberry was speechless.

Aiysha gave her first smile of the day. "Well, I'm glad we left our egos behind on Earth. Looks like you're now in charge, Bruce. Strawberry, as you're under Bruce in First Contact situations, I'm officially passing the landing on Phobos role to you." Then she paused and said, "Want to wear the tie?"

"God, no!" said Strawberry.

Everyone laughed.

Mars above them had begun to strobe across the 'sky' as the spinning of Phobos increased. Both Rishi and Strawberry had left the lander without tethers, carefully stepping so that the low gravity wouldn't throw them off into space. Even so, it was slow going as each step meant carefully controlling and settling themselves before the next.

Strawberry had taken the first step out of the lander and made a short speech about humankind of all genders. Bruce, Aiysha and Wei had clapped inside the lander while Rishi had stood silent and respectful on the ladder. When they had finished, he had floated down and joined Strawberry, then they had collected a drilling robot from the side of the lander before heading to where the alien spaceship was buried.

Bruce now watched Strawberry and Rishi attempting to cross the moon without bouncing off into space. "This is painful to watch. If Phobos had just been a bit bigger, I could have used my own weight to compensate. I hope you're not recording this. Earth will think we've chosen a couple of lunatics."

"Appropriate name for people on a moon," said Wei.

"Hey," yelled Rishi. "We can hear you!"

"Yep, radio is working," laughed Bruce.

About half an hour later the astronauts were almost above the spaceship. "It's a 4.5 kilometer walk to the center of the crater," said Bruce. "With all your jumping, you're almost there. You're coming up to some big grooves, so don't twist an ankle."

"Impossible in these suits," said Strawberry. "I can barely move my leg."

"So, the UO created the crater?" asked Rishi.

"Nah," said Bruce. "Crater's at least a billion years old. But Phobos is pretty porous. The ship probably sank." Then he clicked his fingers. "The Soviet Phobos 2 spacecraft in 1989! They lost communication and the lander was never deployed. It must have been magnetic interference!"

Aiysha continued monitoring the situation. "Everyone. 'Fraid there's been a change. Our magnetic shields have gone to maximum due to another solar burst. Your suits have automatically strengthened. Phobos spin has increased further, effectively reducing the gravity on the surface."

"If I could cover my face with my hands, I would," muttered Strawberry. "I need to be heavier."

"Not long to go," said Bruce. "Looking forward to seeing that hole-drilling robot in action."

Minutes later Strawberry and Rishi had arrived at the designated point and they both carefully lowered the drillbot and turned it on before making a small bounce away from it.

"Drillbot activated," said Rishi.

The drillbot looked like a wagon wheel combined with a drone, covered in pointed pieces of metal. Not enough to cut through a space suit accidentally, but combined and turning at high speed the pieces would carve through soft rock. Pins on the edge slowly sank into the regolith then hooked underneath. Almost immediately it began spinning, carving a tunnel into Phobos.

"I thought we'd do our best to NOT damage the environment," said Strawberry.

"Can't make an omelet without breaking eggs," Bruce radioed.

The team watched the progress of the drone drill, dust pouring out of the hole in its middle like a geyser.

Moments later, it alerted their screens.

"We're in!" said Rishi.

Everyone saw Rishi simply jump through the last of the dust into the hole, with Strawberry following almost immediately after.

"If we'd landed closer we could have kept you tethered," said Bruce. "Don't want either of you floating off into space."

A few seconds passed without a reply, then Rishi's voice came over the radio again. "Not sure if you're feeling it, but gravity feels a bit stronger here. It looks like we've landed on a hatch."

In the lander, Bruce released a breath he hadn't realized he'd been holding.

"I was thinking you would pass out from oxygen deprivation," said Aiysha, attempting humor.

"Ha. Ha," said Bruce. "You know, *I'm* coping well with my mental health, but we haven't heard anything from *you*. Now that our roles are reversed..."

Aiysha frowned, then said, "My mental health is fine."

"Our mission is off course," explained Bruce. "Phobos is turning. We've discovered a UO! Surely these can get you to react. A bit more emotion wouldn't hurt, surely?"

Aiysha stared at him; her eyes unreadable. "I think you should put your gogs back on."

Bruce tched. "Off. On. Off. On. Just let everyone leave them on! If you micromanage too much, you're going to wear yourself out."

Aiysha walked over to Strawberry's terminal and tapped the communication icon. A form appeared.

Bruce shook his head. "Send a radio message to those Earth clowns that won't read it for minutes? Another twenty to reply even though the speed of light says three? No thanks. Laser transmission should be back soon."

Aiysha muttered back. "We still have to send a record of what we're doing. There is a team of high functioning scientists down there that can answer anything. You can ignore their reply if you wish. Wei?"

Wei sighed and went over to a console and began entering data. "Aiysha, I think we should alert Malik first."

Aiysha nodded. "We'll alert him when laser transmission is back."

"I'm sure Malik has already worked out what is going on," said Bruce. "We solve this, we can then get the lander back to the MS."

"If we solve this," said Wei.

"Gogs on," said Aiysha.

Bruce groaned and put them back on again. Both Rishi and Strawberry were represented by flickering icons.

"Sending visuals," said Rishi.

The environment lit up with an image of the drilled tunnel. Both Rishi and Strawberry were gingerly perched on the upper side of the drillbot. Below it, through the spokes, was something metallic mostly covered in dust.

"Cool!" said Bruce. "Can you see a way in?"

"Yes," said Strawberry. "That's why we're calling now. There's a hatch on the surface and our tools unlocked it quickly. We can enter. Do we have your permission?"

Bruce almost smacked his own mouth in excitement. "Yes, yes. Go go go!"

"Bruce," said Aiysha. "I realize this is your jurisdiction, but checking out the saucer isn't going to stop Phobos spinning or get us back to the Mother Ship."

"There's a method in my madness, Aiysha," said Bruce. "You'll see soon enough."

Video showed the hatch being lifted up by the astronauts. A puff of dust escaped from under it. Rishi shone his torch down. "There's a ladder but the rungs are a short distance apart," said Rishi. "Whoever owned this ship was half our size."

"Careful not to bump your head," said Bruce.

"Going in," said Rishi and Strawberry together.

They watched as the two flicked on their torches then carefully drifted down through the hatch.

"Surprisingly clean," said Rishi. "I was expecting it to be full of broken parts and piles of…"

The hatch drifted closed behind them.

"Glad they left a camera out there," said Aiysha. "At least we can see when they come out again."

"If they come out again," said Wei.

"Wei!" said Bruce. "Of course they will. Though, maybe not the way you think."

"Ah," said Aiysha. "I now know what you've asked them to do. You're right. You *are* mad."

"With a method!" said Bruce.

Wei looked uncomprehendingly. "I'm still confused why this mission is taking place first. I mean, we should get off this damn rock and come back later."

"What is causing the magnetosphere?" asked Aiysha, pointedly.

"The minerals in the spaceship," said Wei.

"What would be a solution, then?" asked Aiysha.

"We leave, and Phobos should stabilize."

"We don't have the program or coordinates for leaving yet," said Aiysha. "What's another alternative?"

"Well," said Wei. "Obviously we find some way to get rid of that UO!"

"And how would we do that?"

Wei stared at Bruce. "Noooo! You didn't ask them to do that, did you?" Wei looked surprised.

Bruce smiled. "We're a team of mavericks on a private exploration mission. NASA either wouldn't have done anything like this or at the very least have gone with whatever would attract grants and public support. Can you imagine NASA trying to explain to the public how to do a slingshot maneuver around Venus to get to Mars faster? They'd be like "But isn't Venus further from Mars than Earth? Wouldn't the trip be longer?"

"But flying an alien spacecraft…" began Wei.

"Rishi is a pilot and has worked on the navigation instruments of thousands of space vehicles. Strawberry has the math," said Bruce. "If they can get it working, it'll break out of Phobos, almost instantly dismantling the magnetosphere."

"Almost instantly dismantling Phobos as well, I'd imagine!" said Wei.

Bruce shook his head. "Phobos is a bit bigger than New York City. That ship is barely the size of the Statue of Liberty. Hardly likely to break it apart."

"At the first sign of danger," said Aiysha, "You have to get them out."

"No problem!" said Bruce, confidently, pointing at his screen. "A swipe of my finger and…"

"Physically!" said Aiysha, frowning.

"Ah," said Bruce. He pulled off his gogs and looked across the confined space at the hook holding his oversized spacesuit. "Better get dressed for the occasion." Then he blinked and looked at Aiysha. "Hang on. I'm in charge, now!"

"When you're in charge, crew morale and occupational health and safety fall to me to manage."

"Fair enough," said Bruce, grinning. "The suit probably needs a stretch, anyway."

Almost half an hour later, Bruce was beginning to get uncomfortable in his suit. Aiysha looked him in the eye and gave a frown.

"A few more minutes, please," he said, and Aiysha concurred before returning to her station.

Minutes later, the hatch lifted again and both Rishi and Strawberry clambered out.

"Sorry, Bruce," said Rishi. "As exciting as piloting an alien ship sounded, unfortunately I couldn't."

"No controls," said Strawberry. "Probably mind interface."

"But we did find something," said Rishi. "Right in the center, on the third level, sitting on a plinth. A huge ball of some kind of element behind an impenetrable energy shield. Well, we think it was a pure element. Our equipment couldn't identify it."

"We're leaving the hatch up and sending details to you," said Strawberry. "We've left a camera down there."

It was faster for them to return than it was to go, and both Strawberry and Rishi were now sitting in the lander with their suits off and their goggles on. Bruce had, with great relief, clambered out of his own suit and was now back in the environment.

The virtual reality showed the live stream of the sphere levitating in a force field.

"I'm thinking it's one of those *2001 A Space Odyssey* kind of artifacts," said Wei. "They've left it there for us to work out what it is."

"Is there anything getting through that shield?" asked Bruce. "If the shield is failing it could be why Phobos now has this magnetosphere, reacting with the lander. We've never detected anything like it from Phobos before."

Aiysha swiped her screen. "Yes. This is the source. Oh."

She stared at the screen for a moment. "It's totally unbelievable."

"Well, don't leave us in suspense," said Strawberry.

"Scans have just come through. It's a superactinide. Element 121. Similar to actinium but heavier."

"Code name Unbiunium?" said Bruce, surprised. "We haven't even created enough to see yet. The value would be incalculable."

"Is that what is increasing the gravity of this moon?" asked Wei.

Bruce frowned. "A moon can't suddenly start increasing its own gravity. Where would the mass come from? I'm more inclined to think we're getting stronger gravity from Mars as we get closer."

"There was that Doctor Who episode back in '14 where the gravity started increasing because a Dragon was growing inside the Moon," said Wei. "No explanation of where the extra matter was coming from to increase gravity. The science was so bad I had to turn it off."

"Really?" said Bruce. "The kids probably loved it. My grandson would have been tickled pink at the idea of the moon being an egg."

"Alright people," said Aiysha. "Focus, please." Aiysha was staring intently at the object. "Something's happening."

There was a flash, and the shield seemed to flicker and swirl around the object before it settled again. The metal had changed from a dark metal type to a silver one.

"I don't believe it," said Aiysha.

"What now?" asked Rishi.

"Transmutation. It's lost some photons."

"How many?" Bruce croaked.

"It's now Unbinilium."

"I don't like the sound of this," said Strawberry. "I don't want to jump to conclusions but jumping from element 121 to element 120 sounds like a Type III civilization countdown."

"But the amount of energy needed would be incalculable," said Wei.

"Unless you're an advanced civilization that can make any kind of element and control it and choose one that has almost infinite energy output," said Aiysha.

"Like something in a spaceship still powered up after millions of years," said Rishi.

There was flash again. "Yep," said Aiysha. "It's a countdown. Ununennium."

"We have to contact Malik," said Wei. "We have to get off this rock. We definitely shouldn't be here when it becomes Uranium."

"Oganesson is next," said Bruce. "Quite stable. Worth a fortune. If we could get it..."

"It's looking like 20-30 seconds between element transmutations," said Aiysha.

"Well, I definitely don't want to be here when it reaches hydrogen," muttered Strawberry.

"Yeah," added Rishi. "A countdown to what?"

They still couldn't contact the mothership, so it was decided that they had to take the risk to just enter orbit away from Phobos, and hope that whatever was planned by the alien ship wouldn't affect them.

The AI had calculated a flightpath away from the spinning moon that would use the force spin to 'parabola' them into an orbit that would eventually intersect with the mothership. Also, hopefully, by getting off the rock and away from the magnetosphere, they would be able to give Malik sufficient warning.

Having several days' worth of oxygen left meant they could remain in space until their lander's and the mothership's orbit intersected.

"Ready for liftoff in 10," said the AI. "9...8...7...6...5...4...3...2...1...Now."

They all gripped their seats, waiting for the minor jolt that would release them from Phobos, but nothing happened.

"Did the lander fire, AI?" asked Aiysha.

"Confirmed," said the AI.

"Where did the energy go, AI?" asked Bruce.

"Dissipated," replied the AI.

Rishi groaned. "Either the spaceship is absorbing it or it's not powerful enough to move us."

"That was a lot of fuel," said Aiysha. "I'm not sure what we can try next."

They all began unclipping their helmets and getting out of their seats. "This is ridiculous," said Strawberry. "It was supposed to be a simple mission. Land. Samples. Leave. We've been here for hours."

Aiysha frowned then called up the countdown on her monitor. "We've already passed uranium without any considerable effect. So, the shield is definitely absorbing most of it. It's down to lead."

"Then Thallium, Mercury, then Gold," said Bruce. "The dream of Middle Ages alchemists."

"Gogs on," said Wei. "You have to see this."

"What is it?" asked Bruce as everyone started putting on their gogs again.

"You know those grooves?" said Wei. "Looks like they're getting wider."

"That's what it's using for energy," said Aiysha. "Rocks! Probably absorbing what it needs remotely."

"I don't like the sound of that," said Bruce. "If it needs silicon, we're in trouble."

Strawberry pointed to the latest screen in the center. "Worse than that. It's been absorbing Phobos from under us. The moon is already collapsing. We're looking at multiple Phobosquakes any second."

"Phobosquakes," said Rishi. "That's all we need."

"Try Malik again," said Wei. "If Phobos has reduced in size, maybe the magnetosphere has reduced in strength."

Aiysha shook her digital head. "If anything, it's got stronger." Then she looked again. "Bruce, did you say that the ship is the size of the Statue of Liberty?"

Bruce tapped his head. "Engineering guess based on its vague tapered shape. Then the length of time Rishi and Strawbs were inside. Confirmed when they said this element is on level 3."

Aiysha flipped the screen around. "Why this shape, do you think?"

Bruce's mouth fell open. "It almost looks like a screw with pushpin cap."

Wei coughed to get everyone's attention. "You know, you all seem to see things logically and get things, or understand things, a bit faster than I do. I probably sometimes look slow or stupid but my neurodivergence is dealing with a lot more than you are at the same time."

"Of course we don't think that, Wei," said Bruce.

"We're professionals," said Strawberry. "Besides, I thought I had the claim to that title!"

Wei's avatar smiled. "None of us are as normal as Bruce."

"You make it sound like it's a bad thing," said Bruce, pretending to be hurt. Then he smiled. "But I know you have something for us, and you're just chomping at the bit to tell it."

"I guessed what it was when it started showing us all the elements it could make."

"Aha!" said Rishi, slapping his hands together. He looked like he was about to say something, then stopped. "Sorry, I'll try not to spoil your explanation."

Wei pulled the image of the screw ship out of the center screen and placed it above it, then pulled in an image of Mars, placing it under it. "AI, assuming the alien spaceship absorbs all matter from Phobos, and that our current spin and trajectory are planned, where is it most likely to land?"

"Assuming the alien spaceship absorbs all matter from Phobos," began the AI's reply, "and that our current spin and trajectory are planned, and assuming that the loss of all matter doesn't disturb its current path, it will land on Olympus Mons in just under a year. However, it is possible that internal navigation may redirect the alien spaceship somewhere else."

"AI," said Wei. "Is there a most likely landing place, hypothesizing it is a terraforming probe?"

Bruce, Aiysha and Strawberry gasped. Rishi grinned.

"Hypothesizing that it is a terraforming probe," continued the AI, "suggests that the area most suitable would be the poles. However, as Phobos is in an equatorial orbit, this is unlikely."

"It's also unlikely as an alien probe able to create any element wouldn't need to go to the poles to get water," said Wei. "It would just make some, if it even needed it."

"We have another problem then," said Rishi. "We're almost up to

7 hours since we last saw our mothership, so it should be coming up on the horizon now." He flipped his screen to the center. "It's not there."

"Our landing changed the vector of Phobos," said Bruce. "We might have changed its orbit speed, too. The mothership is just further away from us."

"Phobos is slowing down," said Strawberry, frowning. "That's it then." They pointed at the screen which showed the new trajectory. "*Not* a year to crash land."

"Let me guess," said Rishi. "A month?"

Strawberry's avatar stared seriously at them. "More like a day."

The lander was a hive of activity. Aiysha continuing trying to contact Malik on the mother ship, Bruce searching for what they could salvage, Wei standing in a corner weeping, Strawberry looking angry, Rishi napping. Bruce pointed a thumb in Rishi's direction while talking with Aiysha.

"He can't be that relaxed!" whispered Bruce.

"Rishi has found a quick nap can sometimes solve problems. I'm hoping he'll wake up with a solution."

"Not napping," said Rishi. "Deep meditation."

"I thought you were the cynic," said Bruce.

Rishi sat straight up. "Got it." He threw his gogs on and set up a new joint environment. In it was a turning, tilting Phobos with deeper lines and new cracks. He navigated around it, his avatar flitting across all its surface—above, under and through.

By this time everyone had put on their gogs. "The suspense is killing me," said Bruce.

Rishi waved his hand over the surface. "An advanced ship capable of making any element, using the matter of Phobos without even a fusion reactor…It would be using the rock methodically. From one end to the other, or from around the alien spaceship outward for conservation of energy, theoretically."

"So?" asked Strawberry.

"It's not," said Rishi.

"That's it?" asked Wei. "How is that going to save us in 23 hours' time?"

"I'm not finished." Rishi waved his hand over the Phobos image and time sped forward several hours. Phobos had broken into little chunks. "It's creating thousands of highly magnetized masses from the matter."

"No way," said Bruce. Then he began laughing.

"What is it?" asked Wei.

The others had already posted smiley faces in the environment.

"You're the one who realized it is a terraforming probe," said Aiysha. "Think about what Mars needs."

"Yeah, Wei," said Rishi. "If it wasn't for you realizing it was for terraforming, I would never have jumped to this conclusion."

Wei snapped her fingers. "Mars needs a magnetosphere!"

"Exactly!" said Aiysha.

"And with Phobos being a carbonaceous chondrite rock, in particular a CI type, it contains magnetite. Ideal for creating a magnetosphere from space."

"With a spaceship that can create any element, a grid of magnetic satellites would be child's play," said Rishi.

"I have a question," began Bruce. "This ship waited until an alien lander, us, appeared to begin the process. Are we just collateral? I can't believe a Type III civilization would just ignore the alien life that began a process. Surely, it's going to plan for us, too?"

"Looking," said Rishi, moving Phobos several more hours forward. Then he stared at what it showed. "I don't believe it."

Bruce looked at the long-board-shaped rock that was going to form perfectly under the lander in just ten hours' time. Then his avatar grinned. "Surf's up, dudes!" he laughed.

Twenty-three hours later, just as they entered the extremely thin atmosphere of Mars, and Phobos had almost completely broken up around them, its balls of reinforced magnetite entering orbit equidistantly around the equator where Phobos used to be, Aiysha began descent procedures, attempting to slow the lander and its surfboard of rock to 1600 kilometers a second. "We still have fuel for course corrections," said Aiysha. "I'll do what I can."

"Don't forget the parachute," said Bruce.

"Got my eye on the controls," said Strawberry. "As soon as I think it's safe."

"Suits on, everyone," said Aiysha. "I know it means barely any room here, and that we're going to use up most of our tanks, but if the landing is harder than it should be, the suits will help. Glad everyone's used the toilet already!"

Just then a crackling message came through the lander speakers. "Phobos Lander, can you receive? This is an automated message. Wake me up when you get this. Phobos Lander, can you receive? This is an…"

Aiysha gave a small shriek then composed herself. "Ahem," she tapped on her screen. "This is the Lander crew, reading you loud and clear. Are you there, Malik?" She turned back to the crew. "Opening it up to everyone."

"Great," said Rishi. "Just as the magnetosphere releases us, entry into the atmosphere is going to stuff up communications."

"Better hope Malik wakes up quickly," said Wei.

A sleepy-eyed face with curly black hair and a bright white smile appeared floating on screen. "A few seconds delay," said Malik. "But so glad to hear your voice. Are you okay? The AI here has been following your orbit. Nothing I could do. I thought you'd decompressed. Earth says I'm to head back if I don't hear anything in two more days."

"When our oxygen runs out," said Bruce. "Yeah, fair enough. Well, the good news is that we're alive. The bad news is that we've discovered an ancient alien terraforming device that is about to hit Mars. It's following us down."

Bruce flicked the image of their position, their possible landing place, and the screw-like vessel that was several kilometers above them, slowly descending without any propulsion.

A few seconds later Malik replied with some notes. "I've been regularly updating Earth on Phobos' situation, and they have been sending new flightpaths every hour or so. After Phobos broke up and they realized it was creating a magnetosphere, and they could see you had left orbit, they sent this."

"Gogs on, everyone," said Aiysha. "Do you think this could work?"

Strawberry flicked the map and path around in the environment, looking at various points. "We need to deploy the parachute in about 20 minutes."

Rishi pointed at another section of the flightpath. "1600kms per hour isn't going to cut it. Great for robots, not so much for humans. At this point we also need to fire the last of the thrusters."

On the central screen, Malik's shrug appeared on the monitor, replying to Aiysha's comment seconds later. "I pilot orbit-built slingshot craft around planets. No idea how to land one!"

"Thanks Malik," said Wei. "Wish us luck!" She traced the path to the robot-built prefabricated buildings on Mars, waiting for colonists in 2039. "Nice."

Malik's next out-of-sync message played. "Hope you don't need it! I'll let Earth know. We're going to be out of range in seconds so, if I hear from you after you land, I'll have a one-person party here. If I don't, it'll be a wake." He grinned, then blew them a kiss. "Love you guys! Good luck!"

Malik disappeared and the crew focused on their new mission.

Everyone had left the environment and were back to putting their helmets on. "Standing room only," said Bruce.

Strawberry was already suited up. "Minutes to thrusters. Is everyone secure?"

Everyone confirmed they were suited and ready. Rishi quickly floated over and checked everyone's seals, then went over to have Wei check his.

"A minute to go," said Strawberry. "Hold tight!"

Rishi floated to a spare part of the wall and hooked himself in.

Bruce and Aiysha looked over the team then nodded at each other. "Good to go," said Aiysha.

Strawberry waited a few more seconds then hit the thrusters. The Lander jerked and shuddered as their descent was slowed enough, then hit the parachute.

The crew were instantly jerked around and held their controls or handholds as the lander's descent was slowed further.

Then they saw a flash as sunlight reflected off the alien spaceship passing their window.

"What do you think will happen when it hits?" asked Wei.

"What do you think will happen?" asked Aiysha.

"It took a whole day to absorb and transform Phobos," said Wei. "11,000 cubic kilometers, give or take. One day!"

"Well Mars is 163 billion cubic kilometers," said Rishi. "It might take a bit longer."

"And those tiny ball satellites aren't going to do much," said Bruce. "I think they're just there to get things started. If this alien civilization can instantly create any element as a timer, I'm sure it's capable of creating a new magnetic core for the planet."

"No!" said Strawberry. "Are you serious?"

Bruce couldn't nod in his suit so said yes. "I mean, why be screw shaped? I reckon it's going to go straight to the core."

The astronauts all looked relieved. "So, whatever happens, it's not about to turn us into parts of the elements it needs," said Wei.

Bruce tried to shrug then sighed. "I'm shrugging! It hasn't attempted to do anything biological, so I think that's its main purpose. Not sure how long it'll take to generate an atmosphere, but it's the first step. Maybe our grandchildren will get to enjoy it."

"Aren't your grandchildren teenagers?"

Bruce grinned. "Yep!"

Everyone gave a laugh then focused on their screens as the sound of the roaring atmosphere increased. Soon this was joined by the sound of particles of dust hitting the outside. Everyone braced for impact.

"Landing in five," said Strawberry. "I'll leave you to count the rest."

Moments later, the lander hit the Martian surface. All four lander legs snapped on landing, the empty rocket engine collapsing into the Martian soil. The upper part housing the crew tilted at ninety degrees, then stabilized, with the door buckling and popping out.

Instant depressurization, and one of the windows cracked, but the crew were safe in their suits, if a little shaken.

"Now that's more like a landing," said Rishi.

"Five hours left of air," said Strawberry. "We've got to find those shelters."

Aiysha was already at the tilted door looking out on the darkening Martian surface. A bright light shot up from the horizon and disappeared. It reflected off of the domes that were barely meters away.

The others crowded behind her looking out in awe.

"Well, that's a relief," said Wei.

"You know," Aiysha said. "The door has tilted enough that it is now wide enough that we can all fit and jump down onto Mars at the same time."

Everyone laughed. A relief from their recent stress, and the gratitude to the boffins on Earth that had calculated their descent so precisely.

"Wide enough for you four," said Bruce. He patted the curve of his suit protecting his stomach, then smiled at them through his glass visor. "I think there are enough old white guys being lauded for achievements these days. I'll follow you out. Go make history."

Rishi, Strawberry, Wei and Aiysha linked spacesuit arms, and jumped onto the surface of Mars together.

--

Predominantly a space fiction writer, Neil A. Hogan occasionally dabbles in space opera, YA, children's and speculative fiction. He edits the anthology Alien Dimensions *and self-publishes* The Stellar Flash *and* The Heartness Chronicles *series. His story* Air Cows *in* Stanisław Lem and his Aliens *was published by Guardbridge Books in 2022. His co-authored paper:* Work in Space. The Changing Image of Space Careers in the TV Series Doctor Who *was published in* Outer Space and Popular Culture *in May 2024. He is the current Science Fiction Research Association Representative for Australia, and is also engaged in research as a PhD candidate with the ANU. Read some of Neil's essays and articles, and follow his research blog, at: www.NeilHogan.com*

You might also be interested in

The Monoliths of Redshift 7

Admiral Victoria Heartness is thrown into the 25th century where sun-sized creatures known as The Monoliths are draining stars at an alarming rate. Assembling a team of humans and aliens, she is determined to save the galaxy at all costs.
But she hardly expected some of the most powerful races in the galaxy to accept their fate.

With even the Interdimensional Coalition reluctant to help, it's a race against time to find a way to fight this unknown and seemingly unstoppable force.

A fight that no one believes they will win.

Available in digital and print.

Subscribe to the Space Fiction Books Newsletter

Receive the latest news about Alien Dimensions and other space fiction related titles.

Group giveaways, discounts and more!

Special Offer!

Download Alien Frequency: Stellar Flash Book One for free when you confirm your subscription.

Find out more at

Want to try something a bit different to Alien Dimensions? How about a Cozy Mystery?

Murder on the Rocks
By Eleanor Maplewood

Dive into "Murder on the Rocks" where intrigue swirls like mist over a quaint fishing village.

Follow Mabel Hartwell, a sharp-minded sleuth, as she untangles a web of secrets hidden in the shadows of an old lighthouse.

It's a story of unexpected alliances, hidden treasures, and the quest for justice—a riveting tale that proves some mysteries run as deep as the ocean itself.

Available in digital and in print